Antoni Jach is the author of the novel *The Weekly Card Game* and a book of poetry, *An Erratic History*. As well as writing, he has worked as a teacher, a journalist, an editor and as a creative director in multimedia.

By the same author
An Erratic History
The Weekly Card Game

Acknowledgements

I wish to express my gratitude to Caroline Lurie for her expert editorial advice. I would like to thank Fiona Inglis, for her support and assistance, and Ella Martin for her copy-editing. I also want to thank the Literature Board of the Australia Council for the use of the Keesing Studio, Cité Internationale des Arts in Paris, and I would like to acknowledge support received from Arts Victoria. As well, I want to thank the various authors (mentioned in the bibliography) whose books were helpful in the creation of this novel.

The barbarians had a passion for music and verse.

Tacitus

one | The Library

You are researching the many layers of Paris. You have been wandering around the city for a couple of months and you have written down many notes in a series of pocket-sized *Clairefontaine* notebooks. It's slow and laborious work and you receive a letter written by an old friend who used to study in Paris that says anyone interested in Paris simply *must* go to the Bibliothèque Historique de la Ville de Paris, 24, rue Pavée in the Marais.

You have always been intrigued by what's underground, perhaps because it affects you so. Going underground seems to be the closest link we have with our own past. Contemporary Western civilization is built upon the bones of Romans and barbarians. We're alive only because they're dead; they've passed their genetic messages down to us; though those errant messengers from the past still have the power to disturb.

You have, until recently, been spending every early afternoon in the Pompidou Centre library, returning home via

Monoprix to buy food, and writing every late afternoon in an A4 size *plein ciel* notebook in slow and laborious long-hand about the world of the Métro, the street, the buildings and the ether for a work about the many layers of the great city. You have completed the first two sections and you're thinking about a way in to the latter sections; you are momentarily stuck.

On the first morning of your new pattern, you arrive promptly at 9.15 a.m. at the gates of the Bibliothèque Historique de la Ville de Paris. You are the first to arrive. You wait in the courtyard of the building. The doors are unlocked at 9.30 a.m. You consult the catalogue. You are looking for books on Paris above ground. You find a book that sounds intriguing, write down its call number and present the slip to the librarian. You are allocated a place to sit and you wait for a significant period of time. You must have written down the call number incorrectly because eventually a dusty book arrives about the Romans and the barbarians in Southern Gaul during the first five centuries AD. You open the book at random, and read by chance a section which deals with the coming of the waves of barbarian invasions against the Romans during the fifth century AD in the area around present-day Orange, Arles and Nîmes—the area that is now called Provence but was then called Narbonensis, in the diocesis of Septem Provinciae. You read avidly with a sense that all of this could have some personal meaning. But you return the book to the front counter when you realize the words are starting to have an effect on you.

You depart—out into the comforting sunshine and the

pollution of the city. You look all around at the people: descendants of Romans and barbarians and Gauls. Living, breathing people; anxious, self-absorbed, introverted; a way of defending themselves against the duress of city life. You return home via Monoprix to your flat in the Marais. You can feel the effect of the dusty book still percolating through your nervous system. The book invades your night-thoughts: you imagine yourself first as a Roman, then as a barbarian. You can't let go, much as you would like to, of the images conjured up by the words you have read. You would like to sleep and leave the past behind, but sleep is not available to you. Your night-thoughts have been occupied; you are an invaded country.

The following day you are drawn back to the dusty book about Romans and barbarians, almost against your will. You know the book is not good for you—it has tapped a nerve, a current, you didn't know existed—but you copy down its call number exactly so there will be no mistakes this time. You are seeking that particular disturbance caused by letters of the alphabet, written in a particular order, one after another. While you are waiting for the book to be brought to you, and while you are looking up at the ancient beams supporting the ceiling, wondering what stories this building has to tell, an American comes up to you and asks you in French if you are an 'Anglophone'. You can understand every single word she is saying but the word 'Anglophone' is unfamiliar to you. You answer her in English instead, very quietly so that others won't be disturbed. She smiles. She says she came over to explain the system in the library: there are always long delays and you might as well get a journal to read from the shelves that line the reading room while you are waiting. She is curious about what you're doing there in 'her' library. When you tell her that you are researching the many layers of the city she says that you *must* visit the museum of the archaeological crypt of Notre-Dame which is located under the forecourt of the cathedral. That, she says, is the place for anyone interested in the underground layers of Paris. You say you are also interested in the layers of the street, the buildings and the ether. She drifts away, again with a smile.

Your book, the dusty book of yesterday, finally arrives and as you keep reading about the barbarian attacks in Narbonensis you notice you are starting to feel breathless, your heartbeat is quickening. The writing is affecting you just as it did yesterday, but today you are determined to read on. You want to find out what happened next. But you are starting to feel overwhelmed by the weight of past generations. This is a part of me too, you think. In a very general sense I am implicated in all of this too. These are my ancestors, this is part of my inheritance. You are starting to feel faint. This has happened to you before: words on a page have changed your heart rate, have made you feel breathless, have even made you faint. You know if you don't move quickly to get some fresh air, and more importantly, to start thinking about something else, then you *will* fall over (just like Julius Caesar used to do). You grab your notebook, return the history book to the guardians and rush out into the street, grateful for the pollution which revives you with its pungency. You take a few deep breaths of carbon dioxide mixed with carbon monoxide and oxygen.

You turn around at the sound of a voice. It is the American woman. She introduces herself as Juliet, she asks you if you are all right. You say you felt overcome by the weight of past generations, that's all. She says, that's OK, she understands, she's a historian after all, she lives with the past every single day of her life. You notice she is confident, outgoing, totally in command of herself. You feel like a barbarian in her presence. She says that Carl Jung in his memoirs mentions that he was always drawn to Rome's past but was never able to visit. He was frightened of being overwhelmed, and the one time he went to book a ticket to Rome he fainted in the ticket office of the train station. No matter how much he pushed himself towards the imperial city, he could not in the end subject himself to that sort of meeting with history. Rome had become the symbol of the mythic past for him; it obviously had a symbolic personal role for him as well. Jung, or some other writer, also mentions Stendhal, she says. Stendhal being the first to record this sensation of being overwhelmed by history. She says she needed a break from her work anyway, she needed some fresh air, and she suggests a rendezvous tomorrow in the café on the roof of the Pompidou Centre at midday. You hastily agree, perhaps too hastily, grateful for company, for unexpected compassion. She says one day she will take you to the archaeological crypt of the forecourt of Notre-Dame but right now she has to return to her study. She smiles again and departs.

You stand in the narrow street breathing deeply. Pedestrians walk around you. It's still morning, the weather has closed in. Out in the street you are becoming aware of the noise—human voices, drums, shrill whistles—and the smell of smoke and flares. You move down the street towards the sounds, move out into the rue St-Antoine and step into *une manifestation*; a whole sea of individuals turning into a gigantic swaying sea-serpent. You attempt to cross the street as best you can. You are caught up in the corporality of the demonstration: physical and intense, sensual and symbolic. The signs say they are Métro-cleaners, secondary school students, truck drivers, health-workers, teachers. You are swept forward by the momentum of the crowd. It is only with great difficulty that you are going to be able to get to the other side. As you are swept forward you are curious about this sea of people purposefully making their way forward. The flares are very beautiful lighting up the dampness, the noise is overwhelming, the *manifestants* are energized. You have rarely seen city people look like this before. You're used to the dead-while-alive look of the standard city-dweller. You are being inexorably carried forward. The crowd starts to run to get away from the riot police but you want to get away from the noise and the smoke of the flares. You need time to yourself to think. You keep cutting across *manifestants*: *pardon, pardon...*

You finally make it to the other side of the street; and as you do, a well-dressed grandma pushes a sign in your face asking for money then moves on with a huff seeing your blank expression. A *clochard* pushes his toothless face into yours, and breathes heavily upon you. You feel displaced. You feel disentitled to stand anywhere, to belong anywhere, to occupy any patch of ground, you have to get away, you have to move. You feel dizzy, preyed upon. You

head down the steps of the Métro station Saint-Paul longing for warmth, comfort, security...You rush through the
barriers, onto the platform and walk into knee-deep rubbish. You see a rat scurrying for its life along the rails.
There are well-dressed citizens in thick cream mohair over-
coats and elegant leather jackets either side of you
seemingly impervious to the rubbish, though they kick it
away before entering the Métro-car. This is the world of
the future, you think to yourself. The city as a huge refuse
site. You stand stock-still. A young boy asks you for money
because his baby brother whom he is holding in his arms
has polio. He offers you the baby. You run, up the stairs
and back out onto the street. You run, bumping into people:
pardon, pardon, pardon.

You run down side streets, out of breath now. You enter
the first café you see. You feel agitated. You notice its name
as you enter: it is the Café of All Poles. You sit at a table.
A truck driver in overalls, a large bear of a man, is talking to the owner of the bar. He is complaining to her about
the rise in petrol prices but there is rising energy in his
voice when he talks about this morning's *manifestation*
which has blocked the main arteries of the great city
making circulation impossible. *La patronne* is wiping her
hands with a tea-towel, nodding sympathetically. You feel
better already. Everything is ordinary. Apart from a cursory
glance in your direction, no-one is taking any notice of
you. Everything is as it should be. A street-sweeper at the
bar is listening to the conversation. He is looking blank:
that time-honoured blankness that spells defeat, resigna-
tion, misery, the end of all aspirations, the look of the

already-dead. But then he changes: his face becomes animated, he throws down *un pastis* hurriedly, slaps his money on the counter and leaves with a wave to the owner.

You are ignored by the owner—as you no doubt deserve to be—but you are warm and out of the grey wetness of the morning, out of the carnival of the street, out of the faces thrust in your face, out of the nightmarish landscape of the underworld. Your hair is still damp. Your scarf is wet. You are perspiring. You are asked what you would like. You reply gently, in a whisper. The noise in the café is cheerful. The truck driver, unshaven and hearty, seated at the counter, is talking in an animated fashion. He is enjoying himself. His presence fills the whole room. This is his space. He is a regular. He says over and over, saying it louder each time, that the sapling will not always bend, and follows that up each time with: So when it breaks, watch out, the streets will be full of people, marching and shouting and demanding their human dignity, demanding their right to exist, to be heard, to be acknowledged as having a right to a place in the scheme of things, and when the streets are full of people then we will *all* be happy.

He laughs and slaps the Algerian businessman beside him on the back. The truck driver is cutting himself slices of Polish sausage with a Swiss army knife and placing the sausage carefully on rye bread. He cuts gracefully, and with precision. He cuts slices of Polish dill pickles and adds them. Then he reaches for the ham on the bone and cutting swiftly places slices of ham on top of the dill pickles. He says he will join the strike, and adds that it is fitting for the workers of *mouvement* to stick together.

—Get the pilots to join, adds the owner. A second street-sweeper leaning in the corner of the room drinking a beer, with his straw broom standing to attention beside him, awakes from somnolent self-absorption and agrees by nodding vigorously in a cartoonlike fashion.

You drink your short black. You are feeling much better. You have slipped into a scene from ordinary life, and while not being a part of it, you are at least allowed your place. You are accepted temporarily with a benign indifference. They look at you as a tourist, an outsider. You look on at all these characters, observing them quietly. They are used to tourists who stare, tourists who intrude, and they don't like it. You look around for clues in the café as to who you are, and what you are doing here; you look in the mirrors. You are determined to stay in Paris to get to the bottom of things—unless, that is, your friend returns early from his work with the European Parliament and kicks you out of his flat, in which case you'll move on to Provence and make Avignon or Arles your base.

You finish your coffee, pay, and as those around the zinc counter erupt into a burst of laughter, you step out into the dampness, heading homewards. But instead you decide to go on further and see what water looks like. You remember water from childhood, you haven't had much to do with it since. You have however, a substitute: a whole world of virtual water, of virtual nature on the Internet; facts about water, compressed movies of waves striking empty beaches. Then there are the web sites devoted to sunshine, to sea-gulls and to fields of springtime poppies blowing in the wind. This is your common, everyday accessible nature:

unspoilt, untrampled upon. You hook up to relax, to unwind. In digital nature every blade of grass is in place, the wind always blows from the same direction; it is always sunny. There is nothing disappointing about it at all. You have Nature all to yourself. When you hear the triumphal chord of the Macintosh starting up, you feel suddenly civilized.

You feel the greyness of the day on your face. You look up. There are a few birds forlornly hovering around. You can still hear the noise of the demonstration, and see the trails of the flares. Strangely there are only a few people about, bustling along to keep warm. You head down to the Seine and walk onto the Pont Louis-Philippe until you reach the middle of the bridge where you stop. You look down, over the rail: the Seine is grey, as the Seine should be, moving sluggishly. There is a boat carrying coal. A young boy, unkempt hair, barefoot, inadequately dressed—he could be someone you know, say, your son from a previous life. He is staring up at you, inquiringly, as if he is asking for something, just with his eyes. He has noticed you. The boat goes on. You have made a difference, for a split second. Someone has registered your existence and you have registered theirs. There are other people in the world, you are not alone. A boy on a boat has momentarily made a difference. Going, going, gone. Under the bridge and out of sight.

You look up, from the middle of the Pont Louis-Philippe, at the air above. You see pigeons overhead, but what you feel are the airwaves that are all about you: sound waves, colour waves, picture waves, waves of stored information, waves of transmission. Someone with messages to send is bouncing those messages via low orbiting satellites and then on through you on their way to a trillion antennae which are diligently collecting. No longer the smoke signals of the past but vibrations passing through air. No longer the pristine, uninvaded air of two thousand years ago, but now a *resource* to be carved out and parcelled up and sold to those who have messages to send. Signals emitted from powerful antennae, waves journeying out into the electromagnetic spectrum. No wonder we feel invaded. The air we associate with transparency is full of *broadcasting*. Every direction we turn we are hit in the face by someone's message: here a radio signal, there a television signal; here waves from a mobile phone, there waves from a pager passing through the ether. No wonder we feel so full of thoughts, so implicated in the world's guilt, as the news of the world passes through us in the form of radio frequencies. You look up and see clouds hemming you in but what you're aware of is the uppermost level of the ether— crowded with thousands of satellites and thousands of pieces of space junk all orbiting at a furious pace.

You look around. An organ-grinder is pushing his cart across the bridge, heading towards the forecourt of Notre-Dame de Paris where he will entertain the tourists. An ancient photographer—in his suit and bow tie, weighed down by his heavy old-fashioned camera hung around his neck like an ill-fitting noose—is making his way towards Notre-Dame. He is lost in time. No-one wants his services— instant black-and-white photos at 40 francs each—anymore. Technology has left him behind but he still wants to believe it's 1948 and postwar lovers (the girl from Ivry-sur-Seine and the sailor from Galveston) will want a souvenir of their brief affair. Our photographer, presumably, now makes his living by photographing Japanese tourists who are too embarrassed to refuse. You hear a couple beside you who have stopped to light cigarettes, sheltering the matches from the wind with their hands. They are talking loudly and gesturing towards a faraway point where a car shot off the voie Georges Pompidou and into the Seine early that morning. Neither knew why or what happened next.

—One minute they were in the car, the next minute they were in the Seine, the young guy says with a laugh.

When Paris gets too much—when there is too much *compression,* the layers are squeezing you tighter and tighter—you catch a TGV to Avignon which serves as a base to travel to Orange, Nîmes, Arles, St-Rémy-de-Provence and the Roman ruins of Glanum. You wander around touching the remains of ancient bricks, descending the steps of an underground well, kicking up the dust, feeling the presence of the Romans who made this their township before the waves of barbarians finished them off leaving their civilization in rubble. A constant cycle of building, destruction and rebuilding. Communities re-emerging over the top of other communities. Live bones on top of dead bones. You find it hard to get the ruins of Glanum, with its mausoleum and commemorative arch, out of your mind. You notice in a guidebook that Glanum was abandoned after the barbarian invasions at the end of the third century AD. It's barely sixty-eight generations ago.

The Layers of the City

Something keeps drawing you back there to stare at the mute, poignant testament.

Similarly you revisit Orange in order to stand in the Roman theatre, admire the solidity and grace of the structure and contemplate the past. A majestic city laid waste by the Visigoths at the beginning of the fifth century AD.

The citizens of Glanum would have assumed their city would continue to exist long after they were gone. What was once a proud city is now a ruin. You remember Rilke's line that *the age of cities is nearly over.* One day Paris might be a ruin like this too. You think of the Métro: knee-deep in rubbish, rats running along the tracks...

two | The Métro

Repeat after me:
Louvre, Pont Neuf, Arts et Métiers, Châtelet;
Concorde, Madeleine, Palais Royal, Opéra;
Pont Marie, Cardinal Lemoine, Jussieu, Austerlitz;
Duroc, Invalides, Alma-Marceau, Franklin D. Roosevelt;
Voltaire, Alexandre Dumas, Place de Clichy, Belleville.

Observe the signs:
Place the ticket in the machine. Do not obliterate your orange card. Foot-walkers this way. Exit. Exit. Exit. *Direction*—Mairie des Lilas. These seats reserved for those incapacitated in the Great War, those who have lost their limbs. *Direction*—Mairie d'Ivry. Exit: rue St-Antoine. *Direction*—Pont de Sèvres. *Direction*—ha Courneuve—8 Mai 1945

Regard the male supplicant who enters the carriage and makes a speech in a confident and impressive way under the bluish-yellow lighting. He says:

—Look at me, you well-fed brutes. I too have a right to

eat in a good restaurant. I too am a graduate of the class of May '68. I too was in the streets, as you were. And look at you all now. You have become the bourgeois you so despised! Give me money so I can eat in a good restaurant, as you do.

He goes around with a cap held out; it is lunchtime. Those in suits are going to eat in good restaurants; others are going to eat on the run; some are not going to eat at all. The *clochards* who live on the street corner pull the cardboard boxes over them, eating roast chicken, drinking wine and chatting to the passers-by. The smell of urine and sweat and chicken is so overpowering you have to cross to the other side of the street.

The *clochards* speak to you as you cross to the other side of the street. They say:

—Do you like the colour of the day? Do you want to sup with us today? We have some spare chicken here. Our prices are reasonable. We'll give it to you for free. We are your grateful customers—and your saviours. We assist you to divest yourselves of all those heavy coins that weigh your purse down so. We assist you daily to wash your conscience with the holy water of alms-giving. We are your daily poor. Your highly paid, exquisite jobs have created us. Your investment companies, your banks, your new technology...all of this has created us. You owe us your consciences. We are why you cannot sleep at night. Why your expensive eiderdown so weighs you down it threatens to suffocate you. Why your shirt collar becomes so tight at odd moments of the day. We are your consciences: we sleep out on the street where you can see us—in all kinds of weather. Our smell is your smell. You just use more powder than us, you use more water to wash away the human smell of sweat and piss and shit. Just look down from your first floor balcony. We are always present: you can't get rid of us. We are your consciences. We are as corporeal as you are. We breathe the same air.

Observe the signs:
Fixed price menu. Today, couscous: 49 francs. Or you can eat on the street. Fried chips: 20 francs. Falafel, with the lot: 30 francs. The steam of the frying chips rises. Above ground, it's humid. We are all looking forward to the release of rain. Underground, the humidity becomes even more intense. Millions of bodies brush up against you: laddering your stockings, creasing your suits. The brush of a million thoughts. When you go down into the Métro you put your mind in neutral, until the moment you can arise from the subterranean world, and breathe more easily. In the carriage you are crushed against each other with such force that only a bag standing by itself in the corner can separate you...Everyone eyeing the bag. Five kilos of Semtex waiting to blow us all up, until we are fused into each other's body: the glue of plastic explosives...We will be civilized if we stick together. The *clochards* sit like a giant incubus on our bodies at night as we wrestle with the angle and depth of sleep.

Where does it come from, this strange perfume of the Métro? From those who built it? From the million beads of sweat sliding to the platform of those who use it daily? From those who sleep there all day long? From the ancient guild of fishermen who inhabited the islands of the Seine? Where does all of the dust of the Métro come from? From the millions of cells of dead skin—the epidermis layer—that rub off as we go about our daily round. Warm, fetid air, that circulates only a little; a cocktail of biological soup; something primeval about the smell...A perfume left behind by the Romans when they picked up their kit-bags and returned home. A perfume left by the barbarians, left by Saint Genevieve, left by Abelard, left by Maurice of Sully.

Regard the female supplicant who enters the carriage. Under the pale bluish-yellow light. She says:

—I have three children to feed. I need your money to put shoes on their feet. Give so they may grow tall as fir trees—and as strong as birch trees...

She goes around with a tin, her wild and angry eyes flashing: accusing, accusative eyes, nominative eyes, nominating YOU.

*

Repeat after me:

    Pasteur, Maison-Blanche, Oberkampf, Place Monge;
    Place d'Italie, Tolbiac, Père Lachaise, République;
    Malakoff, Boissière, Pyramides, Ecole Militaire;
    Censier-Daubenton, Télégraphe, La Fourche;
    Crimée, Sèvres-Babylone, Filles du Calvaire.

*

At Châtelet you get off the moving walkway and there are the African musicians once again with their drums thumping out primeval rhythms: the music of underground, the music of leaking pipes, stained tiles, the music of the jungle, the music of beads of sweat tinkling to the ground, the music of muscle and sinew.

Observe the businessman in the smart cream mohair suit with its beautiful collar and elegant cuffs going down the Métro stairs, one foot after the other, down the stairs into the semi-darkness, or down by escalator, down into shadowy recesses, cul-de-sacs of thought. Underground thoughts. A man of business, of busy-ness, of important decisions, of uninterruptable thoughts, of reptilian power...

Leave the daylight behind. Plunge into the semi-nightlight. Out of the brightness, the warmth of mid-afternoon in midsummer to wait on a Métro platform: the humidity surrounds you like someone has wrapped a scarf of rotting red roses around your face. The sounds of the African drums insist themselves upon you, insinuate within you. The compression of the Métro. The terrible perfume of the Métro assails you as if you were a villain. Above ground in our elegant bathrooms we put on our powders, our unguents, our anti-ageing creams, our skin-softeners, our deodorants to wash away the smell of humankind...

Waiting on the Métro platform Cité, waiting above the ancient city of Lutetia, waiting for the barbarians who will eventually come, who will eventually destroy it all. Waiting for the modern invaders to arrive. Caesar saw his role as bringing civilization to savages, and thus the Romans were in Gaul overpowering the guilds of fishermen who inhabited the islands in the middle of the Seine while a couple of thousand years later Hitler said he was occupying

Paris because he needed more *lebensraum* (living-space). He was just stretching out his arms and shoulders—that's all. Every house or apartment needs a living room. His army just walked straight in—into an undefended city. The bridges weren't blown up, as had been planned. The front door of the house was left wide open.

Observe the signs on the platforms that tell you where you are. What ghostly pallor, what unearthly light, what radioactive green seeps through the Métro travellers as they are pulled along in their communal chariots? Travellers: their veins a map of the lines of the Métro. Each city-dweller a walking skeletal X-ray, pumped full of enough radioactivity to light up a hallway; a tracery of veins and arteries and tissue; structured with beautifully dense, complicated wiring; a walking power plant; a mobile knowledge-unit of emotion, superstition and memory; an ambulatory memory hard-wired with the climb out of the primeval slime and the struggle to survive.

Observe the advertising in the Métro corridors: red lips, two metres wide; teeth, half a metre long; a smile as an open cave; a leg, an office block; hair, a shop's awning; an eye, the dead side of the moon. Brightly lit gigantic faces coming at you as you turn the corner; gigantic boxes of toothpaste, of breath freshener, of underarm deodorant. Gerard Depardieu starring in the latest film; a film about lost love, according to the poster, about the impossibility of love—what else? What else would you expect?

Listen to the hysterical shrieking as you turn the corner. A young gipsy woman with her six-month-old daughter, she grabs your coat sleeve as you pass. She says:

—Give me money so my child may eat. I don't care for myself. It's so the child may eat. Look at the poor one. Doesn't she remind you of someone? Doesn't she remind you of yourself when you were young? She has a right to grow up healthy and tall. Give so that my child may grow old. You too were once small and defenceless. Yes, you too had to be looked after. You too had to be fed and burped and have your shit cleaned up...

You stand mesmerized by the unexpected intensity. Your thoughts had been elsewhere. You are now thrust into someone else's misery. Suddenly you are implicated. You want to get away. You do not want to grow old in the corridors of the Métro...amongst the passing mass of feet that scurry by daily—on their way to important affairs...affairs of the heart, affairs of business...many important things to do...a passionate massing of bodies on the platforms of the city. Things to do, people to see, a rendezvous to accomplish. As you descend the Métro stairs—a carnival at your feet. Swaying massed bodies descending to fill the gaping hole of the deserted platform. The quotidian passage from morning to evening.

Qui parle? No-one speaks. Things are just overheard.

The African drums, the African drums, a black man grabs your coat as you turn the corridor in the Métro, he wants a cigarette from you; the drums rattle away until they build up an edginess, a distress, an urban anxiety, amongst the lines, the grid of moving cattle-carriages, the endlessly moving ball-bearings; the oil endlessly applied to keep the whole show on the road. The willpower required to push humankind from here to there.

The Layers of the City

And if you're lost amidst the moving crowd on the moving walkways, consult your map on the back of your *carte orange,* that tells you where you are. Amongst the multilayered platforms...the *flics* are harassing the Algerian in the corner, he is searching for his identity card... the Métro-cleaners from Mali with their straw brooms are sweeping away the debris of dead cells, of lost hair, of broken cuticles. An ordinary day in midsummer...listless, relentless energy...all these particles on the move...restless atoms...mordant thoughts...keep the lid of the pressure cooker on...that we may not sink...and when the pressure cooker blows: Chernobyl—egg on your face. Life underground: do not eat the green leafy vegetables, do not drink the milk—something about the thyroid gland—and when the pressure cooker blows—SKY HIGH...Blue sky here we come...the radioactive green inside...outside, the white light, the streets are deserted, the feast day of the 8th of May: Liberation Day...Even the many-pointed hexagon could not keep the white light, the white heat from entering its borders; invasion via the airwaves; no Maginot Line strong enough to keep out the persuasiveness of the radioactive argument. White light, white heat...

*

Repeat after me:

    Bastille, Hôtel de Ville, Nation, Saint-Paul;

    Bonne-Nouvelle, Porte Dauphine, Michel-Ange Molitor;

    Iéna, Trocadéro, Charles de Gaulle-Etoile;

    Mabillon, Odéon, Saint-Sulpice, Gare de l'Est.

*

A scientific exchange of air in the Métro: 'For your Convenience, and Health—Warm Air Out, Cold Air In...'

At Michel-Ange Molitor the buses come and go; the spirit of the great sculptor presides over the oil-stained pavement. The buses prowl the city looking for fares. The clicking of tickets being validated. Identity passes being checked. Identity being validated. Place your right ear in the validating machine, Van Gogh style.

Regard the look in the Métro: abstracted, vacant, distracted. The bluish-yellow glow changing the colour of the skin to jaundice. Regard the look of the Métro-car driver: distant beyond belief, emptied out, staring at a fixed light in the tunnel, without foreground. The eyes are dead, not a flicker of emotion, the gaze—sphinxlike—fixed on the eerily lighted tunnels ahead; a study in perpetual motion. They say that when the eyes go, mesmerized by the repetition, it's simply the hands that do the rest...Underground thoughts, underground voyages. Above the Métro lines there are floors of people awash in deodorisers living their separate, impermanent lives.

Regard the look of the Métro stations early morning: dishevelled, though scrubbed around the edges, like a tramp in Sunday best. The cleaners in their green uniforms with their straw brooms sweeping up cigarette butts, throwing a bucket of disinfectant over the steps, trying to clean, to eradicate disease. To eradicate tuberculosis, now back in the Métro according to the local doctor. Children are particularly susceptible. Eradicated for ten years, now back. How do you clean the uncleanable?

That we might not sink under the weight of our own shit, said one of the Roman emperors (probably Augustus) of the first century anno Domini. So the emperor repaired the *Cloaca Maxima;* the Great Sewer of Rome that was first built by the Etruscans. The emperor's secular prayer: That we might not go under, under the weight of our own waste. That we might not bury ourselves under the weight of our own by-products...And then the pressure cooker blows sky high...What a waste: you cannot eat the green leafy vegetables that are open to the sky, you cannot drink the milk; the beaches are weighed down under the weight of oil spills when it rains. It rains acid from factories from Dusseldorf, from Nuremberg...The four horsemen of the Apocalypse come riding from the East...*blitzkrieg!*

In the corridors of the Métro: regard the well-dressed middle-class woman of fifty, obviously somebody's mother, sitting on the steps begging. She holds out a plastic box full of 10 franc coins with dignity and with her other hand she holds up a sign which says: I don't sing. I don't dance. But I do have to eat.

A young girl in a torn yellow silk dress sitting in the rain holding out a tin outside Monoprix; a dog on her lap. Her sign says: Please, we both need to eat.

Nearby: the carousel—not with horses and nostalgic music but miniature cars going around imitating the traffic; *la circulation,* which hardly circulates. On the periphery of the city—the architectural boxes rising upwards: on the streets, the shelter of cardboard boxes. In the early hours of the morning the flattened cardboard boxes open like the petals of a flower accepting sunshine to reveal... humankind.

That we might not sink under the weight of so many feet, mercilessly pounding the footpath, creasing the surface that holds us all together. In the apartments of the great city we have...humanity living on top of each other.

The Métro-cars snaking below, we walk the grand boulevards; the air above, filled with Harrier jump jets, Mirage fighter planes, Concordes, Sikorsky helicopters, the white light, white heat of failing nuclear reactors and the pink exhaust trails of the stream of never ending Boeings.

That we might not sink through all the layers of apartments and through onto the Métro platforms. The compression of the great city. The declension: compression: *une pression*: beer on tap: lives on tap: a pressure: a depression: a repression that keeps it all going in an orderly fashion. So many hopes and dreams. That we may not sink under the weight of all those hopes and dreams. That we may survive—to breathe again, when we climb out of the Métro. That we may not be condemned to life lived perpetually underground in the new Age of Radioactivity. With the white light above, the white light you cannot see. That we may not destroy our civilization with our failing power plants; that we may not die by our own hands: the knife to the throat, that sort of thing; the fatal accident of circulation, the heart attack, the blocked valves, clogged with Camembert and Brie, that sort of scenario; with the film crew just around the corner, waiting to take the irreplaceable footage of the spectacular celebrity car crash.

The Layers of the City

And the city? What does the city think of all this? The city is neutral. Subdivided, built upon, its marshes drained, its innards quarried for the limestone and gypsum to build the facades that sit proudly upon its worn-out soil. Owners bought the land above and below ground level; raping the subsoil to build above. Whole *arrondissements* (the Tenth, the Fifteenth) just waiting to fall into the holes created for the grandeur of the facades. The insides are hollow. The elegant apartments sit, and wait. Time is on the side of the earth that seeks to reclaim its own.

The expensive apartments. Inside: the private space: the Louis Quatorze cabinets and Louis Quinze chairs with the rope across (too valuable to sit on), together with the Louis Seize candlesticks. The apartment (that which keeps us all apart) is getting crowded—until there is no more space for living. There is no *lebensraum,* no living-space, no room to stretch out...The four pilots of the Apocalypse, riding Messerschmitts...

*

Repeat after me:
   Gare de Lyon, Gare du Nord;
   Châtelet, Châtelet, Châtelet.

*

That we may not sink. That we may not fall. That we may not reduce ourselves. That we might not shrink inwards under the weight of gravity. That we may not destroy each other. That we may not be absorbed into the crowd, never again to emerge into the white blinding light of perfumed summer. That we may escape, up the Métro stairs—disentangled finally from the metallic crush of the Métro-car as it rams a pylon. That we may not go under—weighed down by the continual exploratory incursions of the scalpel into the brain—as the experts go about their business of looking for signs of cancer.

The unearthly glow in the Métro carriage. The pale bluish-yellow light as we head towards Saint Denis, towards the *Stade de France*. The carriage is full—a football crowd. Every bag is suspicious. Every unattended bag holds a bomb. Five kilos of Semtex—no smell. A plastic bomb fitting snugly in a plastic bag. No-one will get out if it goes off now. Perpetually underground: our dust mixing in with the generations of living bodies who have gone before us, clutching their identity cards tightly to them as they would to a life-raft in a storm.

That we may live life above ground. That we may not fall over in our daily round. That we may live a life: *luxe, calme et volupté*. That we may not fall. That we may get through the day; and then through the next day, and the next, until we can afford the rent for our apartment: four flights up, the stairs are worn down, all those centuries of feet, and the plaster falls off with our steady breathing, as we climb; the windowed doorway out onto the street is cracked; the concierge has been sacked; the cooperative will not cooperate; this seventeenth-century apartment block is falling down. There is hardly any room to move within each apartment. There's hardly room for living.

That we may live life abundantly. That we may have beef and lamb on our tables, artichokes and endives too;

may have mustard from Dijon, and Roquefort with our wholemeal bread; may have Atlantic salmon, and that it may not be irradiated by the dispersal of waste from nuclear-powered submarines which now lie 'safely' on the bottom of the Atlantic Ocean. That we may have our aperitif before the meal, our glass of red from Médoc during the meal, and our nightcap after. That we may close our minds (and open our hearts) to the many small daily injustices which lie in wait ready to ensnare us. That we may not be reduced to frozen food. At the end of the Darwinian cycle we lie as frozen slabs of meat waiting to be consumed or, better still, waiting to be brought back to life—out of suspended animation—into the full glare of a hospital's birthing chamber and back to life; but only at the moment when they have found a cure for the cancer that has riddled our bones. That we may not be reduced to powdered soup. That our cupboards may not be bare. That we may live life everlasting—preserved in the brine of that first cocktail, the cocktail of evolution which spawned the human race, the insects and the seaweeds which lie at the bottom of the ocean (the mother of us all). That we may remember who we are—and how we got here.

*

Repeat after me:

Bobigny-Pablo Picasso, Stalingrad, Goncourt;
Châtelet, Châtelet, Châtelet.

*

Place names. Names whereby we are placed. Urban travellers, going home to apartments (where we keep each other apart) built above Métro lines. At night the Métro lines are singing. At night you lie awake, thoughts filled with Romans and barbarians; you can hear the Métro carriages beneath you turning a corner with that characteristic high-pitched whine. Your thoughts go down to those below: fellow-sufferers. In the courtyard, a rush of hot air—the exhaust from the Métro. In the dead of winter you have to throw off the covers at night because the air has become mysteriously warm. The pollution of the day has reached its zenith and falls back like an eiderdown to cover the city at 3 a.m.

That we may not fall under the great weight of the aspirations of those who live above us. Their dreams weighing them, and us, down with thoughts of consumer durables, of white goods, of new carpets and curtains, of a new computer; their washing machines and refrigerators about to effortlessly fall through the floorboards onto the hapless below. That their hopes and dreams may not crush us. That their nightmares of being chased, of sinking, of being burned alive in an exploding Jumbo at 33 000 feet may not keep us awake thrashing about in our beds with the insomnia of the blind, the wakefulness of the deaf, the dreariness of the bland politician and the banality of daily life. That we may wake up after a sleepless, frantic night into a full and glorious life. That the ancient sun may shine again with its restorative/deadly rays penetrating the damp and the gloom, the perpetual greyness of the leaden skies above.

That we may not fall through into the lives of those

below us—unsuspectingly carrying on imitations of our own lives: perfect replicas...with their health cards and social security numbers and tax file numbers and Master-Card numbers and employment numbers and phone numbers and identity card numbers etched into their fore-heads in an iridescent pink. They arise from their beds when we do. We hear them flushing their toilets seconds before we do. We share the same pipes: connection via refuse.

That we might look into one another's eyes and con-verse without interruption, for hours and hours, building upon what the other has said until we understand.

That we may not destroy others in our greed for gaso-line. Stealth jets being loaded with weapons; nervous young pilots scratching their cheeks in apprehension of the battle; television technicians taping down kilometres of cable; on Wall Street the stockbrokers go into a buying frenzy; their battle cry, the hymn of the republic, *May the dollar be strong again*; avgas in their nostrils; sweat trickling down the back of their necks; the smell of power is so sweet— like honey and apple blossom. The victory leading inexorably to a humiliation. To win an election you go all out to win a 'popular' war—and end up standing naked in defeat with blood falling from your wrists into warm buck-ets continually being rearranged by young children. The young pilots are climbing into the cockpits of their B-52 Bombers ready to send whole civilizations underground, perpetually; the battle cry *Return them to the Stone Age*.

That we may not end up as stage characters in a tourist's snapshot; mere oddities, amusements, spare parts in some-one else's documentary. That we may not be condemned to being perpetual tourists ourselves; caught in a documented orgy of consumerism. We are buying the sights and sounds and smells of other people's lives; we are intruding, we are capturing them on our Polaroids, we are collecting them as picturesque inhabitants, we are smiling at their quaint customs, laughing politely at their manners, posting pictures of 'the locals' on our web sites. We are the dead class; but the dying takes a lifetime.

That we may end up content rather than as someone else's content in *a media extravaganza.*

That we may not end up as someone else's social experiment. Our water full of poisons, our apples and pears irradiated into a glorious consumable radiance, our bacon continually recoloured to hide the telltale iridescent green. Our livers rotting with endless consumption: the oils and fat mounting in a symphony. Our kidneys working overtime to process the necessary and unnecessary drugs that aright the nervous condition of humankind. Neurosis providing us with our conversation: delirium, our poetry.

That we may escape the nightly incubus that comes to settle on our shoulders, our lips, our faces. That we may not end up perpetually underground: forced down by the weight of numbers; forced down by the crowd; the weight of tourists who come to look at us. That we may avoid the nightly succubus, who comes to steal our thoughts, by emptying ourselves—placing those thoughts in the bedside table under lock and key. We who are looking at those who look: looking to see who will stare the other out. We are all tourists in a fairground of mirrors; we carry our personas to work and back. We carry our passports, our identity cards, so we can check to see who we are. We carry each other's image—reflected in our eyes...We carry a memory of *humankind*.

That we may smile into the security cameras in the change rooms of the large department stores, in the streets of the city, in the banks, at the football grounds. Your appearance—public property: your thoughts—noted, quantified, arranged and filed. We who are insecure film on videotape the entire population of the city. The huge inter-linked databases toiling away into the night, cross-linking random events: a visit to the doctor, a visit to Social Security, a visit to the football, a subscription to a journal, an affiliation to a union, a chance meeting in the street.

Surveillance, Surveillance, Surveillance.

We believe in the modern miracle of science, we believe in the romance of adventure, in the equality of the sexes, we believe in the positivist-rationalist dream, we believe in the stability of words, we believe in the necessity of insurance, we believe in the obviousness of taxation, we believe in the obligation of individuals to pursue the full attainment of a maximum utilization of personal happiness, we believe...If it all gets too much there is always Prozac.

We believe in the crowd in the Métro. We believe in the smell of fear, the smell of compression, of exhaustion, of indignation, of curiosity, of perfume that's gone off—chemicals quietly rotting. We believe in the human river, the circulating bodies, receptacles of warm blood, carriers of flesh, coat-hangers of tissue, portmanteaus of breath, of neurons, of desires, of electrical impulses, of passion...Pass the deodorant. We believe in desire, that night will fall, that morning will come again, we believe in exhaustion...

We believe in the cry of the infant, we believe in the wheaten smell of the head of a newborn baby, we believe in the warmth of the body, we believe in the necessity of words, we believe in the felicity of the child just learning to speak, we believe in the silence of the forest, in the darkness of the night, in the blueness of the sea, in the enigma of the individual...

The crowd in the Métro: apprehensive, listening to quiet conversations occasionally taking place in the bluish-yellow light. On the platforms the crowd stares up at the gigantic faces advertising toothpaste, stockings, dental floss, the latest Hollywood film, invitations to a journey to Noumea—palm trees in the background, oiled brown flesh in the foreground, the golden sun coiled above all...waiting to pounce.

We believe in death duties, we believe in email, we believe in the World Cup, in videos, in CD-ROMs, in the Internet. We believe in department stores, in escalators, in lifts, in light bulbs, in refrigerators, in washing machines, in clothes dryers, in power drills, in television sets. We believe in electricity, in the importance of the individual, in the necessity of corporations to maximize their profits on behalf of shareholders. We believe in the nation-state, the UN and the judicious use of the red card.

We have come by various routes to end up here on this underground platform at this particular time. You look around at your fellow human beings, those with whom you share space, time and collective memory. We have come by plane, by ship, by steamer, by tugboat, by helicopter, by truck, by automobile. We are literally lost: we carry our hopes and delusions in the back pockets of our jeans, next to the crumpled map...Our guidebooks will tell us where to go, what to see and how to feel. We arrive in sparkling planes at Charles de Gaulle, in summer, in winter...pilgrims all...looking for a way out, an exit from self, the suffocation of the individual consciousness...on a personal crusade.

The Métro-cleaners look at their booty, while discussing Ricardo Muti. The Métro-cleaners ask each other how they feel, while discussing conductors at the Bastille. They ask each other who will go to hear the next concert of Rodrigo.

*

Repeat after me:

Europe, Pigalle, Château-d'Eau;
La Défense, Dupleix, Monceau;
Concorde, Concorde, Concorde.

*

There's something humble in the gestures of the early-morning risers who go down into the bowels of the earth to earn their daily bread; down the escalators of the Métro—with heads bowed, thinking innumerable thoughts, the daily anxieties, the bills to pay, the lack of money, the counting of days until payday, the amount due on the credit card—the stumbling forward into the light of the Métro, the sudden explosion of noise, the persuasive African drums at Châtelet. Going forward like humble sleepwalkers—

waiting for a destiny to unfold itself. Going forward with quiet rosewater dreams. The crowds waiting patiently for the doors of La Bonne Samaritaine to open so they can pick up their bargains. The buses pick up and set down passengers and crawl past the Palais Royale. The organ-grinder outside Notre-Dame gets his picture taken a hundred times a day. He orders a pastis at the outside café and recites a list of RATP autobus lines, including their places of departure and terminus points, to pass the day.

*

Repeat after me:

Liberté, Liberté, Liberté;

Châtelet, Châtelet, Châtelet.

*

Waiting on the RER platform of Pont-St-Michel, amidst the roar of the trains and the smell of damp; waiting above the ancient city of Lutetia Parisiorum; waiting for the barbarians who will eventually destroy the city. The city that survived the Nazis, hardly touched at all; the open city; the branch bending, so it need not break in the firestorm. The city springs back to life, supple city, with remarkable ease— the grand city of imperial dreaming. Caesar claimed his role was to subdue the savages of Gaul and bring the sweet light and powerful fragrance of civilization to the savages who were living in an animal state. Hitler said it would have caused him considerable pain to destroy Paris for he had often dreamed of the great city in his youth: Leningrad, on the other hand—no pain at all. And the great city did

not let him down; when he stood on the terrace of the Tro-
cadero looking towards the Eiffel Tower he was amazed by
the sight of the city spread out before him. It was reported
by a scriptor that the Devil took Christ onto a mountaintop and said *All this will be yours if you lie down before
me and worship me*, or words to that effect.

Going down by the moving stairs, onto the RER platform St-Michel, validate your ticket, validate your ticket,
going down into the artificial light, down into Lutetia Parisiorum, slushing around amongst the fishermen and the
fisherwomen of the guilds of the islands of the Seine—a
safe place to be, cut off by water from the surrounding
savages, from the *Others* out there in the darkness, curled
up in the safety of shelter. Caesar will save you, don't
worry, will provide you with central heating, running water.
Those Roman gods of order, civility and system will save
you from the natural state of primitivism. Running water—
clean water in, dirty water out: scientifically arranged *For
Your Convenience*. We are the children of the Romans. They
are the forebears of the supermarket, fast food, plastic cards,
nuclear power and the great war-machines, etc. etc. The
great technologues of their day; inventors of the modern
bureaucratic state.

The Gauls were amazed at the complexity and ingenuity of the Romans' war-machines, such as the giant hook
(the *talon*) that could be swung from the battlements and
into the bodies of those invaders who were climbing the
walls. But what the Romans couldn't fight against were
those who would simply wait; those who did not believe
in order, rationality, convenience and comfort; those who

did not believe in a centralized system of government; those who were ungoverned and ungovernable. The Romans were powerless against anyone who did not believe in what they themselves believed in. Nothing so destabilizes as disbelief.

The barbarians would not play by the same rules. All the Roman predictions of how the barbarians would behave were worthless. The Romans had to try to learn about the state of mind of the barbarian with its apparent lack of past or future; instead, an ongoing present. The barbarians seemed so much *older* than the Romans—as though they belonged to another century. What amazed the Romans was that the barbarians had no respect for buildings or property, and *they did not work*. They did not fill their days with *productivity*. They just existed.

What ghostly pallor, what blank staring emanates from the RER passengers, locked like gladiators from the Arena of Lutetia in the communal embrace of the exhausted city workers, on their way home...The arena is quiet now— only a few students from the nearby university of Jussieu reading *Libération*. An arena for ten thousand; it could be filled with water, for nautical games, for *sport*. War by other means. Sport came about through the inability of a paying public to see a war taking place: they could hear the racket, but could not see the effect. Now if you could only package war and sell tickets you could make a fortune! The gladiators oiling their bodies, dressing in ceremonial robes—for the slaughter. Slaves mainly, or else a few free men so steeped in anomie they were waiting for a chance to lose their life publicly in front of an appreciative crowd...

Fighter pilots in full-dress uniform sitting down to silver service. Civilization means silver cutlery and gold plates on the dinner table: the ceremonial meal before climbing into the cockpit to bomb the hell out of 'primitive' societies. Primitive societies are those without credit cards, without identity numbers, without life insurance, superannuation: all those things that make a society truly great. An integrated society where you can't even sneeze without it being video-taped, annotated and filed on huge cross-linked databases. War: an affront to pride: vanity—the bombing of a retreating ancient civilization: you bomb it because its recorded civilization goes back thousands of years: you bomb it because you read about it as the birthplace of civilization in primary school textbooks. The great democracies can't survive without villains: can't survive without the OTHER, without the nightly incubus on the painfully rising chest...

That we may breathe without obstruction, that we may eventually wake from the nightmare...That we may not black out on our daily round...That we may not bore ourselves to death with our own meaningless conversation and banal dreams...What a civilization we have constructed: order, regimentation, discipline...

Waiting on the platform St-Michel...The air is evacuated from the underground station just before the train arrives—to avoid the vacuum effect: a sucking in of people towards the train, to fill the vacuum of departing air. A vacuum cleaner on rails cleans the underground lines during the five hours in the morning which are reserved for maintenance of the tracks. An expelling and inhaling of air: that's the way we all keep going, in 5-second intervals. We inhale the air from Saxony, from Gothenburg, from Salzburg and expel it over Mont Blanc, over the Amazon, over Tetuán...

Maintenance of a city: when the Nazis invaded, it was instructed that life in the great city should go on as normal; there were just new masters, that's all. The Métro ran, the markets were open, the music halls were open; everyone had to be careful, that's all.

The Romans in Lutetia were seduced by a love of water—not to contemplate, but to use: to recline in, to drink, to carry away waste products. At the same time as the barbarians were setting up camp outside the walls of the great city, the Romans were in the process of moving from the gymnasium into the steam room, then into the hot baths (the *caldarium*), the lukewarm baths (the *tepidarium*), then into the cold baths (the *frigidarium*) before moving on to being massaged and anointed with seven different oils.

Successful barbarian invasions had already taken place in the north-east of Gaul and there was no shortage of information about the numbers killed. There was much speculation about the nature of the barbarians camped a few kilometres from the walls of the Romans. Speeches were required for every occasion and the forthcoming invasion was no different. One of the tasks of the local senators was to compose and deliver speeches. Speeches can accomplish many things: they are, after all, the foundation stones of civilization.

Behold the traffic as it weaves its way around the place de la Concorde, around the Luxor obelisk, in a spirit of autonomous movement. Over ten thousand people die on French roads each year. Writers in particular die on the roads. In a spirit of individualism everyone has the right to die for their country on the roads. Just like anywhere, though...Regard the genial bus driver, cracking jokes as he crawls at a snail's pace during the morning peak hour (slower than the horse-and-cart public transport of the nineteenth century). He is taking you to the Tuileries so you can catch a glimpse of life lived above ground.

Waiting outside the gates of the city are the barbarians: the Romans' dark selves—the flip side of the Romans' rationality, love of order, love of fine speech, love of clean clothes, of perfumes, love of water. It's like wherever the Romans go they have to drag these barbarians with them: they're the Romans' night-selves. When those Roman men and women of Narbonensis finally fall into bed exhausted, take off their fine silk togas, and let those exquisite perfumes (frankincense, myrrh and the essence of gold) fade away, it's like the barbarians hop into bed with them, sharing their warmth (for they themselves are creatures of the cold), sharing their luxury (for they themselves are creatures of hardship), sharing their communality (for they themselves are creatures of spartan individuality who come together by chance), sharing their cleanliness (for they themselves are encrusted with layers of dirt and blood and sweat).

You are aware of the loneliness of the past. You are aware of how far you have travelled. Strings of DNA replicating themselves peacefully, chromosomes building themselves in the night air, nucleotide letters creating a gene complex—the building blocks of humanity, of civilization. Blocks of monuments created; built stone by stone by patient builders; like the Luxor obelisk created for Rameses III, now standing in the place de la Concorde; covered in writing, telling a long and complicated tale, of what? Of love and romance? Of kings and queens? Of the numbers of battalions in the army? The ownership of real estate? Or of succession, dynasties, instructions on power, how to get it, what to do with it when you've got it? Strings of messages handed down by generations of familial members—codes wherein we're written. Blue eyes or brown? Green perhaps. And where did we learn to kill each other? Which code in the DNA string says we have to blow each other up in some final apocalyptic Wagnerian crescendo? Radioactive dust blowing in from the East. Radioactive strains seeping into the water table. Is this our destiny— for the sake of *electricity*? The warmth, the entertainment, the usefulness. Vast power plants by the side of the Rhône as you effortlessly glide past in the TGV on your way to St Rémy-de-Provence and the ruins of Glanum. The Rhône in Roman times was the temporary dividing line: the barbarians on one side of the river, civilization on the other.

You go out into the street. You wonder where everyone is for it is a weekday after all. You know the radiation cloud passed overhead a week ago. But then you see a poster and you realise it is May the 8th—Liberation in Europe Day, so you descend into the Métro once more, emerging on the Avenue des Champs-Elysées in time to see the national riot police (the CRS) on the roofs of the buildings, semi-automatics loaded and ready to fire; the presidential parade driving past at quick speed—anyone could be inside those black bullet-proof Mercedes with the laminated windows; the bored gendarmes observing a motley crowd; a policewoman wearing burgundy lipstick and beautiful shoes coquettishly chatting up an officer, girlishly twirling a blonde curl with an errant finger, shifting her weight from one foot to another to hold his attention, pushing back another lock of hair which has slid over her left eye; he, meanwhile, is trying to watch the parade—his walkie-talkie poised by his lips, ready to communicate a message.

After the parade you stand on the edges of the place de la Concorde and wonder which way to go. The day is your own, you can go in any direction you choose. You stand immobilized by the necessity of choice. The tree exists because it branches two ways at each tip: one divides itself into two; each of the two tips divide into two and so on. Human beings only exist because each cell divides into two. The building process is unavoidable. Cells dividing, cells dying. You notice another flower-seller and you remember all of the others you have seen today, all selling the same flowers—must be the flower of the anniversary, whatever that may be—you do not know its name.

*

Repeat after me:
    Replication, ceremony, sacrifice;
    Concord, harmony, renewal;
    Forgetfulness and memory.

*

Nightfall, you enter the carriage at the Métro station Châtelet and stand because it is so crowded. Wet umbrellas lying about. Steam rising from wet coats. Near you, two thirty-year-old Americans—a man and a woman—speaking loudly:

—She left her plastic surgeon husband to run off with an HIV-positive jazz musician who can't speak English. The husband tracked them down, found them in a little one-star hotel near the St-Martin canal. Tried to turn them both over to the gendarmes for a supposed crime against humanity.

—Don't talk so loudly, people can hear.

—Don't worry about them. *They* can't speak English.

All the heads turn with disdain to look at the speakers. The connecting tissue, the fabric of life, the breath of the crowd, the circulatory intensity; above-ground the fear of the herd, the bottles and rocks thrown at the advancing security forces, the charge of the security forces (whose security is at stake?); below ground in the safe womb of the Métro the emptied-out faces of a holiday crowd off to the football in a state of childlike delight. Your heart pumping, now looking around at the benign faces you are suddenly calm, you have left the agitated crowd behind, you have left the blood on the pavement behind, and the few trampled bodies. When a crowd of three hundred thousand decides to run you decide to run too. You cannot argue with that force, you cannot stand still any longer. Mindlessly running your eyes over the many faces amassed in May Day solidarity in the place de la Bastille: a crowd of workers, of students, of academics, of painters, standing around in the early May sunshine under the July column, under the rotor blades of the circling police helicopters, in range of the cannon and machine guns of the tanks of the security forces. And then the panic. The pushing, the shoving, the almost joyful release into locomotion.

We are all connected—the crowd, the security forces, the Métro-train driver, the helicopter pilot, the President of the Republic behind his tinted windows: all connected by lines of DNA—a shared linkage of genes, of ancestry, branching out into many different pathways but sharing the same basic genetic structure. Our ancestors came down from the trees, came out of the mud and slime of the Cambrian era; shellfish and corals leading to insects, tetrapods, dinosaurs, hominids, modern humans—what next? Periodically the dominant life of the planet is wiped out—to be replaced by other life forms which then become dominant. Have we had our turn on Earth yet? Should we make way yet? Or wait another thousand years or so? Can we put in an ambit claim in order to stay?

We are all connected by the place we live in. We breathe the same (radioactive) dust, we throw away the same (toxic) waste. We shop at Monoprix, humbly bringing along our own plastic bags. We buy our CDs at FNAC, our books at Gibert Jeune. We read the same tragedies in the same newspapers, listen to the same dulcet tones of the nightly newsreader. We age in seconds as measured by an atomic clock. We are dis-eased. Out of ease. Ease is something left over in the vestigial memory. We live over and above and beside each other, stealing each other's air, sneezing into

each other's faces. We are impinged upon by, and implicated in, other people's lives. We share this space with all
who have gone before us. We breathe the fumes of exhaust
created by someone else. The modern city, the great caul-
dron, the crush of bodies, the place of comfort and of
despair. Unsustainable; lacking in sufficient sustenance.

You step off the rue de Rivoli and enter W.H. Smith's
English Bookshop. You are looking for a particular book.
Perhaps one that has not yet been written. You are bumped
accidentally by a handsome woman with a boyish face and
a mass of curls who apologises in French, but she has
knocked a book off the shelves which lies at your feet. It
is a paperback: *A Thousand Nights and a Night (Alf Laylah
wa Laylah)*. A wife (spelt Shahrazâd in this version) tells
stories to a Persian king. It is a modernized French translation—published this year—of a nineteenth century
English translation of the notoriously unreliable 1548
French translation by Antoine Galland. You open it at
random and read to yourself while standing in the bookshop with the full sunlight flooding in from the side
windows. As always you become lost (totally, hopelessly,
inextricably) in reading. You want to find out what happens at the end of a short tale within a tale before being
moved on by a shop assistant. You feel her accusatory eyes
peering at you from behind a counter and you reluctantly
return the book to its shelf, making a mental note to return
tomorrow to read the denouement.

You are about to go but you notice a book out of the
corner of your eye which asks to be picked up. You turn
to its back cover. You read: *This is a novel which at first*

glance doesn't appear to be a novel. It seems, at first glance,
to be all true. It's only later, after you have read each and
every word and thought about each and every word that
you will realize you have been reading a contemporary folk-
tale, albeit one written in an enigmatic way, which does
not give up its forking paths easily.

You are intrigued and want to know more, but at that
specific moment the book you are reading is knocked from
your hands by the handsome woman with the boyish face,
either accidentally or on purpose, you cannot tell. The book
lies in ruins on the floor, its spine broken, its pages scat-
tered as if there's been an automobile accident. You shuffle
the debris together, in any order, and take the dead book
to the counter to pay for it, feeling somehow responsible
for its fate. Your curly-haired assailant takes the book from
your hands, apologetically, and insists that as it was her
fault entirely that the book was destroyed it is only fair
that she pays for it and takes it home 'for mending'. She
speaks very quickly in that familiar-sounding educated
Parisian accent. She pays and disappears out the door in
an instant—as if she had never existed. Amazing, you
think: something has just happened, but you're not sure
what. It's time for a coffee.

You emerge from the darkness of the Métro, climb the
stairs to your apartment and switch on your Macintosh.
You access the Internet: the virtual world is more engross-
ing than the real world. Nine hours later, in the morning
you emerge into the real world feeling disorientated. You
shrink away from people. You have Internet sickness. You
are hyperventilating. The real world is insubstantial, vague.

But your feet are carrying you back to the computer, and your communications, across the globe, small as it is.

The weight of the past weighs heavily on all those concerned with the present... When your past is invasion that's how you feel—invaded, degraded, compromised. When your title is 'Displaced Person' that becomes your identity: you inhabit your title. The habit of each successive generation is to rewrite the rules by which the previous generation is judged. There is not necessarily anything fair about this, but why should that be the case anyway? One invades, the other is invaded. Luckily, memory is so fragmentary, fragile, so short and transitory, just like caches of information/emotion skimming across the high seas at a great rate of knots... The past accumulates and rubs off in the form of dead cells as we push up against each other in the crowded Métro carriage. We are in this together, whether we like it or not.

Hitler felt the weight of the Holy Roman Empire lying across his shoulders. Seeing no-one thought he could paint as well as Claude Lorrain or Poussin, he decided to do something that couldn't help but be noticed. And what is more noticeable than fire? Everyone loves to see the flames leap. Not in one's backyard of course, but a fire, someone else's fire, is spectacular. And what better way to make a colourful, splashy statement than through the old Roman way, with brand new technology and iron-clad discipline? *Work makes you free.* And that sort of particular freedom makes you dead. Brand new aeroplanes: Messerschmitts. Like a howling wind. Blowing in over Poland like a swarm of honey-bees on a summer's day.

The Layers of the City

The Roman war-machines—like the *talon*—were so exotic that the Gauls used to stand with mouths agape. But not the barbarians. They were so old, in mind, that nothing impressed them. They were born old, like Neanderthals. They had no need to scratch themselves endlessly to see what their origins were. You could tell by taking a sample of tissue and putting it under a still-to-be-invented microscope. All those helixes and double-helixes, those long strands of genetic string tying us up in loops. What can't be grasped rationally can be grasped intuitively. Blocks are to be played with, after all.

Hitler needed a painting teacher to tell him he was a genius—then everything would have been all right. He needed a patron to buy his watercolours and tell him he was the match of Claude Lorrain, and then everything would have been all right. Or would it?

When Prometheus asked himself how he could raise Man to the level of the gods he decided he would steal fire, risking his own destruction in the process. Hitler saw the world as comprising Gods and Beasts, majesty and slavery. Those who lived above, on the mountaintops, and those who lived below, in the underground. Those who represented the light and those who represented the dark. As many commentators have noted, Hitler made war on himself, in the first instance: on the darkness of his skin and hair, the shortness of his stature, on his own physical weakness. His praise—for the strong Nordic Germanic ideal—was reserved for what he was not. It was as though Hitler, despising that part of himself who was the failure of the beer halls and the doss houses of Vienna, declared war on all who reminded him of himself. Out of a self-hatred comes a willingness for everyone to die.

Bloodlines: veins, valves and pumps; straddling the world, connecting all to all. The mixing of bloodlines—a communication of all the world's past. Interrelatedness.

Much written about, Hitler the barbarian becomes the twentieth-century enigma, the riddle, the sphinx. Residing at the core of the century he is the centripetal force around which all politicians and governments revolve; all who come after have to deal with his legacy. Picking up the pieces. Sorting out. Cataloguing. Arranging the files. Burning out the evidence.

Given to fits of nervous illness and being anxious at turning fifty, Hitler invades Poland. A mid-life crisis brings on World War II; a fatal neurasthenia. A death-wish that is as primordial as the destruction of the dinosaurs—those overweight, unhealthy, unhappy creatures who grew so heavy in their conquering swagger that they could no longer chase their prey and were forced to recline on the ground, melancholically; but even supine, they were still above the height of the trees which provided them with no shelter from the sun. When Hitler had just about given up hope he decreed that the enemy should find only 'death annihilation and hatred', and that anything of use to the enemy should be destroyed. Albert Speer—the insider, the intellectual, the court artist—was given orders to burn Germany. Like Sardanapalus before him, if the ruler was about to die then everything would die with him. Even his rhetoric. The speechmaker would pass into oblivion leaving millions dead and millions upon millions more with blood-curdling nightmares and a loss of self, a loss of belief in the essential goodness of their fellow human beings, a loss of security in the beneficence of progress and of science.

When the atomic bombs were dropped on Hiroshima and Nagasaki, when the concentration camps were discovered in Dachau and Auschwitz, it signalled the end of the age of confidence in technology. The Romans' love of war-machines finds its apotheosis in the atomic bomb. The same inquiring mind which produces clean running water and penicillin makes it possible to turn cities inside out so they are left as ruins. All done in the name of civilization. The modern gods—of science, of political and industrial power, of wealth, of influence—have made it possible to return inhabitants of cities to underground cave-dwellers with omnipresent radiation at ground level that they cannot see or taste or smell.

With the invention of nuclear power and the subsequent 'unavoidable accidents' everything ingested could be fatal—even air. The future of humankind lies underground amongst the sewers and pipes and Métro stations. Henceforth, it has come to pass that the citizens of the world would be fearful of air. This is a relatively new phenomenon. Nerve gas was used during World War I but apart from that the air itself had not been used before as a weapon of war. Murder by gas in the concentration camps. Henceforth citizens would fear the air in the same way their forebears had feared the barbarians and feared the plague. Fire, of course, had been long feared as a means of warfare. Cities like Rome and Paris have been burnt down and rebuilt many times in an endless cycle of destruction and renovation.

The gods became bored with overhearing the petty jealousies of women and men. They, the gods, after all, had their own tiresome squabbles with each other to contend with. They became the first storytellers—endlessly boring each other with stories of how fleet of foot Hermes was, how sexy Diana was, what a scamp that Pan was—until they ran out of stories and checked out of the All-Nite motel on the mountaintop they called home and slouched off somewhere to die a hero's death—in some crocodile-infested swamp somewhere, far away from their homelands and the essential comfort of a familiar place. Despair, endless travelling to get away from a suffocating and nauseating sense of self: the Twentieth Century of Dis-placement.

When they quarried out the Métro lines in Paris the excavators found piles of bones, human skeletons, here a head, there a foot. And how did they feel—those excavators? Did they feel grand? Connected? Happy to be alive? They felt inconvenienced. By thoughts of mortality? No, the skeletons were slowing down their work. They would be late home for lunch. The daily baguette would already have been eaten, the coffee in the cup would be covered with motes of dust, the wife's kiss would have a stale taste, like she's been in bed all morning with her cigarette-smoking Spanish lover. In quarrying they come across an ancient graveyard: the past rearing its ugly head again. They feel annoyed. Why can't the past leave us alone? they say to each other. It means nothing to us. We who are the moderns. We who are without superstition. We who have killed our king, and murdered his wife. We who have dismantled the authority of the Church, until even its officiants feel embarrassed by their place in the scheme of things.

*

Repeat after me:

Work makes you free;

Excavation, Evacuation, Equivocation;

Concentrate, concentrate, concentrate.

*

The waste. On the Ile de la Cité, a block of apartments has just fallen in—underneath was hollow—while we were walking by. The debris is being carted away. Just a vast hole remains. We are looking down like explorers in a Jules Verne novel for signs of prior life. If indeed Jules Verne was right then we should be able to look through the reverse end of this dusty old telescope and see the remains of old Lutetia. We look and see bones in the water, a centurian's helmet, a pinch of salt, lead pipes (a convenient excuse for the downfall of the Empire). The Romans just got tired; the responsibility of running the known world became too much for them. They succumbed to migraines, fits of nervous illness; the pressure got too much for them; it blew them sky high, like a gas leak finding fire and a point of combustibility.

Water made the Empire great, water lead to its downfall. When the barbarians destroyed the aqueducts of Rome in 455 leaving the good citizens dependent on the Tiber, they had clearly attacked the lifeline of a civilization.

Jealousy, envy, revenge: how the world turns on its axis. Rome burns for lack of water while Nero sings. The Romans ran out of salt to pay their soldiers and ran out of water to comfort them, and thus the collective will faded. The inhabitants could no longer believe in the meaning of 'empire'; nor could the emperor, who had the most to lose. When the master architect ceases to believe, then all is lost. Multiplicity, duplicity. It's all a matter of belief. You can keep saying that you won't be let down, that the people would rather die than be defeated, but in the end the people have a thirst and a hunger and a desire to be safe that won't go away...won't be soothed away by words.

We come out of a space—we are placed by birth in a nexus of currents, a confluence of streams that unite: fore-bears travelling from opposite ends of the globe randomly encountering each other in the best surrealist fashion, by chance. How many connections do we individually each hold within us? We are connected to a civilization that pre-dates us; we use a language we did not create; we borrow a particular set of words for the duration of our passage; we go to and fro with our ship's clock strapped to our backs so we can plot where we are; multiple lines of origin intersecting in each of us; a maternal line and a paternal line intersecting in a cultural soup—the mixing of strands of being, strands of meaning. We hold the Romans and the barbarians within us, unable to throw them off even if we were capable. At nightfall we long to be free. In the morn-ing we seek captivity. We go gently, humbly to our allotted desk in the workplace and go submissively home at evening into the dusk. We go down to the port and watch the ships prepare to sail (the embarkation state of mind). We are perpetually preparing to journey, to set forth, to renew a primitive pattern of wandering. We look anxiously, enviously at the Airbus overhead laboriously rising with fully laden tanks of avgas to cruising altitude. What set us on this journey in the first place? We did not ask for the ticking to be turned on, but now we have been set in motion like a wind-up toy with red chromium plating and a destination in mind...

The future of civilization is in digital form. Zeros and ones: value added and raw material; the absence and presence of an electrical charge. The word goes zinging across the world's telephone wires, goes bouncing off the world's satellites skimming above our heads in mellifluous patterns illuminating the night sky. The primitive message-post is now a hunk of junk flying around in low orbit. Once you had to strap the wings of Mercury on to your feet in order to pass on the message, or else run the twenty-six miles and 385 yards to Marathon and then drop down dead, but now you can feel your own messages pass overhead at the speed of sound.

The future of civilization is in apartments. We will all end up living above and below our nemesis. Their footsteps above us, their effluvium rushing past us down the wall next to the Macintosh computer and the CD-player and the banana lounge and the stack of videos of old Humphrey Bogart and Lauren Bacall movies with the radio-dial tuned to the soothing tones of France-Musique. As long as we are kept apart by a pastrami-thin slice of prepressed concrete everything will be all right. So our thoughts don't have to tangle (like so many strands of hair) with those above us. So our hands and legs and arms don't get in the way: the inconvenience of bodies. Inconvenient how they rot. We all return to dust, via a corruption of the thought process; a scrambling of the zeroes and ones. The elegant solution of cancer: it is only through the multiplication of cells that we are alive in the first place; quietly working away while we sleep; a multiplication of the perverted cells. A copy of *Rear Window* sitting by the video-player in a patch of early morning sunlight, near the binoculars. We are part of our neighbours' present: those above us and those below us; we are integrated vertically into their lives. Insert one or more humans between prepressed concrete, squeeze gently until the insides come out, and serve.

The future of civilization is in the movies. If we just keep acting everything will be all right. All shall be well. All manner of things shall be well. We can act as if the cameras weren't turned on. Act spontaneously, so to speak. Act with our mouths shut. Or crammed full of blueberry tarts, of foie gras, of Camembert and Brie; visceral fat stalking the organs, like barbarians at the gates. We shall act nonchalant, as if it doesn't matter. We shall act cool until the high-beam film lights are turned off and we can fall in a heap and unravel in private, dissemble in private, with just a fifty-strong camera crew to keep us company. The brilliant sunshine outside, the sounds of the country in our memory banks, the memory of a running brook loaded with unfreezing snow, the delicate etching of wind through the pine trees on the nervous tracery of the mind. The logic board is up and running; parts all imported.

The Layers of the City

That we may not expire due to over-consumption; our arteries clogged with Roquefort and *fromages de chèvre*; our veins awash with salt, our brains clogged with binary oppositions.

We walk over bodies as we go about our daily business; the bodies of previous generations, buried deep within the ruins, buried deep within the subconscious. We carry our forebears with us as we travel over the communication/navigation lines of the planet; we are without hope, without trust, we forge on regardless, with our little bibles—our passports and identity cards—clutched grimly in our hands, our email addresses stapled to our ears, fastened for perpetual safekeeping. Lose your identity card and that's it, you're gone—no identity; erased electronically from the great database of life which embraces us in omnipresent digital space. End-of-the-millennium, start-of-the-millennium malaise. It happens once in a while—a particular tiredness in the bones, a certain calcification, a certain numbness, hayfever, migraines. Marcel Proust cocooned in swathes of fur venturing out in the dead of night to the Ritz, to feel a sense of family, of belonging, borrowing from the head waiter only to return the money instantly as a tip, repaying him the next night with interest.

The future of civilization is in your head. You are playing a nightly movie with a broken-down score on a screen not much bigger than your retina. Flashbacks from your personal past come back to you in the form of intertitles. The film-stock is covered with scratches and brandy stains. The child-star has been shot, for 'genetic reasons'. You've been called in at the last moment to give credibility to the whole. You've been told that your contribution is valued and it is *so good you could make it at short notice.* But at the last moment you've been tapped on the shoulder and told you're to be an 'extra' in a so-called 'feel-good' film about the end of civilization. The film with the child-star has been deleted: too awkward, too difficult. The producer wants a happy ending for the new film, not because he believes in any of this—he doesn't believe in anything any-more—but because he knows what sells. So you screen this film, nightly, in your head about fifty times before going to sleep. While you sleep your fax machine propped up on your bedside table whirrs quietly away with messages from Dante's Inferno; nightly updates on who's been admitted into the seven circles of hell. Someone is desperate for you to know. Lately your fax machine has become a *smart* machine all by itself: the number you punch in is randomly changed to another number and your private, cryptic messages end up on an anonymous machine where you interrupt someone else's sleep on the other side of the globe.

The future of civilization is in our genes. We pass down our genetic codes in all sorts of accidental ways. Late one drunken night, between the ending of one forgettable day and the beginning of the next, in between many glorious bottles of wine and a warm Camembert you create a child, in that hapless way of all generations past. We all look for-ward to a bright new shining millennium with ecstatically happy consumer durables to wash over us and make us clean. When we drown we do so gracefully—looking like Esther Williams. The vanished era of fifties' TV: *wholesome* values, *happy families* set within a patriarchal milieu sitting down to watch the TV together. TV as the only remaining cultural glue—binding a globe together, enmeshing a set of beliefs with desired, modelled behaviour patterns. Test patterns late at night as the content fades...or is that a program? Is that the music from 'Seinfeld' in the background? That our consumer goods, at least, may have everlasting life...

The future of civilization is in atomic energy (so said a leading Soviet academician recently). He didn't say a thousand rads will kill you within hours or days.

Acting: thinking: action—and back to thought again. The poverty of thought. How do we all get up every morning—like automatons—and go to work? Like *robotniks*. Look at the freeways at seven in the morning choked with cars coming in from the *banlieue,* unable to move, individuals locked in private space. In the end it's all quite remarkable that it all keeps ticking over. It all works so (relatively) smoothly. The bus lane has buses in it, the elevated train tracks are compressed with trains, the footpaths are jam-packed. All are going about their allotted task; little bodies taking little minds along for the ride. The music from Walkmans is loud and brash. Doing the cakewalk...Looking up at the messages...Looking for a sign: how do I get off this ring-road? Who's ringing now on the mobile phone?

*

Repeat after me:

Mass age, message, massage.

Communicate, communicate, communicate.

Prozac, Prozac, Prozac.

*

There is no longer the village square to comfort us, to distract us. The local café has been turned into a convenience store. The *clochards* lie above the warm air from the Métro vents. *What is to be done?* (The great Russian question of the late nineteenth century.) Massage the mass age, with advertising; massage the message: the message is selling. What's left to be said anyway?

Another bomb goes off in the Métro—in a crowded train during evening peak hour at St-Michel station. Someone is trying to send someone a message; five kilos of plastic explosive as the message stick: beating out a deadly song via sound waves. Ironically, the protest message is usually one about injustice: a minority group is talking to the majority about how unfairly the former has been treated at the hands of the latter; it is a message designed to gain maximum attention (and sympathy?) for the message. Pity about all the spilt blood; the glass in tissue and sinew and bone; pity about the child with her left arm dangling forlornly out of its elbow socket; pity about the teddy bear with its head blown off exposing its straw innards.

*

Repeat after me:
Correspondance, correspondence;
Métro, work, sleep.
Châtelet, Châtelet, Châtelet.

*

The Layers of the City

Names and naming: street names we use daily, Métro stations we use daily. Named after people, after places where people died. The amazing resonance of 'Austerlitz': how many died there? Napoleon, 1805, Russian and Austrian armies, snow covered with blood...We use it as a train station; a point of convergence. We use it as a switching point, to change lines—but its meaning lies buried; or else its meaning keeps changing as time changes. We incorporate it into our daily routine. 'Bastille': once again, a train station; its meaning? Shifting in the wind. The past implicating itself in the present. Insisting itself, upon those with memory. To be empty of meaning: to be free? To be an empty vessel. Freedom makes you work? Work makes you *free*? The blood-stained twentieth century.

*

Remember after me:
Repeat Repeat Repeat;
Remember Remember Remember.

*

And forgetting, and sleep as the connecting passage from one to the other. Sleep as the video-eraser of the mind—getting rid of all of those unwanted frames-per-second; all those strange meetings where not a word was transferred successfully; all those illicit conversations where the words kept slipping, just missing the right timbre, the right beat, failing to find their mark in the disorientation of sunlight; leading to the anger that razes whole cities to the ground until not a scrap of construction is left, until the name of the place itself is erased from the map with frightening speed. Whole armies of cartographers working through the nights by lamplight, with mosquitoes flying around looking for an opportunity to draw blood, redrawing the boundaries of nations, removing place names from the map. The colouring in of new countries—this one can be mauve. A melancholy task if ever there was one. Move the course of a river before lunch, put it back afterwards. Remove the following words from the map before you leave for the day: 'Yugoslavia', 'USSR', 'Peking', 'Bombay'...Take Carthage off the map—it's just been destroyed. Razed to the ground. Brick by brick removed. The famed library of Alexandria burnt to the ground. A bomb on the platform, where children are gaily going home from school, a bomb with a religion attached to it, a note about difference...

And more forgetting. To enable us to get on with our daily round...all that movement from breakfast to lunchtime...that terrible gnawing hunger...in the middle of a crowd of blank peak-hour faces going home, in the middle of vast over-consumption...the aqueducts supplying water, the forests supplying paper...the slippage between meaning and contiguity...nuclear power plants supplying the electricity that drives all those self-replicating zeroes and ones.

When the Jacobins wanted a mode of civic propriety to model themselves on, they found the perfect motif by looking into the excavated parts of old Paris. By looking down through the cracks in the earth they found their forebears— the Romans of Lutetia—staring back at them with a steady and direct gaze. Having been assaulted with the catchcry that they had behaved like barbarians in guillotining their king and queen their retort was to dress and manner themselves in the fashion of Romans and spread rumours about themselves that they were indeed Romans reincarnated. Purple togas were all the rage. Short skirts—looking gorgeous on the young and frisky; delicate leather sandals, letting in the air. The hair had to be attended to: coiffured in Roman style: for women the hair was up; for men severe, Brutuslike. You had to give the right appearance. It would not do—politically, socially—to be seen in last year's outfits, last year's hairstyles. Furniture became severe rather than decorative. Purity of line came back into play rather than the riot of the rococo line. Serious and earnest of purpose, they set about their task of changing their fashions for the sake of the revolution. No sacrifice would be too great, on behalf of the common good. They had a brilliant propagandist in the painter David, organiser of magisterial parades; master of dramatic lighting that filled the night-sky. The court-artist in the service of revolution which elides into orthodoxy and the new conservatism. The question on everyone's lips: how could the terrorists be barbarians if they dressed like Romans and spoke of the Rights of Man? Sometimes it is very helpful to have a past: you can pluck a rabbit out of the hat at the right moment.

Initially, everyone who wasn't a Greek was a barbarian. There were, said Plato, 'Hellenes' and 'Barbaroi'. That neatly summed up the world: civilization in one place and darkness in the other; reason and unreason, with only the flick of a switch between the two. When wars are fought it's always couched in the same language: the difference between lightness and darkness, between the civilized and the barbaric. It's all a matter of perspective.

Four radionuclides: iodine 131, caesium 137, barium 140 and zirconium 95. We live under a radioactive shell. Abandon hope all ye who enter beneath the portals of the reactor hall; a fiery consummation awaits you. Fire and brimstone: dust to dust, ashes to ashes. The mortal shell: sloughed off like the snake's unwanted skin. Freud's great insight: the body wishing to return to its initial inert state; wishing to fulfil its destiny, to keep its appointment with death.

Tonight, you return home to a brand new item—an insinkerator: to get rid of the waste. As long as they keep coming to take away the waste we shall be well. We shall all be well—as long as our food isn't irradiated, as long as the apartment above doesn't come crushing in on top of us, as long as we don't fall through onto these citizens way beneath us under ground level in the Métro-car going about their gentle, sincere, humble activities of travelling from point A to point B. That we may survive the long nuclear winter. That our fallout shelters may become our wombs not our tombs. That we may become finally civilized.

*

Repeat after me:

Iodine, barium, zirconium, caesium;

Zirconium, barium, caesium, iodine.

*

Correspondence: the transferring of information, emotion, inflection. All of Paris passes through this point of

correspondance—Châtelet: on their way to work, on their
way home from work, to meet a lover, on their way to a
job interview, to buy shoes, to have a haircut, to arrange
a rendezvous. Worker bees swarming through the hive of
the Métro (songlines, bloodlines, spaghetti, petroleum pipes,
a spider's trail, a hammock).

We're all just waiting to get home to watch the nightly
news on TF1, the football (Marseilles against Strasbourg) or
the movie on Canal Plus: tonight it is Jerry Lewis as a bell-
boy in *Grand Hotel*, living out the American Dream. What
is envied is that youthful naivety, that brashness, that lack
of self-consciousness: the difference between the Old World
and the New. The Old World wears tattered leather gloves
smelling of naphthalene, and an old fur coat smelling of
animal, of mink: the New World has dispensed with the
glove, the hands are calloused, and are doused in petrol;
the TV sets are on in every room—an eternal, perpetual
hum; somewhere or other a space shuttle is lifting off
towards the future; your email box is full; your mobile
phone is switched on; your pager is turned on; and we are
all going about our minor underground activities with the
purposefulness of sleepwalkers.

three | The Café

Juliet arrives, breathless, bringing the modern world with her: all that resoluteness, confidence, love of life. She orders a coffee, lights up a cigarette and tells you she's from New York, she's been studying in Paris for three years, she knows the city like the back of her hand and she's writing a PhD on late-nineteenth-century amusements and entertainments in Paris, but she knows all about Gallo-Roman France as well, having studied that era, in Boston in fact. It all comes out in a rush. She is open and generous and warm. You feel there is nothing she would not tell you about herself, if you gave her the chance.

You do not know what to say in reply. It's like you're emerging from months of thought, of introspection, of reflection—you have been un-peopled—and you are now back in what used to be a familiar public arena. You struggle to focus on her, to get a sense of who she is, over and above what she has said about herself. You finally say you're pleased, which she finds an unsatisfactory answer, turning up one corner of her mouth.

The Layers of the City

—What are you doing here? she asks.

You reply that you're just sitting, catching your breath, drinking coffee.

—No, I mean, in Paris? What are you doing in Paris?

You reply that you're minding an apartment for a friend.

—No, beyond that, what else?

She's so persistent that you tell her your story, at least as you imagine it to be at that particular moment. You've run away from your life as a hack journalist and a failed poet for four months, and you're writing something about the many layers of the city of Paris, just for the hell of it. It's not for other people, it's just for yourself. You've been writing about life underground in the Métro and now you're currently writing about the level of the Street. Your former pattern was to sleep in the mornings, go to the library in the Pompidou Centre early afternoon, write in the late afternoon, go to a café to eat alone in the evening and roam the backstreets and alleyways of the Internet at night. You've become a *flâner* of the airwaves. And two days ago, due to a chance encounter—both with the Bibliothèque Historique and with a particular book—you've just become unreasonably interested in the barbarians and Romans of the past because you realized with a jolt this morning that they too are part of the topographical layering of the city: the declension starts with the ether, and continues downwards through the buildings, the street and the Métro; but then comes the twist with the sting in the tail as the layers below are historical layers: the Revolution, the Renaissance, the Middle Ages, the invasions of the barbarians, the Romans and the Gauls. What has become apparent is that your attention has been dragged away from contemporary

Paris and is being dragged towards the layers of Romans
and barbarians whose lives underpin those of us who
belong to the Graeco-Roman line who are alive today.

—What I've only just realized most forcibly, you say, is
that here in Paris we live physically above the past and yet
as Marx has said it is the weight of past generations which
bears down upon us. It is the *weight from below,* if you
like. It's a matter of resolving that weight from below
before we can resume living. Until we can do that we're
trapped in an unresolved cycle of personal disturbance. We
are prevented from living in the present by this weight from
below. No wonder Hell has been characterized as belonging to the nether regions.

—So you're a journalist?

—To tell the truth I was a journalist in my former life
but now I'm burnt out and so I'm here in Paris. I'm on
leave. I may or may not go back to it. For the time being,
I've pushed the pause button. I grew sick of writing temporary and transient information as if it was factual and
thus ready for transmission. I grew sick of colluding in a
business where everyone presumes they've got it right when
all information is essentially tentative and undefinable in
the present without a knowledge of what has happened
before, which is *essentially* unknowable, and what happens
next, which is unpredictable. After all, we read backwards.
The ending redefines the beginning of any story—and you
usually don't know the ending when you're writing news.
It's always just a slice in time, incomplete by its nature.

—Do you know Paris?

You reply that you don't.

The Layers of the City

Juliet says she will be your guide, your guide to the many layers of the city.

—On top, she says, it's like a wedding cake. Underneath it's a sewer. She smiles, suddenly pleased with herself, showing a large amount of perfectly formed teeth. She says she prefers nineteenth-century Paris to contemporary Paris. She would rather live back then.

—You must see at least three things, she continues, while you're here. You must see the former Roman thermal baths in the Musée de Cluny on the boulevard St-Germain, the Arena of Lutetia just off the rue Monge, but above all you must see the archaeological crypt of the forecourt of Notre-Dame.

—Why must I?

—Because they're your key to the Gallo-Roman city. In my role as guide the crypt is our first port of call. It will explain a number of things for you. There you can start to appreciate the many levels of the ancient city. What's underground gives you the inverse of what's above. Let's meet there in a few days.

You leave the Pompidou Centre together. The forecourt is crowded with fire-eaters, magicians, comedians. There are people everywhere, applause, shouts, noise. She leans over and tells you something which you can't hear amidst all the noise. You gesture that you can't hear and she whispers again more loudly, but you still can't hear. Even so you nod in agreement because you can't continue to ask her to repeat herself.

She smiles—you have agreed to something, but you're not sure what.

four | The Street

The street itself. A little street, not a grand thoroughfare, in the great city. Hot and dusty in midsummer. Thirty-five degrees. The schoolchildren singing their way home at lunchtime. Plaster-dust from nearby renovations swirling around in the light breeze. The smell of lemon, and fish frying. The smell of sunshine flooding in through open windows...the indolence of summer. The posters flutter in the breeze: catamarans skid along the surface of the surf; Gauguin, palm trees, dark women peering out, a white horse with a boy on top. Inside: luxury, calm, voluptuousness. Outside—the street. The baker-boy with his basket of baguettes. The Spaniard with his slim women in silk—one on each arm. His moustache bristles. The cleaner from Camaroon leaning on his green straw broom. Content. To rest. The parish priest clutching his breviary—saying his prayers out loud as he walks: *Forgive me father...Now and at the hour...O blessed virgin...* Sunshine knitting everyone together.

Everyone is out for a stroll in the sun: a grand parade. Here we have the butcher, the baker, the supermarket owner, all out to take the air. Behind them we have: three strolling chefs, two ancient combatants, one fashion model and a Dutch football team...All the balcony-doors are open. Everyone looking down from their first floor, from their second floor, from their third floor, from their fourth floor. Everyone home for lunch. Everyone on display, like in a shop window. The watchers being watched...And still the parade continues. Here we have: five laughing schoolgirls, four limping bus drivers, three sopranos singing, two tri-colours fluttering and a robin upon a parked car. And behind them: Monsieur and Madame Doucemère—jolly, content and elegantly dressed—out for their daily stroll. A copy of *Figaro* in the man's hand, a rose, newly plucked, in the woman's hand; a dash of Chanel No. 5 dabbed behind her ears.

Let us watch them, from the first floor balcony, as they approach. She is petite, he is hefty. She swings her hips, he swivels his neck. She licks her lips, he brushes off bread-crumbs. She dreams of trips, he does up his fly. She avoids the dogshit, he steps right in it. They are in their sixties. They are reasonably happy—in a manner that is common nowadays. You can tell they used to be a fashionable couple in the fifties, when they were young and the world was their oyster. Lifetimes of talking too much, of smoking too much, of eating too much salt and sugar and saturated fat. Cholesterol levels are way too high, but they are enjoying themselves anyway. Enjoying each other's company, enjoy-ing the day, the peace and contentment of the day's sunshine, the easygoing ambience of the dusty summer street when most people in the Fourth are away *en vacance*. They've both booked themselves in for heart surgery in the new year—to unclog the veins. All their best friends are dying, or going crazy or separating from their partners of forty years. Nothing can deter them from their daily strolls. They would have sweet skin, if only you could get close enough to tell. A poodle running after them trying to reach them. You hear the name: it's Fi-Fi. You hear: *Ecoute Fi-Fi*...but then the rest fades away as you start to feel sleepy, standing in the sun on a first floor balcony. An iced Perrier water on the nearby table.

Lunchtime smells. Coming through open windows, and open full-length glass doors where you can step out onto narrow balconies. The smell of olive oil from Granada, of oranges from Seville, of cod from the Atlantic. Let us share a glass of red wine together...Someone is baking bread, either next door or over the passageway. Everything swelling with anticipation in the poignant, sweaty afternoon. The rotund priest—poured into the prophylactic sheath of his black soutane—returns. Circling the block, he carries a plastic milk bottle now as well as his breviary: *Forgive me father...Now and at the hour*...Five Japanese businessmen pass by, carrying four cameras, with three handkerchiefs showing from top pockets, holding two *Plans de Paris* while one carries a dachschund...*At the hour of my death.*

Lunchtime. The smell of frying flounder, dripping lemon and Spanish olive oil, returns. The baker-boy with his basket of freshly baked baguettes casually slung over the shoulder is running to the restaurant for the midday meal.

The Layers of the City

Don't be late...don't be late little baker-boy...or your daddy will give you a hiding. Here is an American in a harlequin jacket looking for a *real* tourist attraction. He holds his street map up high to get a better look. Over there is a plain-clothes cop waiting by the Métro exit for someone to throw a bomb; he smokes away for hours—until he too is content in the sun. Here is a tennis player, over there is a jogger, here is an ice cream seller and there are the nannies with their pushers containing precious cargo. All this and more you can see from a first floor balcony with the sun streaming in. The golden sun...A Dutch milkmaid carrying jonquils floats serenely past; her jonquils melting in the midday sun. A helicopter overhead, the Métro below, and between? All these people...A few nuns go by, chattering away, good-heartedly. The concierge briskly setting out to collect the mail. A man wearing an eyepatch reading *Le Monde* walks by. The neighbourhood cat arches her back. The friendly mini-supermarket owner, Monsieur Peaumou, is out for a vigorous walk. It looks like he's on an errand. The sharp-faced girl with the bad temper from the cake shop, Mademoiselle Gabrielle, is asking the gendarme to stop the schoolboys from running in and out of her shop...He can't be bothered. He has more important work to do: directing traffic. She scowls at him through the frilly curtain, from behind the gleaming mounds of patisserie. He raises a lazy hand to stop a four horse-power Citroën, out of spite, just to show his power. Everything is slowed down, tenuous. Even the insects move slowly. The sound of Gershwin ('It Ain't Necessarily So') from a third floor balcony, and right on cue a skinny painter wearing a beret, a sailor shirt and a pencil-thin moustache looks down to see what all the commotion is about. It could be the set for a light comic opera.

The gentle breeze, the plaster dust, the sun streaming through the full-length windows heating up the sand in the TWA poster of the Costa del Sol, frying the backs of the well-tanned naked sunbathers. Thirty-five degrees. A 747 above taking gaily painted holiday-makers to Majorca. Perspiration trickles down the side of your face. Even the neighbourhood *clochards* are amused, emerging from their hastily erected cardboard-box sunshades, to face the mid-afternoon sun and plan their summer vacation. It could be the late 1950s—something distant and faded; a post-World War II innocence.

The street, as painted by Balthus. A side street to the main action (say, the passage de Commerce Saint-André in the 1950s), inhabited by daydreamers, adjusting sleepily their nineteenth-century minds to a twentieth-century post-Freud landscape. Locked into their own separate thoughts, like children's vessels sailing on a lake in the dry flat sunshine of consciousness, they go about their daily round. Self-possessed, playing out a private set of automatic actions. The reveries of the nostalgics in the summer heat. Playing out childhood patterns: repetition, security, order. Altar-boys from the nearby church go serenely by; one boy with a mass of blond curls stands out from all the rest due to his seriousness. He is carrying a pile of heavy candles; the wax is starting to melt like a clutch of Dali watches. Two schoolgirls run by, one with a violent tangle of red hair—swearing at each other. A crisp young businessman, in a suit of blues and greens with yellow socks, clutching an alligator-skin briefcase marches past. A maid leaning on her broom in a nearby apartment, daydreaming of retirement. A dripping tap behind her. The blond plumber from the suburbs will arrive in a week, if she's lucky. The police helicopter hovering overhead, looking for terrorists planting a bomb in the Marais. Just last week a bomb was thrown from a speeding Renault into a crowded Jewish restaurant on a Friday night. A Lufthansa Airbus leaving its white exhaust trail behind it as it flies off towards the Matterhorn. It flies off towards the future. The past is underground. The weight of present generations, above. The crush of anxieties, desperations, pushing by force of gravity whole *arrondissements* into the carved-out substratum. In the forecourt of Notre-Dame, under the stones: the remains of old Paris, of Lutetia, home of the guilds of fishermen, then home to the Romans, the first tourists who came to stay, until the second wave of tourists, the barbarians, forced them out.

In front of us the parade continues. For our benefit, we have: four smiling tourists, three snarling terrorists, two water-polo players and a street-sweeper with a straw broom. How quickly they all pass by. How elusive is the moment. They won't return. We have had our time with them. There goes the concierge, always so good-natured, off on another errand; probably to call a plumber—a shower blocked yet again. Underneath her footsteps the Métro goes about its daily business. A moment as light as a lemon sorbet. How quickly they all pass by...Just as quickly the passing day recedes into the filing case of memories, never again to surface. These cast members in our private play have flickered across our consciousness; it is unlikely we will ever see them or think of them again. We have had our moment of theatre with them. Our time has been spent either wisely or unwisely, who's to say?

The tourist buses invade the sunshine like a flock of sheep waiting to put themselves down somewhere. There is nowhere to park. The guide at the front of the bus is speaking into a microphone about those who walk the streets as though we are all extras in a historical film being shot on location. You notice she smiles and speaks animatedly about the old man wearing a beret and holding a baguette who is crossing in front of the slow-moving bus; he is suitably 'in part'—a local as promised in the brochures. Finally, the well-scrubbed German tourists with perfect teeth and cinema-quality smiles are let loose; swarming over hills and through the pretty streets in search of mementos of their stay...

This morning up at five, walking the streets, peering this way and that, the half-glow of early morning, the street lamps still on, the neighbourhood *clochards* asleep on the sidewalk under the carpet they have recently found, the baker working since four comes into his shop half-naked carrying a tray of croissants with the steam rising. He is all skin and bones, with a carrot-top. He does not eat his own products. You buy a copy of *Libération* and wander the streets waiting for a café to open. It's the right moment to see the city: hushed, expectant—like the men's waiting room in a maternity hospital. In an electrical store a TV is on: it's showing 'The Three Stooges'. There they are, at it again—Larry, Curly and Mo. Right out of childhood. Poking each other in the eyes. All that curled-up aggression—just waiting to be let out of the bag. It must be a video: all they do is poke each other in the eyes, slap each other in the face, and recoil. An endless loop—like the double-helix of DNA. All that encoded genetic information, working away, painstakingly, copying, recopying, engineering an identity, creating a pattern: poke, slap, recoil, poke, slap, recoil.

The working day will be delivered soon. The sleepy gendarme holds up his arm to the few cars to allow the schoolchildren to cross, the construction workers start to climb up their scaffolds, the *clochards* awake and throw off their carpet as the day warms up and start to good-naturedly abuse those who pass by, the schoolchild with satchel strapped to his back lights up a Gauloise, the co-owner of the Café of All Poles puts out her few tables and chairs and opens the door for the thickset butcher who will stay for a coffee, a pastis and a chat—for as long as she will allow it. She is imperious in her little domain. In here, amidst the coffee, the Polish sausage and the Polish cucumbers she gets her way: out there, beyond the glass windows, she takes her chances like anybody else.

The neighbourhood *clochards* ask you why you cross the street when you draw near to them. Do they smell? Isn't it human nature, after all, to smell? They were, after all, put on this earth, like you, for a purpose: by handing them some coins each day you can feel less guilty about your own fortunate station in life. *C'est tout!* They are happy *clochards*, content in their social usefulness. Like modern-day priests, or shrinks, really; ready to hear your confession at any time of day. They explain that they are always with you—like sin—in whichever *arrondissement* you wish to visit; even in the fashionable Sixteenth. They are there, just for you. Just out of the corner of your eye. You are of course trying not to see them. There is one famous *clochard*, they tell you, who has even been on TV, on an afternoon chat show, explaining his craft by way of theories of guilt and expiation. They were immortalized, they say, by Samuel Beckett, though he of course romanticized their way of life. And now as you walk away they say, Do you think we're uneducated? It's not true. We are educated. We went to the local Catholic school. Do you think we smell? It's only the smell of humanity.

Are these *clochards* the grandchildren of the vagabonds in Rilke's fifth *Duino* elegy? Those transient spirits who by their nature form a bridge between heaven and earth, between the pantheon of the gods and we mere mortals who lie beneath the diamond-encrusted night sky? Who are they? Indeed, who are we? Where do we come from? Where are we going? Those great unanswerable questions which lie around ready to ambush us in some thoughtless, ugly, complacent moment.

The street itself, in midsummer, all the full-length balcony doors in every apartment are open to let in any bit of breeze, sunlight streaming in. The private world is made public. Thirty-five degrees. The heat knitting everyone together; putting everyone in a good mode—relaxing, sensual, invisible threads tying strangers together. The cold spring—just a fading memory. The street is in harmony. Even its guardians, the *clochards*, are momentarily happy.

The morning: possibilities. Lunchtime: probabilities. Mid-afternoon: desirabilities. The silk stocking draped languidly across the sunlit chair. The life of the mind. The discarded pink bra. The midsummer indolence. The cooling breeze. The smell of perfume. The smell of sweat. The indolence of the mind. The fantasia of the mind. The possibilities of conversation. The smell of lemons, of fish frying. This ancient dusty street. The Matisse print peels off the wall and floats gently to the floor whenever it gets this hot. The painter from Dusseldorf in the opposite apartment painting naked; her strokes are vibrant and muddy. A tubby pianist in another apartment practising in his underpants—playing the same scherzo over and over. The painter, now in a red dressing gown with a Chinese dragon on the back, entertaining different men as the afternoon wears on. The drops of sweat on the linoleum. Iced water by the bed. Gusts of piano music enveloping all in a public embrace.

Outside, and below the first floor balcony, the parade of citizens and tourists continues...All of the great city is out for a stroll: the butcher, the baker and the candlestick maker; the pilot, the bully and the croissant maker; the terrorist, soprano and plain-clothes cop; the laundryman, thief and the supermarket owner; the politician, his mistress and the real estate dealer; the diver, the tennis player and the gateaux maker; the nun, the priest and the humble street-sweeper; the cook, her assistant and the newspaper seller; the nanny, the baby and the Danish au pair; the fortune-teller, the roué and the video-maker; the scoundrel, the judge and the minister for culture; the plumber, the sheik and the Australian model; the basketball player, the gamin and the printmaker; the jogger, the jockey and the oil-well driller...All out for a promenade with one destination in mind; across the bridges of the Seine, along the boulevard St-Germain and the boulevard St-Michel, all the way to the Gardens.

In the Jardin du Luxembourg all the world is out for a stroll: the bankers, the lawyers, the painters, the nannies with their charges. The world's retired dictators are here too, minding their own business, ruminating over what went wrong—the wrong phone-call on the wrong day, that's all. Endlessly checking their jacket pockets, finding bits of Semtex in their fingernails: careless moments. Stomachs ballooning out with the weight of all those pastries. Looking like generals as painted by Botero (the melancholy is palpable): the same feminine hips, the puffy face that descends by force of gravity onto the shoulders, the fluid-retaining fingers, the shiny military-style boots. Finding a way to fill their days, now that their flunkeys have deserted them; dreaming of Napoleon, dreaming of the 'impossible' come-back, the dramatic arrival by Iroquois helicopter to the cheering masses waving palm branches. On the mobile phone occasionally to Washington to see if America can back their return—masquerade it as a return for the sake of *democracy* and all shall be well, and all manner of things shall be well. Reduced to three mistresses, two Swiss bank accounts and a *pied-à-terre* in the Sixteenth. The American heiress over there under the tree—just off the QE2; checking her lipstick in a hand-mirror, looking for a

definition of long days, looking for a reason for her dis-
quiet. The young nannies with their charges on the lawns,
waiting restlessly for the day to end, waiting for their
boyfriends to take them out dancing for the night. All the
world's fading movie stars strolling through the lawns—
waiting for the dice to roll their way. To get another
part—even to be the voice talent on a documentary would
do. The Spanish starlet, the Indian soapie star, the Swedish
bombshell, the Chilean dandy. All the world's film directors are here too—searching for a tree, a bush or a path
that hasn't yet been filmed by some other filmmaker.
Anxiously looking up at the weather. Alert to minor adjust-
ments in the quality of the light: maybe go down another
f-stop? And if the light's just right then the expression on
that actor's face is just wrong. If the bush is unfilmed, then
the rotunda in the backdrop certainly has been shot and
reshot, until the whole of the city resembles this giant
movie lot, except the light is often pure drizzle rather than
pure Californian. Though not today. You couldn't find a
more perfect day if you wanted to. The sun alighting on
plants, the water in the lake just lapping it all up, drinking the reflections of the passers-by who momentarily stare
into the water, looking for a sign of their own existence,
bouncing back at them through long and short waves
of light.

Perhaps, as Rilke asserts, existence *is* singing and all of
this breathing and heaving, and pouting and gesturing, and
sweating, sighing and crying, and striving and despairing
is just a way of putting off the moment of embracing, the
moment when the very particles of air vibrate with a cosmic

harmony. Perhaps life *has* a purpose after all—when you are immersed in the shape, the feel, the texture, the density, the grace, the calm, the solitude, of the heat and warmth of the Gardens. The past commingling with the present. The former headquarters of the Luftwaffe only a stone's throw away. Obscenities, atrocities fade away in late afternoon. The longueurs of the season. Operetta escaping from an indecipherable source. Even the gendarmes are relaxed. That animal violence of humankind put aside for the duration of the day; that eternal viciousness dissipates in the warmth of the sun; the sound of Franz Lehár coming perhaps from that Walkman over there. The citizens, for once, at peace with one another. The striving, despairing, put aside temporarily. Those lost years effaced, removed from the mental map. Your personal topography of remembered incidents, wrong turns and serendipitous moments appear as extruded points in the technicolour screen of your mind. Putting off embracing because we can't cope with it; we can't find a path to it; our defences have been up for too long; the tortured night-thoughts; the suffering of our ancestors rippling through us in one long involuntary shudder. Perhaps all this regurgitation of memory is merely bad faith; that just relaxing into the day, and trusting the warmth, the heat, the good-naturedness of the crowd is the way to go. Perhaps, some essential giving up, surrendering, is the way to go. A going with the flow. A watery slide into...silence, into...calm existence...into acceptance.

That clown over there with the painted smiling face bristling with humanity: for what purpose was he made? Or did he make himself? Some sort of implosive drawing

together of swirling separate particles. Like a universe—
inventing itself in one overwhelming shuddering act of
self-impregnation. Expanding in an instant, with a purposeful insistence that we are meant to be here, that we
are travellers in a cosmic journey that starts with a big
bang. If humans are the model for all things, as the Enlightenment asserted, than the universe too takes on human
characteristics and it comes into being in a very human
way—as the result of a conception, a violent intercourse
of swirling particles and unstable elements (isn't that very
human in itself?). And if we are meant to be here, then
won't our anxieties, our insufficiencies just float away like
the seeds of those gum-pods that explode in heat and get
carried away on the westerly winds? At heart, we know so
little. We are incomplete, unfaithful daughters and sons of
the Enlightenment.

The clown in his commonplace costume—almost a
parody. Better by far to be wearing a Pierrot costume with
a whitened face—much prettier; a better song in silk; a
deeper link with the past; a more complete embracing; a
wordless moment from the world of pantomime, of imitation, of dumb speech. Presumably he is here to entertain
the children. Or maybe he is just advertising hamburgers;
with those long shoes and anarchic painted face. Come to
think of it, he looks like Ronald McDonald. He has that
same purposeful air, that same expression, of a man deliv-
ering a message, a modern-day John the Baptist, awaiting
his Salome. That must be it: he is a thoroughly modern
walking sign. He stands for Commerce and the promise of
Modern Happiness—through the stomach.

Everyone has a role in the Jardin du Luxembourg. All bit-players in someone's else's fantasy. Pieces in a jigsaw of light, density, texture, colour, weight...We are conjoined by the dry heat of the day, the day we share, the air we share, the music from the brass band in the rotunda we share, the pebbles on the footpath we share, the ants making their trails we notice, the tennis-players in sparkling white we notice, the old man, with rotten teeth, wearing a blue beret and limping past whom we notice... *Un ancien combattant,* no doubt. We are the observed as well as the observer (a wandering camera taking snaps)... The gendarmes avoiding all signs of trouble. Just strolling, enjoying the sunshine, enjoying the enculturation of the moment, the pasteurization—with the sun as the agent— the homogenization. The brass band strikes up more loudly from the rotunda: a nineteenth-century waltz. Something by Strauss: merry, cavalier. Life as a picture postcard—a momentary willed-for delusion. The world as painted by Watteau: ever fragile—an evanescent bubble of happiness about to burst into...hysteria, mordancy. But a gentle breeze blows all of that away. The crowd is swaying in conjoined movement. The sun gives a benediction, at this moment, in this place, to all who shelter beneath her. It is a moment of inclusion—the peaceful crowd. *Luxe, calme et volupté.* An invitation to a voyage.

Perhaps, as Heraclitus asserts, the universe *is* imbued with a hidden harmony—those ties that bind us together... those moments of peacefulness...those moments of calm... those moments when the crowd is not an angry mass surging together but rather a long uninterrupted skein of cotton—and all of the bloodshed and reptilian viciousness of the twentieth century is part of the pattern, part of the elements (fire, earth, air, water) we breathe, part of the jigsaw? That the harmony is a pattern, and yet that pattern is not necessarily harmonic.

Humanity. Adrift. In the sunlight. A vague purposelessness. A small lake in the middle of the Luxembourg Gardens covered with tiny sailboats being pushed from the sides by cherubic children. Some of the boats are motorized and are being controlled from shore; some are made of paper and are floating of their own accord.

If we are all puppets, then where are our strings? Our toys of childhood lie under the rusting car in the backyard, or under the dilapidated sofa, the child within us lies dormant, those plastic Barbie dolls with their elaborate outfits, those rubber dogs and soft rabbits we invested so much meaning in lie waiting to be picked up again: they did not ask for meaning. Orpheus played his lyre and the animals came to sit at his feet, enchanted by the sweetness of his music. Was it not the most beautiful thing they had ever heard? Was it not why they had been born? To listen to music. Gods make their own meaning, out of bits and pieces, scraps, anything that is at hand. Being gods they do not have to force the issue.

The children in blue and white sailor suits crowd around the puppet theatre anxious to get a better look. A pantomime is about to begin. The gentle breeze ripples the miniature sailboats on the lake. The island of Cythera—a space inside the brain. The journeying of the spirit. The wished-for delusion. Life as an excursion on a barque, in the sunshine, with a gentle breeze blowing. The encircling, soothing voices. The smoke that rises from behind the rotunda. The haze in the imperial purple of sunset—the city's residue. Nightfall in the Luxembourgs. The attendants asking, sotto voce, everyone to leave. The return home, via the crowded streets, via the humidity of the Métro. Expulsion from the Garden of Eden. Naturally, the world's a stage. Bit-players all of us. The cameo entrance via the birth-waters followed by the dramatic exit in the ball of fire of the automobile accident in the middle of the eight-lane freeway. Exclusion. The body extruded into the bitumen, such is the heat of the fiery collision.

Nightfall, last thoughts, unrequited thoughts, the running down, the turning off, the impulsive shiver of your body's natural electricity turning off.

It was an idea of Heraclitus that in sleep we lose contact with reason (*sweet reason*) and we are connected to the world-fire of life by a slender thread of breathing. As every anxious parent knows—as they watch their week-old child struggling tenaciously for breath, for life—the grasp is still tenuous. Half-dazed from lack of sleep, from anxiety, the mother wonders if her child can hang on to that furled piece of silk which knits together heaven and earth; that place of the spirit and the mortal, earthbound space wherein we reside. The breath that in unreason, that in unknowingness, is still struggling to maintain contact; to hold on to life; to not throw it away casually; to find the balance between inhaling and exhaling.

Emerging from a winter of confusion, of bitter winds, of persistent darkness and frozen lakes; a winter of turning

inward for warmth and comfort; a winter of disillusion-
ment. Turning towards a spring of compassion, of
contentment, of generosity; new life shooting upwards with
grace and precision.

You wish to breathe as one who lived in Nature would—
to breathe without thinking about it. To return to a
preconscious state where you exist as naturally as a tree
in a footpath, immune to the fumes of the cars.

Early morning, before the sun has risen, in the Café of
All Poles the workmen in their blue overalls talking about
Ricardo Muti at the Bastille: is he as good as he was? Turning slightly towards each other, over a short black, talking
about *Les Bleus,* the national football team, a powerful
running team. There's a scandal down at Marseille,
though—something about money. What else? In the Café
of All Poles, open early till late, vodka in the glass cabinets, Polish sausage on the sideboard, a few tables on the
street, only a few tables inside. The local teacher brings
his own croissant, sits reading *Libération,* drinking his short
black, occasionally looking up at the workers in their blue
overalls, talking loudly. The street-sweepers in their green
overalls holding their brooms come in out of the darkness
at 6.45 a.m. to have the first beer for the day... *une pression,* the pressure. There's something humble in the gestures
of the local teacher, surreptitiously pulling his croissant out
of his bag, drinking his coffee in the window, hunched over
the paper. Outside in the darkness the schoolchildren with
bags strapped to their backs head for their schools early
as their parents have to work. They gather outside the

school in the rue Charlemagne pushing and shoving and laughing...

So this is civilization, this is what we've become, backwards and forwards, endlessly capitulating and recapitulating, struggling forward with best intent and little means...So this is civilization...evolution, revolution, terminal despair...Thought it might have turned out differently...So this is what it means to be living in a technocratic state, a technocracy...So this is what is meant by good taste, by refinement, by manners. So this is how we've kept the barbarians at bay. So this is why we have kept the barbarians at bay. So this is why we use perfume and deodorant: to keep the smell of decay at bay. Some kind of new golden renaissance. A renaissance founded on money. All those traders bartering away through the dusty streets of Siena. The bankers of Florence, founders of a new civilization. The traders sailing out of Genoa—in search of spices. So these are the buildings we have chosen to build; this is how we wish to live. So this is the structure we have embraced. Once again a set of hierarchies—as though there was no other model available. We've become encoded in our own skeletal maps. We are neither coming nor going. We are in stasis. We reproduce ourselves—over and over, sending our little icons out into the world...to become traders and merchants, bankers and financiers.

So this is our culture. So this is what we've made: the air above—polluted; the streets at middle level—crowded; the buildings at middle level—on insecure foundations; the Métro below—swarming with cellular activity.

The Layers of the City

So, this is it...There ain't no more...Just as long as they keep coming to take away the (toxic) waste...

So this is what a crowd looks like. This, the inside of the crowd. And this, the outside. And this is what a running crowd looks like. You look around and all you can see are elbows knocking you and feet trampling you, police helicopters overhead and tanks in the streets. So this is what fear looks like. So this is the power of the crowd. So this is the modern state: heavily protected. So this is what humility is: the medieval monks transcribing manuscripts in the scriptorium, their necks aching, their wrists getting tired, their thoughts getting scrambled.

So this is how the wheel turns. Monkeys come down from the trees, slime oozing out of the primeval sea, all sorts of larval energy bubbling away to create tissue and bone and blood—eventually. Protozoa and plasma...the long chains of DNA, encircling and linking, by circuitous routes—ending up with some sort of HUMANITY...Neanderthal, Palaeolithic, the primitive person, the origin of the species, all sorts of sperm and eggs, all sorts of sticky stuff, coagulating plasma on the kitchen table...By these means, by this route we have become human, we have become civilized.

Inorganic chemicals in the blue-green sea-soup swirling around—the cocktail of life...fizzing away to create new forms, new life...the adaptation of the species, in order to survive. New life forms to emerge from the Métro—after the long nuclear winter: humans perfectly adept at living underground. A series of changes designed to equip the new species with much needed attributes: larger eyes—to see more powerfully in the darkness; larger ears—to hear the onset of enemies; a greater distribution of body hair—to withstand the increased cold; diminishing cognitive powers—to enable one to survive the boredom. Life perpetually underground...That we may not wake into one eternal irradiated winter, our genes corrupted, the snow piling up at the entrances and the exits of the Métro.

Raising the dust, the dust of centuries of Marcus Aurelius—conqueror, philosopher, fiction-writer, Stoic—the dust of Lutetia...the dust of Seneca, of Cordoba, of the Patio of Oranges...The dust of centuries past rising from the (Freudian) mouth of the archaeological crypt of the forecourt of Notre-Dame...

Our Lady of the blue rinse hairdo, Our Lady of the advertising billboard, Our Lady of the Minitel, Our Lady of the sensual desirable voice, just airwaves after all, a mouth and an ear conjoined via the wires that tie us together around the world, Our Lady of the Internet, global traveller: concubines of the airwaves. The streets of Paris almost deserted now—the month of the *vacances*. The locals are in their Provençale country-houses eating bread and honey, watching their cherry trees ripen in a Balthusian haze of post-pubescent sexuality, watching Eric Rohmer videos about other Parisians on holiday picking up schoolgirls in Mercedes coupés, just the shimmer of viewed content. The great god of the sun shining on the olive trees and the cypresses that have seen so many Greeks, Gauls and Romans come and go. The great sun shining benevolently on St-Rémy-de-Provence, on Glanum, on Aix-en-Provence, on Arles—shining with compassion, glinting off the nuclear power plants. In Avignon the tourists come and go—counting out their money: deutschemarks, liras, euros, pounds, kroners, zlotys. And up flies a blackbird to peck out your eyes, up flies an axe to chop off your head, and (on the autoroute) up flies the wheel of a semitrailer to knock over your Renault. The King is in the Papal Palace rinsing out his purple robes and reading *Combat,* the Queen is on the Minitel blowing out her snuff and powder, the knave is on the Internet rewriting his father's will. All manner of things are here—in midsummer, in Avignon, in a state of mind, on holidays, in suspension, in limbo...

The edginess of the early morning, unspent energy, coiled figures, such a long day ahead, plasticine figures, bendable as the day goes on. It will warm up when the sun rises...In the Café of All Poles, talking about FIAC—the contemporary art fair—the two in the corner of the café, habitués of the art world, two painters, one with a bald head dressed in black leather, his face covered with stubble, smoking a Gauloise, drinking a short black; his stout companion arguing heatedly about the merits of painting anything at all. This year it's the Germans at FIAC, the huge canvases with bits of the Berlin Wall emerging and the guards' caps jutting out at odd angles, amongst the video screens lodged into the canvas displaying late night TV—a panel discussion with smoke swirling everywhere. The Japanese galleries are selling Picassos, Pissaros, Renoirs, Monets, Manets. The two painters discussing the value of art: a bad year for painters: nothing sells. It seems the merchants with fat chequebooks only want recycled bits of the past nowadays. The huge Berlin Wall canvas by

Vostell will sell though—everyone wants a bit of History, to hang on your wall, easier to see that way...You can touch it and feel it and fondle and turn it over.

A bit of History, a bit of Geography: when the Berlin Wall came down there was incomprehension—what seemed solid, immutable had just shifted; the dialectic had just lost one of its halves. We can't get by without opposition, we can't define our identity without knowing who we are not. We are not here for nothing—or are we? Gauguin's three questions: Where do we come from? What are we? Where are we going? We come from dust, we are matter, we are going home (if we have one). Or Rilke's three questions from the *Duino Elegies:* Who are we? Where do we come from? Where are we going? Freud's comforting thought: that at the end of life the molecules of the body are struggling to return to their prior inert state; they are struggling to return to dust; they have a pre-inscribed organic rendezvous to meet.

In the Café of All Poles the workmen arrive early, chatting up the woman—let's call her Katyrsyna—who runs the bar; her husband—we can call him Tomek—looks after the café in the afternoon. They are both thoroughly Parisian now. They hold their own with the locals. They discuss the nightly news as brought to them by Patrick Poivre-Davoir. They discuss the collapse of foundations on a building site in the Ninth *arrondissement.*

The whole of the great city is riddled with hollows— quarried to build the imposing facades that stand above; the citizens are impervious to the absent middle below. It's only when a whole apartment block falls inwards into its absent substratum that the populace crowd around, look surprised, and wonder what foundations their own apartment blocks are built on. What mere shifting thought-patterns hold them up in the sky? Their inhabitants looking out beyond the Eiffel Tower to the gloriously polluted sunset (Samson renting apart the pillars of the Temple), looking over the heads of pedestrians to the Mediterranean. At times like these on warm midsummer evenings they feel their Latin ancestors in their bones.

The integration of a society on all levels: we share each other's pollution as if it was our own; we pay our taxes and wait for the garbagemen to haul away the waste; we admire the purple haze of sunset; we look for the hero on the hill; we crowd around the man with his portable lyre, Greek tunic and sandals who plays outside the Beaubourg, next to the man with tattoos eating fire. The *carnaval*: that which can't be held can't be repressed, can't be organised into neatness. The fear of politicians everywhere: the crowd in the street; the uncontrolled, uncontrollable display; the random, unpredictable event that punctures the facade of normality, the facade of power. The same fear of contemporary art—better by far to have it dead, distant and buried.

A trip to Monoprix to buy some provisions: past the church of the Jesuits, with its clock in the shape of a Latin American sun, golden flames emerging everywhere: the colonizing priests, bringing the news of Western salvation to the natives under the sun. Avoid the dog shit on the street, avoid the fishmonger throwing out buckets full of melted ice across the pavement in front of you as you walk.

This is your possible story being told to you, in an absent sort of a way, somehow disembodied, like all tales that just go round in circles, sort of lifting and swaying, becoming clear at moments, opaque at others, constantly shifting with the nervous energy of early morning, the sun just coming up, all the possibilities of life in a vast and profound city, a city of layers, a city of beehives, of worker ants and drones, and shopkeepers, a conglomeration of many villages, of lives mapped out and navigated.

When you gaze down from the Eiffel Tower (7 million rods, 15 000 girders, 2.5 million bolts) all of the great city is laid out before you, like a take-away smorgasbord. Humanity as far as the eye can see; people crowded in Airbuses; crowded in Peugots and Saabs and on the footpath; and crowded underground in the carriages of the Métro. Humans mutating, mating, gaining their night eyes, their underground eyes. Civilization as far as the eye can see, habitations as far as the eye can see; the rude dwellings of the original inhabitants of Lutetia, the fishermen and the fisherwomen of the islands of the Seine. The hazy smog of early morning knitting all of the dwellings together into a gigantic quilt—the air as a gritty glue holding we humans together, conjoining our buildings into a jigsaw puzzle of massive proportions—where everything fits together with an inexorable logic.

The dinosaurs exterminated by a shower of comets—as futuristic a theory as anything out of science fiction. Comets with far greater power than any atomic blast; mass extinction facing us just around the corner. Dinosaurs disappearing to be replaced by mammals. Without the extinction of the dinosaurs there would be no speech, no writing—and no-one to read. Words would have no meaning—not even the rudimentary and shifting meanings we assign to them. Words the most slippery of all creatures; evolving all the time; the survival of the fittest words.

From the Eiffel Tower you can see the rectangular gardens of the Champs de Mars, the blue and white toy train, the clockwork pigeons, the cartoon rivets and bolts, the chocolaty Seine, the nougat bridges, the Lego courtyards, the plasticine figures walking the streets; Noddy's TOYLAND; arms and faces bending in the breeze, the endless flexibility. The buildings: mere splotches of greys and greens and steel blues.

So this is how easy it would be to bomb a city: the mere abstract colours from a height of twenty thousand feet. The mass extermination at the end of an outbreak of anger. The real or imagined sense of dishonour, humiliation. The death-of-Sardanapalus complex—if he has to die everyone around him will die also. The gender corrupted through multiple sins of the past: sins of aggression and regression to a reptile state, a reptile brain where survival means to struggle and fight and conquer. Darwin's evolutionary message: the whole of emerging civilization reduced to the desire to ensure the survival of one's own genes; through display or aggression to win the right for the male to implant his seed. No wonder there are wars: no wonder the twentieth century was such an unquiet, unholy, unloved century.

Hitler standing on the terrace of the Palais de Chaillot admiring the Eiffel Tower, whispering to an assistant, calling the great city *a wonder of civilization* that should be preserved. Its aura, he said, had preoccupied him for a long time. The open city; the empty city; undefended; time on the side of the city. Occupiers come and go. Forest will revert to its natural state once the predators have gone. The barbarians at the gates of the city. What do you do in those circumstances? Get it over with quickly without the foreplay of the siege? Just open the gates and let them in?

Napoleon a novelist, Hitler a painter, Nero a singer, Mussolini a playwright, Helen of Troy and Goebbels both poets, Speer the architect...Creativity and destruction: two sides of the same face—the left and the right side; the body and the shadow; the sun and the moon; the active and the dead; fire and water. The creator stuck immobile in front of the canvas, the blank page, the score, the pen/paintbrush dripping with ink. Goebbels, with his gift for words, the Catholic intellectual, the amateur architect, dark, small, with a crippled foot (like Talleyrand); a representative like Hitler of the master race (where was the athleticism, the blond hair, the blue eyes?). Hitler dreamt of the Caesars. Nero admired the culture and civilization of the Greeks. Why can't Romans be like that? he would say over and over. Why can't we think as well as the Greeks, he would ask his boy-assistant before singing songs of praise to the glories of nature. And the Greeks looked back admiringly to the Egyptians, who looked back in appreciation of Mesopotamian culture. And so on it goes. Through a declension of looking back—as a way of getting our bearings, as a way of navigating. What is it about the past that holds us in its thrall? We are enslaved by our shared history and in awe of the past. It is quite natural to regard current times as lacking in substance, in colour, in blood. It is as natural as eating and drinking to look back at a golden age when women and men lived *more fully*.

Hitler confided to those few he momentarily trusted that the power of a speech lay in finding the apt word. Not any word would do. It had to be the exact, shaped, demonstratively and measurably powerful word. He had a feeling for a crowd as distinct from individuals; individuals he could not fathom; it was only when each and every person was submerged in a huge mass that he would start to come alive, as a robot might kick into action at the flick of a switch. He came alive through the colour, the corporality, the bloodfulness of words. And pauses. He understood silence. The obliteration of speech. As a young man (according to various commentators) he learnt the piano, drew countless designs for various architectural projects, was enthralled by Wagner's *Rienzi* and applied unsuccessfully to join as a student the Academy of Fine Arts in Vienna. He started to write an opera, tried to write a play, designed public buildings, ended up as a tramp, a *clochard*. He had artistic ambitions: he wanted to shape and reshape; he did not want to be bored. He characterised himself as coming out of the masses to speak as one of them; to speak as the *unknown soldier* to the man and woman of the street; the ordinary person who would be caught up in wave upon operatic wave of emotion. Always searching for the right word. And when the words deserted him he was done for; a crippled shell looking for a way out; wandering around an underground labyrinth designed to keep the preying world out looking for someone to talk to. When he realised it was time to die—to go over to the 'other side'—he married. In the end he expected his 'double', the soldiers, the nation-state to die too. Vials of poison were handed around like they were goblets of champagne. The poison would take a long time to leave the system. What had started in a public library in Vienna reading about Ancient Rome ended underground. The web of poison once let loose could not be contained—the branches of a spider's web are too strong.

The city is made up of five layers: the air above, the buildings, the street, the underground and the past. The body is made up of five layers: the skin, the flesh, the skeleton, the organs, and the blood/nerve supply. We view the city via a cross-section, but we're always looking from *inside* one of the layers; there's never enough chance to get *outside* the wedding cake effect and see it for what it truly is: a collage, a bricolage. We can't just step outside and see it side on, to appreciate the sections. Even from outer space we've lost the effect because we're looking from above rather than side on. And of course from the underground perspective there is nothing much above that we can see. We can feel the weight of human hopes above, however.

Sleepwalkers function best in darkness and silence. There is a steadiness to their movements; a steadiness which does not undermine their sense of urgency, their strange sense of purpose. When we sleepwalk, sleeptalk, we enter into an ancillary or extraneous relationship to the world. We do not think of 'the world' as being part of the 'night-world' but belonging rightfully to the order and propriety of the 'day-world'. The night-world belongs to the realm of the barbarians; those strange creatures that come and sit on us as we sleep. Of course, when we wake up we become, again, *civilized*. It's as if we throw off the mantle of our barbarian selves to stand upright and walk rigidly out into the full force of sunlight with the assurance of a Bach cantata upon the stroke of morning.

It was not by pure chance that Hitler saw himself as a sleepwalker: what he was in touch with did not belong to day but to night; he contained the spirit of the original barbarians within him. Wanting desperately to be the new Caesar he became the reawakened Vandal sweeping from the East across the snow-strewn plains to put to the sword the lovers of the grape and the steam bath. He had the same measure of intolerance, and yet curiosity, as the barbarians had towards the pleasure-loving Romans. His relationship with Mussolini, we are told by those who might have known, was one of suspicion. Hitler feared Mussolini might have been too soft—in exactly the same way the Roman rulers of the fifth century AD regarded their water-loving citizens as being no match for barbarians—although he was impressed with Il Duce's ability to speak French and English. Old habits of mind die hard. Conquest becomes a template, a maze out of which there is no escape.

Fritz Lang confided to someone, somewhere, sometime, that he directed as if he was a sleepwalker. The creative, and the destructive, comes out of the same place: out of the subconscious, being guided by intuition rather than by rationality. A process of montage, of bricolage, of collage.

No need to question what the slow stray thoughts mean; it's what they add up to that counts. Always searching for fireworks. The complexities of multiple sensation. Intuitively the barbarians knew when to attack, and when to wait by the frozen river, chilled to the bone and asleep on the necks of their horses.

Do we need to choose between being a barbarian and being a Roman? What makes us seek out barbarians? Why do we go looking, impulsively, for that which will end up destroying us? Is it Freud's brilliant notion of the death-wish (*thanatos*); the desire of the animate self to return to its origins as matter, to return to an inanimate state; to return to earth as we decompose or to return to air if we are cremated or to return to water if we are thrown over the side of a ship? Is it a collective return to origins? From dust we come and to dust we return, leaving behind mental electricity, a shivering of being, a remembrance of self. To return to the slights and anxieties of childhood? A life constructed in seeking retribution for a casual slap across the face received as a two-year-old, for abandonment as a ten-year-old, for betrayal as a twenty-year-old? What forces us on? What makes us get out of bed in the morning? Get out of bed in the middle of the night, sleepwalking around the streets of our city? Pale in the moonlight, the steam trains moored to their stations, silent women waiting for something to happen—like something out of those quietly insistent paintings by Paul Delvaux.

In sleep we long for oblivion. An oblivion of self. We long to turn off the motors. In sleepwalking we aim to act, to remedy a situation we cannot change in the diurnal sphere. Where are we walking to with such insistency, with such certainty? Who will be our guide to lead us back to sleep? In sleeptalking we enunciate our fears, private, allusive. A collection of solitary sleepwalkers we march on resolutely through the night, past the town hall, past the river, past the post office by the unearthly glow of the moon. Our bodies cold, our heartbeats slowing, our respiration falling. Do we have to choose between being awake and being asleep? Is not sleepwalking the perfect synthesis of opposites? Are we not both simultaneously in the land of the cerebrally alive and the cerebrally vacant? Hands guide us back to our beds gently, forcefully. Later we are informed when we wake that we were sleepwalking with a restless urgency during the night. We wake exhausted from fitful sleep (transformed from the drama of dreams into gigantic dung-beetles who go to work by day).

Sleepwalkers move with diminished responsibility. Wrapped in pure purple silk sheets we stride out of unlocked doorways into the warmth of a thirty-five degree night. The cats of the grand city are whining, rubbing their backs and pissing against posts. The sleek cars of the city are momentarily still. The night air is thick with the residue of the day's mental activity. A city of ten million goes to sleep with troubled thoughts and perspiring brows, concerned about their livers, their respiration, the pain in the gut; the dulcet tones of the announcer on France-Musique, the last sounds heard.

What we need is a compass that points to inside and outside, what is underground and the air above; something that is more than just directional. It could point to states of emotion as well: anxieties and insecurities. A compass able to point to the implications of History waiting to ensnare us.

With the invention of tourism, that great sea-traveller Mark Antony (born 83? BC, descended on his mother's side from Julius Caesar) crisscrossed the Mediterranean as many times as a modern businesswoman with her Chanel briefcase and an army of frequent flyer points. At the end of his long career in politics and beset upon by a scandal-hungry popular press enquiring about his love life, Antony retired to the island of Samos where his army was quartered, bringing with him musicians, jugglers and buffoons. There, he comforted himself with the balm of aesthetic stimulus and with the thought that there, on an island, he might protect himself from the barbarians, who had no understanding of how a thoroughly modern, civilized statesman such as himself might behave, that is if in fact he hadn't already turned by slow degrees into a barbarian. He had no way of knowing. There were no mirrors on the island (the locals being suspicious of their power). Representing initially a trans-urban civilization, due to his patrician origins, he had had no previous need to question his identity. At the end of his life he despaired, and fell upon his sword. He had been told, erroneously, that Cleopatra had killed herself; the soldier was too trusting of the message—the power of the word—in the final analysis.

Interior space. Rough approximations of the human head. Outer space—surrounding the buildings like plastic wrap. The skin: concrete, wood with a shiver of electricity running through the entire shell. A *frisson*. Take down the paintings, remove the carpets, take off the heavy damask curtains, remove the gilded chandeliers; there is just a thin veneer of civilization between the interior and the exterior of the apartment building.

It's like when you take off your make-up late at night, removing the many layers with the pad of cotton wool soaked in a cleanser; all the dust and grime and conversation of the city comes away, with enormous force. Your personality is coming away too: fractured by too many encounters; too many representations of self as seen through other people's eyes. You have nothing left—naturally you see yourself as a modern, civilized person; you are part of a cosmopolitan world. You are not a prisoner of one country. You have been charged with the world's input. You are media-sodden by the end of the day. The rain clings to your mackintosh in the same way as the world's problems get tangled in your hair. You are truly a world citizen now.

Memory: charged particles bouncing around the brain like a broken pendulum clock. The carousel you remember from childhood still turns. The dancing bear keeps dancing near the brazier of coals while the snow falls in the Tuileries. The smell of roast chestnuts. The half-in-love boy-child watches the girl-child in the care of her nanny as they all stare at the frozen pond where no toy-boats sail. The boy-child has a runny nose and a profound cough. The girl-child has a crimson ribbon in her hair and an olive green mohair coat fluting downwards in a nineteenth-century military style. She is twisting an errant honey-coloured curl with her right index finger. The boy-child wears a white and light green fleecy-lined parka made, according to the tag, in the People's Republic of China. He is infatuated with the girl-child; he cannot take his eyes off her. She cannot see him. Does not know him. Does not think of him. Does not care for him. He doesn't exist for her.

The boy-child is in the care of his father; a balding heavy man sitting on a bench reading the *météo* section of *Libération*, as if his life depended on it. Tomorrow: rain from the north-west. The day after: more rain, with more snow to fall at night. Pull the eiderdowns made of goose-feathers closer to keep the pall of nightmares, of conjectures from invading, to prevent the self from totally dissembling. The scale of the daily invasion. Barbarians scaling the parapets and ramparts of self. Your personality is held together with paper clips, reminder notices and half-remembered bits of Freud and Jung which you wrote out in blue ink along the inside of your arm. Every now and then you get glimpses of yourself as seen by a stranger; you put together a composite picture made up entirely of these half-glimpses and run screaming away from yourself at a million miles an hour, with the velocity of a stone leaving a slingshot, with the force of an atomic explosion, with the power of a space shuttle re-entering the earth's atmosphere... Your personality has six rooms: the kitchen where you are hale and hearty, the living room where you are severe, the master bedroom where you sink down, the children's bedrooms where you regress, the dining room where you wait expectantly, and the bathroom where you dismantle yourself by degrees, as you take off your clothes and your make-up. Pure domesticity.

The Layers of the City

After Napoleon conquered Egypt he commissioned a dinner set presenting an explanation—in pictures painted on ceramics—of what he had gone through. The dinner set now sits in the Victoria and Albert Museum, thoroughly neutered in its exhibition space—it has beauty but no longer power. Both Hitler and Napoleon accumulated paintings and sculpture for their own private collections. It was part of the imperial role. Art had a talismanic value disassociated from its content. It was what conquerors did: they took away the sacred objects of the defeated tribe; whatever was valued—be it gold, or crucifixes, or paintings or sculpture from the Parthenon.

Beauty draws you to itself with the security and precision of an invitation. Sleepwalkers, in their preverbal state, can understand the invitation to beauty; they are drawn to her as if they had an elastic band around their waist, as if they were metal filings drawn to a magnet, as if they were the freezing drawn to fire. Both Hitler and Napoleon were drawn to Russia like moths to a candle. It was almost as if they had no will of their own. The large land mass of Russia exerted a force so strong—like the force of gravity pulling us individually down towards the centre of the Earth—that they invaded against their better judgement.

Prometheus showed his audacity in a spectacular fashion, and will be remembered ever after for bringing light and warmth to the world, but he paid a terrible price: chained to a rock on the Caucasian Mountains, assailed by a vulture which devoured his liver by day, while allowing it to regrow each night so the same inexorable pattern could begin again the next day. The same turning of the psychic wheel, the same malevolence springing up in the healthy, the same increasing anger leading to the locking in of the set of action-reaction, action-revenge: Hitler avenging the defeat of Germany in World War I; Napoleon avenging the occupation of Gaul by the Romans many centuries before, ending up becoming Consul, then Emperor (both Roman titles) and naming his son the King of Rome. Napoleon dreamt of an empire to rival the Holy Roman Empire. Mussolini wanted to recapture the glory of Ancient Rome. The imperial Romans set in train many patterns that would play themselves out over later centuries. They surely did not realise at the time what the pull of their achievements would be for later generations. Nor could they have known that the importance they gave to the seductive strength of oratory and the will to power would be rediscovered in the twentieth century; that the speechmaker would indeed let loose furies, spurred on by the intoxication of listeners willing to devour every utterance.

Plagued by debilitating physical ailments, and having grown as a true son of Prometheus, Napoleon absentmindedly left fire wherever he went. Taking Moscow on the fourteenth of September, 1812, the great city started to burn to the ground the next night, as if by an alignment of the stars, or by magic. Conceived in a fiery carnal moment, Napoleon let his mind wander across his memories of reading Tacitus in school and in particular the episode of the burning of Rome: the blaze, commencing in the area of the Circus Maximus, quickly catching hold in the shops and bazaars, sweeping over the level spaces then climbing and descending the hills until the ancient city was a sheet of flames. The rumour, according to Tacitus, was not that Nero fiddled while Rome burnt but rather he went on to his private stage and, out of an immense loneliness, sang about the destruction of Troy. He too, along with Napoleon, having a sense of History with regard to the many uses of fire.

All this would not have been possible if Prometheus had not stolen fire from the gods in the first place. But why the gods allowed it to happen, no-one knows. Unless there was some collusion going on: that the gods actually wanted humans to be on more of a level footing with themselves— the humans squabbling and feuding amongst themselves as to who had the ownership of fire—and thus the gods could avoid feeling so isolated. For the gods knew that if they gave the humans a marvellous gift it would corrupt them— the humans would want more and more; would even see themselves as 'little gods'.

Fire, smoke and dust—the residue of a cataclysmic shower of comets striking the Earth—totally wiped out the dinosaurs. The first *blitzkrieg*. Death by fire. Annihilation. No wonder the Bible states the end of the world, Judgement Day, will be a day of fire. This is what Prometheus has to answer for, for his crime of theft. No wonder Purgatory and Hell are made up of sheets of fire. But then, all those soldiers died for the lack of warmth in the quest of a profitless journey.

When it was time to die, Hitler shot himself in the mouth, as though it was his mouth that was to blame. He wanted to annihilate the source of all his trouble, humiliation, suffering and despair. Eva Braun took a cyanide capsule, a less violent way to go; through the mouth (the source of all nourishment) once again though. What would we be without mouths? Without an ability to eat and drink? We would be nothing. Hitler made annihilation a password for his journey through life. Annihilation feeds on itself like fire-sucking oxygen; it can't be undone; you have a continual compounding. Heraclitus saw the world as an ever-living fire: the burning kept the world in balance, in harmony.

A building becomes a space in which we are placed. We live out a period of time within an apartment block or a *domus* and then move on. We crave a view; something larger than ourselves; something grander, more overwhelming. We want vastness, a sweep, as the Romantics did. Modern life: as disciplined as the streets are wide. The sound of a piano escapes from the fourth floor in a street you've found yourself in by chance—Miss Stein's rue de Fleurus. You re-enter the nearby Luxembourg Gardens to breathe. The buildings have started to become oppressive; their charm is fading; you seek out 'Nature'. You find: paths, lawns, ponds, buildings, chairs, gendarmes, nannies, lovers. The couples are oppressive; their intimacy as oppressive as a humid afternoon; the wrought-iron chairs and those sitting on them remind you of Renoir; his paintings of mothers and children in the Gardens—portraits of bourgeois stability. Here is the centre of the Gardens; the centre of the sociable city is here also. Everything else belongs outside the city walls.

The five-storey apartment block of nineteenth-century France with its medieval courtyard surrounded on four sides becomes the centre for the familial home—the fortress within a fortress; with its ground-floor restaurant the locus of activity, of conviviality, of storytelling, of ritual, of repetition, of domestic drama—in short, a neighbourhood where everyone has an inkling into other lives. Scheherazade had to keep telling stories because the Sultan was lonely and bored, wanting more than he could find in the ordinary world, wanting distraction at any cost, wanting entertainment, wanting to lose himself in the sound of a voice telling him a story, lulling him to sleep with a sense of the ordering facility of the storyteller. He was greedy for stories. He wanted to be stimulated, comforted, reminded of his mother and father, his ancestors, his line of descent, his cousins, nephews, in fact the whole of the human race. He could never get a surfeit of stories, because the *next one* was always going to be the best story he had ever heard...We have to keep telling stories to ourselves—about who we are, who we have been, who we will become—to keep us from boring ourselves to death.

Within the plastered, wallpapered walls of five-storey ceremonial buildings all sorts of *family business* takes place. The comings and goings of everyday intercourse. Paul Valéry, the poet, talks about every family generating its own inward boredom which drives its members away. So they have to become travellers. Endlessly uprooting themselves in an attempt to get away—to get away from self; to burn out the family from within. So they can forget who they are, what their inheritance is, and consequently what destiny lies at their feet. And yet within the family walls (Valéry again) there is created a space within the building where you huddle together in the dim light over the evening soup, listening to each other breathing and breaking bread. Eating in silence, aware of the other's presence.

Your past becomes your future with effortless ease; and the other way round is equally true: your future slipping inexorably into your personal past. Breaking bread together you sit around with people you've just met within the cafés of the great city discussing how you've managed to arrive at this point at this time; swapping stories as if your livelihood depended on them. These little papier-mâché constructions we throw together out of verbs, nouns, phrases, pauses, masonry, cement, plaster, wood and dust, sweat and blood; conversations swirling around in the stale café air. To not tell stories: inescapable. To not hear them: unavoidable. To keep out their meaning: unthinkable. In the city every building is a folktale, every citizen a folktale teller.

In the last months of the Third Reich, Heinrich Himmler was arguing for a final resistance to the invading armies; he was urging that they stand and fight 'like the Ostrogoths on Vesuvius'. His metaphor had shifted: he had changed from seeing his role as leader of the Knights of the Round Table to seeing himself as one of the barbarians.

Tall commercial buildings carve up space into three dimensions; most other art forms exist in only two dimensions: surface and depth. The storeys of pressed concrete hold the thin skeletal frame together, holding out possibilities for imagination to be extruded between the layers to give form to the mind's meanderings. Inside and outside.

Confusion, projection, reality: what is the 'thing' and what is the perception of the 'thing'. Intentions, actions; morality and immorality; the keeping of madness at bay.

As long as they keep coming to take away the (nuclear) waste. What do we do when we have mountains of the stuff in our own backyard? Send it back to where it came from? Send it back to the uranium producers of the world with a little note saying thanks for the memory, saying thanks for the brief bright incandescent spark (of energy), saying thanks for the half-life of dreams. Or do you just throw the whole damn lot in the ocean? Do you send it to the Third World as a present? Here is our detritus. Do with it what you will. Turn it into housing if you like. At least it is wrapped nicely. Sorry we didn't have time to write a card.

It was reported in a newspaper of the great city that seventeen more nuclear power plants have been found to have serious problems with their filtration systems. This situation has been described by the authorities as having a degree of gravity of 2 (on a 6-point scale). The problem will be remedied within a) three weeks b) three months or c) three years depending on the availability of funds.

All along the banks of the Rhône, the glittering nuclear power plants gleam. From a parking lot next to the river Rhine you can see the central nuclear station of Fessenheim shine. A station is where you wait; a shrine is where you pray; a plant is something that grows. The radiation from Chernobyl is still growing inside the cells of certain inhabitants. Cells multiplying in an ironic statement on development. The word 'nuclear' re-arranged equals 'unclear'...In the end all the nuclear waste produced by decaying fuel has to be put somewhere. Where else but in the Hell of Dante—deep underground? Or buried beneath the sea's floor, or else stacked upright in covered mountains. We have developed a mythologically-induced hatred of the underground. It is the one part of Nature we can't abide.

Iodine 131 finds its way into a country's milk supply. Mad cows graze beside nuclear power plants. The question for the future: how much exposure to radiation is acceptable? Would iodine with its half-life of about eight days be acceptable? Be half-acceptable? Roentgen's X-rays are currently acceptable. The usual line is that the benefits outweigh the risks; the risks are thus muffled and buried beneath mounds of paper.

We live in a mass age: mass production, mass generation, mass rationalization. When the crowds of the former East Germany stood up ready to be mowed down like dry grass on a summer's day the borders started to open up holes, the Wall shuddered, the rulers questioned their own legitimacy to rule and the whole shebang changed shape. Generations grow older; the former certainties dissipate in the same way water seeks by any route to find its way off the Notre-Dame roof. Water seeks to find its natural equilibrium, it does not ask itself why, it just moves of its own accord. Mass energy, mass observation, massacre, massage, mass media, masquerade. The principal actors assemble in false outward show. The politics of the crowd. The *communards* set fire to the public buildings of the great city hoping to bring down the centres of power and prestige in

one incandescent fugal march of fire. The idea was to burn
out the past, to cauterize the wound of indignity, of feeling inferior to those who swaggered around the city as if
they owned it, as if they alone had an intravenous drip
attached firmly to the past and to the future. The inhabitants of the small and narrow, ill-ventilated streets had had
enough so they set alight the Tuileries and a corner of the
Louvre. The rationale: what you cannot have you seek to
destroy, beauty is overpowering in itself. Have you not felt
this yourself?

What if Adolf Hitler *had* been accepted into the Fine Arts
Academy in 1907 in Vienna? (His drawing test was 'unsatisfactory'.) Would the history of the twentieth century now
be different? Instead he had to find a different way of leaving his mark, his signature upon a canvas. He decided to
reinvent himself as a new Caesar (the past suffocating the
present) rather than as a new Claude Lorrain. He wanted
to create a new German Roman Empire. He confided to the
sculptor Arno Breker that if it wasn't for politics he would
have liked to have lived the life of an artist in Paris. What
if he had in fact passed his entrance examination? Or would
another orator—part-time composer, part-time corporal,
part-time architect, part-time poet—have risen up out of
the ashes like a reconfigured phoenix to take his place?
Could Hitler have continued on, instead, as a modern-day
Claude Lorrain, recording the antique classicism of a
German past? Could he have subsumed the nagging question of his personal identity under the typically schizoid
identity of the artist? Could his battles with himself have
been turned into art instead? Why didn't he do what all

artists do—turn neurosis into art? Why did he need to drag so many willing and unwilling participants into his scheme of *building*? His scheme for *town-planning*, for architectural renewal. Which, in time, dragged its shadow with it and when he found himself frustrated as a *builder* the same impulse turned to its flip-side—that of *demolition expert*. Water finds whatever route it can to go down the hillside.

It is said that as the war raged all around him Hitler became increasingly preoccupied with the architecture of proposed buildings—it was all to be built to a monumental scale—and the town planning of Berlin. The corporal finally had the opportunity to follow his early ambition of becoming an architect. With Albert Speer, the 'court artist', hunched over maps of the city, he would discuss the transformation of Berlin into a truly imperial city and even muse upon what the planned monumental buildings would look like as ruins in the far distant future when Europe was ruled over by either 'Huns or barbarians'. The issue of buildings, their shape, form, function and placement would occupy part of his waking mind; the progress of the war would have to be given a lesser attention. The artist in him wanted to shape; the soldier in him wanted to obliterate; the neurotic in him wanted to cauterize himself.

The urge to build; the urge to destroy; the urge to leave alone. The painter takes up a piece of charcoal in order to leave a mark on the primed canvas, two and a half metres square. The purity of the canvas will never be the same again. The canvas itself is so beautiful, it has so much potential; it seems wrong to put a mark on it at all. The light is falling from the west onto a corner of the canvas.

Dust motes are rising from the surface of the canvas. The warmth of an evening in midsummer. The church bells of Notre-Dame calling the faithful to worship. The smell of fish frying in olive oil. Someone in the apartment above is preparing the evening meal; the smell wafts downwards. Light wafts upwards. Life goes on, whether it's remarked upon or recorded, it just goes on.

Twilight: the loveliest time of all. Madame and Monsieur Doucemère are going for their pre-prandial walk along the rue Saint-Antoine. Fi-Fi trotting behind. Midsummer. The temperature dropping after the heat of the day. Now twenty-seven degrees. They are reacquainting themselves with their street, with the couple of blocks that have bordered their married lives; in love with their cruel twentieth century, which in spite of everything, has managed to pull and push them together. Strolling through their own few blocks, listening to the wisecracks of the shop owners, they are content in their role in the scheme of things. *Ecoute Fi-Fi!* But no-one can hear what follows; the remaining words float away on the gentle breeze. Insubstantial words: we try and pin them onto things—a look, an emotion, a gesture—as a way of trapping the moment, but even the words themselves slip away leaving only a faint residue, a delicate shimmering of airwaves. The couple are almost done with the day. Baked fish and salad for the evening meal, together with a glass or two of last season's beaujolais, or a *vin blanc,* before turning in to bed and lulling gently into night-thoughts.

The couple walk past the office of a firm of world-famous architects. On the drawing board the first sketch of a part of inner Paris that will be razed. The architects are talking of a building that will outlast all of them; a building made of materials that will be strong enough to last a thousand years; one that will rival the buildings of the Pharaohs. The architects are talking about a building that will be truly modern: one that will express the spirit of the times: the urgency, the insecurity, the anxiety, the 'belief-lessness'. They are wondering if it can be done. What shape would it have? Should it reference both the past and the present, or stay indubitably in the present—whatever, or whenever, that may be. The problem, they say to each other in hushed tones, is the fundamental problem of creating a possible architecture for *today*. What structure can carry the hopes, fears and sentiments of a generation? What building can adequately represent mass neurosis? What can you create which is undeniably in the present tense?

We cannot avoid the past. Every road has been built by someone. Every apartment block is built on the skeletons of those who have gone before; every river washes away the blood found on the side of the road. Every carpenter and stonemason and architect creates with the hope that the structure will last; that an unforeseen error of judgement will not reduce the whole to ruins, covered with weeds, sentimentalized into art. Better by far to leave the canvas, stretched and primed on its easel, ready for its viewer to imagine any picture on it at all; for any added mark will only ruin its potential, disfigure what might be said. Better not to attempt the unachievable.

We invent our memories. It's easier that way. Let them percolate away for years until one day we can construct a whole mountain made up of a personal past. Cities have memories too. Is it better to forget or to remember? Which is more psychologically necessary for the city to survive?

The earth giveth and the earth taketh away, blessed be the name of the earth...Where do we hide, asked Seneca upon hearing of the destruction of Pompeii, when the earth itself causes ruin? When what is stable, that which 'protects us, upholds us, on which cities are built' turns against us. The buildings crumble. Lava engulfs. The tide becomes molten, and will not be beaten back. The natural world rises up to retake what belongs to it; which doesn't include buildings. Fire becomes the natural state of things: Prometheus unbound.

The above ground—crowded with aircraft, with acid rain blown in by the wind-currents along with the white light, white heat of radiation. Ground level, festering with people, with the massed crowd on a Saturday night, burning to find entertainment, diversion, the traffic (*la circulation* which does not circulate) grinds to a halt along Haussmann's boulevards. In the buses everyone is jammed together, so much so you can smell the perfume, the aftershave, you can feel the warm beating hearts either side of you, you can feel the twitching pulses, the raw nerve ends of emotion exposed for all to see, the good humour of the ride. The acceptance that we are all stuck together for the duration...That's what the great cities have become: glue yards sticking everyone together: Siamese populations. Above ground: the sky, its inhabitants in their Concordes, the flying buttresses, the zeppelins, the Eiffel Tower: all comprising the one space. Peering down from the Eiffel

Tower the city looks like different parts of the brain (the cerebrum, the cerebellum, the optic lobes and the medulla oblongata): all neatly divided into thinking/feeling like so many on/off switches, so many electrical impulses, our modern digital embrace...

Our analogue life slips away to be replaced by digital being: no more a continuous pulse; henceforth a violent alternation, opposition of states; we are either on or off, awake or asleep, male or female: a binary view of the world, instead of a transgendered existing. The alternative: an effortless analogue flowing between male and female, between sides of self, between being awake or asleep. To be at harmony with the self, to sing a harmonious song wherein to fall asleep, perchance to dream...

Not a new idea, but an old one. Heraclitus' notion of the necessity of opposites. Opposition falls away, in the flow of the river. The binary life starts with two arms, two legs, two eyes; we model a world around our physiology...The new order, the new monotony, celebrated throughout the land as a movement forward with a clarion of bells, driving away the forces of discontent with the random complacent smugness of the politician newly elected...The street: the shouting shopkeeper, the shouting cop, the shouting bricklayer: all these sounds going up and down and around and in and out of ears, vibrations noticed by eyes...

To go out on a warm Saturday night. Twenty-seven degrees. To see the swarming masses, the mobile crowd, the feverish crowd, on a warm night, rushing hither and thither, by bus, by car, by foot, by Métro. The stirring mass, happy to be out on a Saturday night, going to visit a lover, a friend, a family. The moving footpath of humankind. There's not much room to move in the middle of that crowd and yet on nights like these it's not the edginess of the crowds that you notice, but the comfort, the harmony of the crowd—one elbow fits neatly into another's ribs—and the compact nature of the crowd. The compression of the city: a benign presence—when the weather's benign, when the stresses of the working week have dissipated. The compression of all great cities: forcing people out at the sides: like a toothpaste container squeezed simultaneously in all directions at once—and yet at times the overwhelming good-naturedness of the squeezed individuals. The crowded bus taking one hour from the Hôtel de Ville to Châtelet—the bus driver cracking jokes to the passengers to fill in time. At this slow pace you can watch the crowd on the footpaths of the rue de Rivoli moving past you in ceremonious elegance. A pace slow enough to take in the glittering monuments. How can you live in a city of monuments? All those residues of the past threatening to strangle the present.

The sound of African drums as you walk slowly towards your normal familiar bus stop, near the Hôtel de Ville (the one that takes you to Boulogne via Michel-Ange Molitor). A small circle of demonstrators (of street-sweepers and street-cleaners holding brooms) in blue and green overalls with megaphones, blowing whistles and beating drums surrounded shoulder to shoulder by the CRS (the army of the city), dressed in riot gear, their helmets with perspex visors pulled down over their faces, with tear-gas canisters strapped to their belts, with tear-gas shotguns and machine guns slung casually over their shoulders.

Four hours later when you return at dusk they are all still there, the same frenzied repetitive drumbeats, the riot police unmoving—turned to stone by the primitive drumbeats. What are they frightened of? They are only frightened of the sound. Nothing else. They want to stop the sound. They are not frightened of the demonstrators who are merely made of bone and blood, water, tissue, flesh and nerve endings. They can be disposed of, dispersed, disentangled or dismembered, but the sound...the sound is elusive, it can't be shot, it can swell up anywhere, even in night-thoughts.

Even if you shot the soundmakers, after four hours of listening to it, you would still carry the sound away with you; it would become part of you. It is the sound of a heartbeat. And yet the riot police with their submachine guns at the ready stand there, for hour after hour, shoulder to shoulder. Who has more freedom? The encircled or the encirclers? Who is keeping whom captive? Who are the agents of civilization, who the agents of barbarianism? When the Americans bombed the unguarded retreating Iraqi soldiers by the waters of Babylon at the end of the Gulf War, who were the barbarians, who were the civilizers? Pity you have to destroy a country to save it. Pity (look at Vietnam), pity...That we may not sink under the weight of our armaments that we build so our economies may stay in order, so we might not collapse under the weight of hungry people, that we may not slip into barbarianism; it's only a slim thread away, only the other side of the brain...only the other pulse, like the on/off electrical pulse driving our digital brains.

With what jaundiced expressions do the locals gaze upon the representations (realismo/heroico style) of the storming of the Bastille that are painted on the walls of the Bastille Métro station. The representations show what a good-natured, cleanly dressed group they were (with school-children amongst them). With what degree of uncertainty (but with a sense of necessity) must the State have faced the prospect of the bicentenary of the overthrow of the State? With what uncertainty must the representatives of the State have rolled around on their tongues those curi-ous words *liberté, égalité,* and *fraternité:* each one a potential bullet from an assassin's gun.

A crowd of 400 000 secondary school students filled the streets of the great city the other day. They were demand-ing: 'the power to study, the power to choose, the power to speak'. The crowd when stirred to protest is always demanding power; it is the nature of the massed group; it is what the individual lacks...The congregating point for the demonstrators when they had finished their march was the Champ-de-Mars—the field which had such symbolic importance during the French Revolution. At least the sec-ondary students knew their history. How can you celebrate a revolution without encouraging another one? You try and turn the celebration into Disneyland, so that everyone's fan-tasies can then be encouraged; all wrapped up in the safety of fairy floss...The crowd of 400 000 was dispersed with tear gas and a baton charge. When the crowd ran, quite a few were trampled. If you've ever been part of a frightened running crowd you don't forget it: your hair stands up on the back of your head.

There were only seven prisoners in the Bastille who required freeing. They would have been happy to take part in the enactment of the overthrow of the symbolic order by walking free and disappearing into the cheering crowd only to resurface years later as part of other crowds who cheered on the public deaths of other prisoners (the latter ones, though, washed and richly perfumed). The mode of the new crowd becomes the new ethics: the language is that of the group: everyone mirrors everyone else. Symbolically slogans are repeated to reinforce the group: chanting is mandatory: the buzz of the language, repeated, magnified is hypnotic—like a Hitler speech: listen for the buzz. The revolutionary crowd in front of the Bastille paused just long enough to ask themselves: Are we barbarians now too? But their leaders had already supplied them with an answer: We live in barbarous times, with a need for barbarous solutions. (An answer that would be used again and again.)

Thoughts of those first barbarians never far from their minds; they had, after all, been drinking the same water for generations. The crowd knew they were doing something different. They weren't just hanging around in the cafés or making shoes or knitting socks...They were inventing themselves as actors...After all they had cut off the head of their king. They had something tangible to show for their existence. They had been humiliated enough. They woke up one morning and said, That's it! and their queen went to the scaffold.

The Layers of the City

A roar and the Bastille fell down. Another almighty blast (the trumpets of Jericho) and the Berlin Wall fell down and the crowd streamed in to look at what they had always feared...to look at their own Stasi files, to look at the head of the Gorgon in the hands of her deliverer...to look up their own past to see if they had forgotten anything of interest about their own lives...to see if their lives could be made into a pattern on paper...to see if someone else understood more about them than they did themselves...to see if they had lived lives worth owning up to.

The tyrants were suddenly in retreat. The citizens could get on with their lives, with the cleaning, the scrubbing, the disinfecting...If the tyrants had to go they would make sure they took plenty of citizens with them: tanks, mud, tear gas and poppies. The troops go backwards and forwards regaining, then losing ground—until everything is laid waste. One hundred thousand dead in retaking a muddy stretch of earth; an extra one hundred thousand dead in losing the same muddy stretch of 'strategically important' ground. Though how could anyone be sure it was exactly the same stretch of ground 'absolutely necessary' to defend when every piece of ground looked exactly the same?

Back and forth until everything is laid waste. Except for Apollinaire roneoing off his poems to sell to his fellow soldiers as the shells came in at the front line. Except for David drawing up plans for a revolutionary parade through the streets of Paris. Except for Napoleon writing his novel, the little corporal, Hitler, with his watercolours...When Chernobyl blew, the tops of the poppies, once covered in blood, were covered with radioactivity.

Invasion and re-invasion: Vikings in longboats sailing up the Seine, putting townships to the torch; crusades setting off from the Île Saint-Louis. The essential toing and froing across a continent, across the sun-and-salt encrusted Mediterranean.

We huddle together in cities...to keep out the cold, to keep out the barbarians, to keep out the plague, to keep out the loneliness of the endless plains and the darkness of the forest with its roaming wolves. We huddle together, so many of us at one time, extruding the city into a wedding-cake, a tower of Babel, a coliseum...of many layers.

If you wish to understand the many layers of the city then you need to picture in your mind's eye a cross-section of the city. Above ground we have the air as we look up, the buildings around us and the street we stand in. Below ground there is the Métro and below that we have in descending order Revolutionary Paris, Renaissance Paris, Medieval Paris, Barbarian Paris, Roman Paris (*Lutetia Parisiorum*) and the Paris of the guilds of fishermen of the islands of the Seine (the *Parisii*). Naturally, we are only alive because of those who have gone before us. We live on top of their bones, on top of their aspirations and dreams. We were dreamt up by our forebears in a fit of optimism, in a hot and sweaty moment.

To go down the ramps of the crypt of the forecourt of Notre-Dame de Paris is to descend through the many layers of the city. Descendants of the Graeco-Roman line, we have within us, waging a battle of imperial dimensions, a war between barbarism and civilization, between gods and humans, between fire and water...

The Layers of the City

Night-time. Nine p.m. Twenty-seven degrees. All of the great city is out in the street (or else looking out onto the street from their windows and balconies) just going for a stroll: Spanish men holding hands, the teddy boys in leather jackets having stepped straight out of the fifties, a couple fumbling at each others' buttons, at a recalcitrant bra-strap, bodies in a doorway, young girls dressed up like Marilyn Monroe—trying to re-create a sense of innocence...

Let us share a meal together...Let us go out into the great city together late at night and walk the streets in the heat of midsummer and browse in shop windows and nod to those who pass us by. We will hold hands and walk under the light of the full moon. On nights like this the great city reminds you of Rome—especially when the cats are out, the air is still and the heat wraps around you like a mohair blanket. Let us wander without knowing where we are going and we can mumble to each other intimate and rambling thoughts as they come into our heads. We can talk about the past and wander through the smaller streets, looking into windows, seeing our reflections in the moonlight come back at us with the force of an intercity train running into a bridge pylon.

We can search for our younger selves, in doorways, in alleyways, over the cobblestones and amidst the spider webs hanging from lintels, by the pathways lining the Seine. We can run into our likenesses as we turn a corner, absent-mindedly. That youngster over there staring into a shop window: isn't there something familiar about the way the head is held to the left? about the pensiveness, the self-absorption, the self-referentiality? We collide with our

likeness, apologize, brush ourselves down, murmur something else and disappear into the open arms of the street
in twenty-seven degree heat. Let us talk about our past
loves. In one incoherent ramble we can tell each other...
everything...and yet nothing. Nothing of importance.
Nothing of value. Ulysses when questioned said, I am
nobody. He had disappeared into a spiral of self-doubt, of
anxiety, of insecurity; he had become...undone. Self-
effaced, he slipped into the landscape, into the scenery, like
an act of nature.

Let us talk for once of that which matters. What matters? We shall wander into cafés and pick up books that
have been left behind, to leaf through torn copies of Baude-
laire and Balzac and leave them covered in coffee and red
wine stains for the person who follows. We shall avoid the
bomb blasts emanating from the neighbouring *arrondissement*. We shall share our thoughts as naturally as water
falling down steps. We shall search through our memories
as we ransack the quays and the boulevards for clues. We
shall chase our likeness down the Métro steps, and catching up with the exact one swing her/him around to face
us just as she/he is about to board the carriage and say,
Haven't I seen you somewhere before? And then it hits you
with maximum force: you are staring at the same mouth,
though younger, the same lips, though younger, the same
eyebrows, though younger, the same nose, though younger,
the same eyes, and you then say in soap opera tones: Where
have you been all my life? I have been wondering when I
would run across you...I want you to tell me what you've
been up to. I want you to confess to me, about your life,

your loves, your fantasies, your misadventures...Tell me who you are.

And the answer comes back, as though from a long way away: I am nobody.

Do you remember that night in Milan? It was so hot, we were walking along the tram-tracks in the early hours of the morning, all the cats were out, arching their backs, and whining away. There was a full moon behind the ancient Roman columns in an inky-black sky resonant with meaning. The cats had taken over the ancient city. All exasperation, worries, anxieties slipped away in the face of the monumentality of the past and the urgency of the moment. You could see clearly all of a sudden, as if for the first time. It was like another night in Barcelona, again the heat unifying the crowds walking together along *Las Ramblas,* setting up a cosmic hum, emptying out the million and one conflictual thoughts that go nowhere... couples drinking sangria in the streets and dancing tipsily, food on bench tops, the cats sniffing around, the smell of the majestic Mediterranean, of olive oil, of sherry and salami. The warm wind blowing down from the Middle Ages...from Roman Paris...from our ancestors.

Night-time. Ten p.m. The temperature slipping now: twenty-one degrees. Monsieur and Madame Doucemère asleep now under their ivory-coloured sheets, lying peacefully under their summer-weight eiderdown. Content. Just to be together. To be old together. To be in company. The comfort of letting go. The tentative security of sleep. The peacefulness of letting your identity slip into another's, of giving up all of the seeking, the striving, the searching, the multiple dissatisfactions of the day. To slip into another's ego for the duration of the night. A complete letting go of self.

Qui parle? Just some passers-by whom we overheard. There are so many voices in any street that it's hard to hear any distinctly. Everybody talking. It could be Manhattan. The heat, the steam rising from the Métro vents. Just enjoy the confabulating. The city—land of confusion, of muddled thoughts, the land of Cockaigne...Tell each other—everything.

Three a.m. The day's pollution having ascended now begins its descent, encircling all of Paris in a warm and loving embrace.

Who watches? Who speaks?

five | The Crypt

You arrive at the archaeological crypt of the forecourt of Notre-Dame. Juliet is waiting for you. You go down the steps, pay for two tickets and walk downwards. Your guide leans close towards you, with a smile, and says, as you both descend:

—Here we can see the many underground layers of the city. Here is the eighteenth century at this level. As we descend we are going backwards in time. Here is a pillar of the foundations of the iron gates of the ancient Hôtel-Dieu. Here are the remains of the Renaissance, these walls date from the Middle Ages and here we finally arrive at the age of the Romans in Lutetia. And just outside the city's walls, in a space we cannot see but we can imagine, are camped those Siamese twins of the Romans—the barbarians...This space here, dating from the time of the Romans, contained an underground furnace. Heat was transferred via those bricks into all of the rooms of the house: central heating, in other words. Julius Caesar invaded this island in 52 BC. He was forty-eight years of age, balding, thin and pale with black eyes, of uncertain health...

The words are too much. You have to leave, you are feeling claustrophobic, like you have no personal space left to live in because of the crowded nature of the past. It's not just being underground—you could live underground if you had to—it's just the weight of the past pushing you down; the ramifications, the reverberations are overwhelming. You have to get out. A panic grips you. A fear of being suffocated by the past, by the responsibility of the past. You feel overwhelmed by the generations who have gone before: their hopes, fear, insecurities, dreams and suffering—above all, their suffering. You've got to get to the surface and lie down on the damp ground in the open air, before you fall over. You quickly run up the ramps and stairs, knocking into a small group of schoolchildren as you go: *pardon, pardon*...Thoughts flash through your mind: a slide show of Julius Caesar the epileptic, Jung fainting at the train station, barbarians camped by the side of a frozen river, Speer fainting at moments of stress, Romans in their public baths...

You lie down on the grass and slowly start to relax and breathe normally again—the fear of falling has subsided, you know the familiar warning signs; when you can breathe normally the panic goes away.

There are people looking at you. There is an organ-grinder looking at you, a young bare-footed boy, a photographer wearing an old-fashioned portrait camera around his neck is watching too. You're embarrassed that you've perturbed these good people. You mumble that you are all right and, feeling self-conscious, you pull yourself up and sit down on a public bench.

The Layers of the City

The thought passes across your consciousness that you have to become more forgetful in the future, you cannot afford to any longer be so conscious of the many layers of the city, of the many layers of human bodies who have lived and whose bones are piled on top of one another. You are only still alive because they have died to make room for you. You are aware that if you don't forget you will go mad. You tell yourself that it's only by constantly forgetting, a conscious insistence on memory-loss that you, we, can all keep on going; insanity, only the flicker of an eyelid away.

The organ-grinder and the boy melt into the surrounds. Your guide comes over slowly, looking at you suspiciously, as though you've come from another planet. Your day is over, you've just destroyed it with your weakness, your incompetence, with your need to get away. You apologise. You say you can't explain. It's too hard to find the right words. You say you're embarrassed. She says it's OK. She says you can find her in the library every day, except Sunday. As she leaves you call out that you just had a touch of the Stendhals that's all. You wonder if you'll ever see her again.

When you have sat on the bench for half an hour or so and your breathing has returned to normal you decide you are going to return to the crypt. You know it is foolish, you know it is bad for your health, bad for your nerves, you know you may have another fainting fit but it is the smell of the past, your curiosity that draws you back; you want to photograph the past. You suspect there is an important message for you, personally, down there, in the dust of past civilizations. You take out your new digital camera that you purchased duty-free before you left home, which you have not yet used. You want to photograph the past, photograph any errant Romans and barbarians still lying around in the dust. You were only there briefly but even so your intuition tells you that in the crypt your own personal past is more present than anywhere else in Paris. You place the camera back in your travelling bag as you realize that photographs will probably be prohibited and you return, buying your third ticket for the day. You feel somewhat doomed and nauseous already as if it's a past you don't want to face. What if your past throws your whole equilibrium into a total spin? Perhaps it is better not to find out. Better not to find out if you were a Roman or a barbarian.

You quickly descend; the crypt is deserted, it is almost closing time. You take your camera out of the bag. You are going to photograph dust and a few bricks from Roman times, from the time of Lutetia, the time of the fifth century AD, the time of the waves of barbarian invasion. You lean further over the railing to get a better shot. The old nausea is coming back again. You are starting to feel overwhelmed once again by the weight of the past and its personal meaning. You are at the mercy of your personal history, your history before you were born, the history you had no hand in shaping—but it has shaped you, it is unavoidable, inescapable, we are paying for the sins of our forebears and they had to pay for the sins of their forebears. You take a number of photos in rapid succession then as you lean over further to get a better shot, the camera,

The Layers of the City

your new Olympus digital camera, slips from your hands
into the dust of Lutetia. Without thinking you slip through
the rails and jump down after it, the drop is about two
metres, your camera is covered in ancient dust, the smell
of the past is overpowering at this level, you feel faint, you
know you are about to pass out, you have been here
before...

six | The Barbarians

A Roman officer noted during the fifth-century invasions of Gaul that the invading barbarians knew no fear, lived in an animal state, were cold, hungry and thirsty, slept and grew old on their horses and spoke in an obscure language charged with metaphors.

The metaphors were often so colourful and poetic that the barbarians had trouble understanding each other. The allusions to a river, say, were so vibrant and resonant that half the men would cross the valley instead of fording the river as had been intended. The poverty of their lifestyle was compensated for by their passionate search for two things: for gold and for the perfect metaphor, with its allusive yet exact richness.

A river, say, might be referred to as an armpit filled with sallow, flaxen hair, which would convey to half those assembled the intended meaning—as they too saw a yellowish stream in the sickly winter afternoon light when they looked—while the others would see a picture of a valley of wheat as corresponding to that image. A range of hills might be referred to as the breasts of supine women while the haze created by the full heat of a summer's day might be referred to as a shimmering of crooked scars. A grove of ancient olive trees might be called a place of twisted snakes while a brook became a handful of saliva nestled in a beard. Dusty tracks would become the cracks in an old man's face while a fortified town would become a pustule, to be squeezed at leisure.

The barbarians on the whole would not speak much, preferring to be left by themselves with their own private and substantial thoughts so as to have the time to better formulate an appropriate metaphor which would impress their fellow barbarians with its colour, its richness and its aptness. Silence ruled for the most part except for those nights of a creamy full moon when no-one could sleep and the men reclining on their horses would ruminate about the nature of life and death, discuss the arrangement of stars in the sky as a portent of things to come and discuss those who had gone before them and would speculate on those who would come after them—all in a profusion of lush and dense metaphor. Misunderstandings proliferated, but at least they knew they were living.

The barbarians spent their lives on their horses. The view from the horse became the normal height from which they saw everything. They were so at one with their horse that they would sleep on their horses (to be better prepared for battle, so no-one might surprise them) with their legs astride and their bodies slumped forward and their foreheads moulded into the neck of their horses.

The ability of the barbarians to sleep on their horses

provoked fear and amazement amongst the Romans in Gaul and Hispaniae. It was both a matter of ridicule and concern and made for endless hours of discussion amongst the Romans in the great bathhouse in Lutetia as they moved from the waters of the *caldarium* to the waters of the *tepidarium* to finally the waters of the *frigidarium* amidst the smell of overpowering perfumes. The barbarians became extensions of their horses in the same way in which branches insinuate themselves into the crevices of stone walls and become the wall.

The life of the barbarians was justified by a relentless and remorseless movement forward, coupled with an equal desire to alternate this feverish movement with periods of stillness when they would encircle the fortifications of an isolated Roman settlement in Gaul or Hispaniae and take time to reflect upon the world. Their desire was always to see new things and they refused to go back over territory they had already covered. They would rather travel for an extra seventy days and nights than to re-see something already seen. They were just travelling forward in an endless progression and while they were moving they were relatively content. But in order to fully feel the surge of renewed movement they forced themselves to stay still in laying siege for long periods of time in order for there to be a contrast. After extremely long periods of feverish movement they could no longer feel anything because there was no other state to contrast it with.

However if they stayed for too long in one place and the grass grew between the feet of their horses and the birds planted nests in their beards and the winds grew too familiar in their twists and turns then they would yearn for a change to the regular rhythm of life and become bored and listless. It was only at times of siege that they would be halted for long periods of time and usually they would try to camp by a river so that the movement of the water would parallel their preferred state and by this sleight-of-hand they would be less discontented than otherwise. The barbarians would stare silently from their horses into the moving stream and would become nostalgic for the certainty of the endless onward-going movement—where the goal was clear—and would become restless at the thought of the sounds and sights and smells that they were missing due to being stationary. For they realized that the leaves that were falling today in the lands they would have been visiting if they had kept on at the same pace forward would not be the same leaves falling when they eventually arrived and there would be different people forging through the villages today than the ones they would eventually meet. This sense of loss was always with them. To remain stationary they had given up movement. In order to decide which way to go they had to forego the chance of arriving in one of the destinations sooner. But while their bodies remained stationary their thoughts went onward envisaging the nature of the terrain they would be crossing, internalizing the regular metronome of their horses' hooves.

Occasionally while stationary one of the barbarians would mention, by way of a vivid and daring metaphor, a Roman settlement in Narbonensis which none of them had seen but which had been described to him by one of the Levantine traders (those transitory storytellers who moved between the Romans and the barbarians exchanging goods and feeding the store of speculative knowledge about each group, but in such a fantastical way that neither group knew what was true and what was fiction) as being the most beautiful, serene and lovely place that anyone could imagine and they would decide then and there to obliterate it from the face of the earth. A Roman town locked behind fortified walls was by its nature designed to stir up their hatred and contempt as walls were something that the barbarians found hard to understand and thus hated with a great passion; walls were barriers to movement and thus deserved to be torn down brick by brick. A Roman town that was so serene and lovely and civilized would be a pleasure to destroy, and a stone bridge across a river provided even greater satisfaction in its demolition; it was, after all, an affront to the river. The river had not asked the bridge to be there; the river did not conspire to assist the bridge to remain; in fact, it actively ate away at the foundations of the bridge.

The barbarians on the whole, however, were not completely inured to serenity, loveliness and civilization; it was more that they had decided long ago that if they could not understand this particularly settled, measured and ordered Roman way of life within walls then they might as well destroy it. At heart, they found the Romans prosaic rather than poetic and thus held them in contempt. Destruction and the accumulation of gold provided twin reasons for perpetual motion alternating with stillness (for then they had a chance to catch up with their thoughts—left behind as it were in the whirlwind of activity) and stillness provided an excuse for the meanderings of the mind. They would fret if there were not sustained periods of enforced stillness, such as the siege of a town.

The barbarians had become wanderers out of boredom, always desiring to see what was over the next hilltop and what was hidden below in the next valley. They had no real desire to settle down until, that is, age grew upon them like moss and their bones ached and they longed for the comfort of a warm river in the sunshine. The Abyssinian traders had told the barbarians about the sensual luxuriousness and the voluptuousness of the Romans, with their command of water, their rich grapes, their fine purple embroidery and their love of sonorous, eloquent speeches— that had its own appeal for the older barbarians. Though they knew with certainty, as did the Romans, that luxuriousness went hand-in-hand with weakness and softness of mind and body while ferocity and a vicious purposefulness of mind and body had made the barbarians so successful so far.

They had destroyed many towns with their reputation alone. When a particular group of barbarians grew older and their bodies were not as iron-and-fire hardened as they once were, they could use the Levantine or Abyssinian traders to pass on to the Romans the message that the barbarians were coming; a message so powerful that the Romans and the native Gauls of Narbonensis would sometimes flee in horror of their own free will. It had happened before, in isolated settlements, that just the word *barbarians*, on its own, had made the Romans sick and unable to fight. The inhabitants had succumbed to *word-sickness*.

For the female barbarians, with their carts and animals and children camped kilometres behind their menfolk, their lives were generally lives of privation though they had a community around them that kept their minds distracted. The major tasks of each day were to find enough food to live on, which wasn't as difficult in Narbonensis as it was in other less fertile areas, and to try and build rudimentary shelters to keep out the biting winds that would spring up. Uncertainty ruled their days for they never knew when they would have to uproot their camp and follow the dusty trail of hoofbeats up ahead. Suspicious of each other by nature they were nevertheless forced to collude and become implicated in the lives of the other female barbarians and barbarian children who proliferated under the conditions and never seemed to feel the cold or find a want of something to amuse themselves with.

Occasionally one barbarian or other might wonder what it would be like to be a Roman: to be one who was passive, rational, soft, water-loving, given over to perfumed sensuality. Perhaps it might be agreeable, especially in one's old age, to settle down by a brook with a small range of hills behind you, watch butterflies and swallows in the sunshine and lazily throw stones into the water and watch the ripples spiral outwards in concentric rings, painstakingly concocting the most vivid and exact of metaphors which might be rewarded by one's peers with honour and respect; to be motionless in body but, by way of compensation, to be remorselessly, relentlessly in perpetual mental motion.

It only needed one exact and resonant metaphor to be accorded the respect of one's fellow barbarians; something that became more necessary as one grew older and lost all delight in one's own physical abilities. You could bask only for so long in the role of being a barbarian—seeing the abject fear in the eyes of the traders—before becoming bored by it all and desiring new stimulation. The persistent risk, however, in the search for the perfect metaphor was the possibility of the inexact or foolish metaphor which would lose the respect of one's peers, as you all reclined on your horses in the darkness and the cold by the frozen river. There might even be a sniggering, a malicious gossiping behind one's back which you could only counter, or redeem, by a metaphor so jewel-like, so stunning, so apt that all your inappropriate metaphors might be forgiven you. The greatest honour was accorded to he who could anticipate the new favoured style of metaphor (be it Grecian, Damascene or some other newly imported form such as the Persian) before the new style had been established as the predominant one. The risk, of course, was that one never knew which style of metaphor was ripe for renewal— that style which perfectly matched the spirit of the times. If you chose incorrectly, however, you might be seen as hopelessly old-fashioned for all styles had been tried and enjoyed a brief ascendancy. There were never any rules in this regard. The most respected metaphorsmiths worked by instinct and would utter their metaphors without fear. Such a display was worthy. (To utter without confidence was to risk everything.) It took courage to pronounce a metaphor in the depths of the still night while all the barbarians were assembled, reclining on their horses by the frozen river, lost in their private thoughts, for the barbarians were essentially a silent people. So different in nature from those voluble Romans who liked nothing better than to spend weeks and months composing elegant speeches with which they hoped to dissuade the barbarians from attacking. A few well-chosen words might have been so much more effective.

The barbarians could not write, nor could they read—which did not pain them overmuch: it suited their migratory nature; spoken words flowed around and were lost in the same way that they moved from one place to the next—without looking back. To look back was to be lost. The only way was forward. The endless forward motion; punctuated by long periods of rest—time for contemplation, for private meditation. Motion lost its meaning if it could not be contrasted with stillness. Essentially solitary, alone within themselves, the barbarians would camp by the frozen river in winter or else by the swiftly flowing, honey-scented stream in summer, amidst the birds and the sunshine. The solitariness of the barbarians put great fear into the traders, who duly reported this quality to the Romans who found it hard to understand and were therefore afraid of these self-contained vessels from another, a more primitive civilization, if it could be called that.

The barbarians would lay siege in huge numbers, for months and sometimes years, just a short distance away from the walls of the Roman towns in Narbonensis, which would completely unnerve the Romans. The barbarians are waiting outside the walls, the Romans would say to each other while reclining in the perfumed comfort of their warm baths. The barbarians cast a shadow across all their days;

there was always darkness lying just on the other side of comfort.

The barbarians would use the Abyssinian and Levantine traders to do all the work necessary to completely unnerve the Romans; plying as the traders did between the two camps, giving scraps of information to the civilized ones about how the barbarous ones, dressed in rough animal pelts and slumped over on the necks of their horses in the freezing cold, were waiting for them. The rich food and honeyed wine no longer had the same luxurious splendour for the Romans knowing as they did that their fate lay outside themselves, lying as it did with the uncivilized, indeterminate mass of part-humans waiting to destroy them.

The Romans had enough machinery to withstand an attack; they had enough men, their walls were high enough; they had an impressive array of tactics; they were the technological giants of their age...and yet...and yet... gnawing away at them while they reclined in the *caldarium*—while their feet were being anointed with rich oils and dried with the hair of the serving girls—was the fear that it was the uncivilized part of themselves that was on the other side of the walls just waiting to destroy them. They knew if they gave in to the dark side of their own natures then they would destroy themselves without the barbarians lifting a finger.

The barbarians knew no fear. When they attacked they attacked with certainty. And they attacked without leaders—and without a plan. Nothing was more horrifying to the Romans than this, for their own hierarchies were rigid and immutable. Everyone had a place within the society; the sense of place accorded security, self-definition, order, harmony; and for those at the top—luxury, calm and voluptuousness.

These barbarians were truly uncivilized men (according to the Romans), attacking on horseback with a dagger in one hand and a sword in the other. They would attack so quickly, and so fiercely, with such a complete disregard for their own lives, and with such a complete disrespect for the Romans' technology (the catapult, the swinging hook) that the Romans were stunned. These uncivilized ones, these barbarians, would attack with such ferocity, it was inhuman. They would attack with a randomness that was unnerving. They would attack after having been camped a short distance from the walls for either a short or long period of time; though always letting the minds of the civilized have enough time to fill with self-doubt. The randomness and apparent lack of forethought was particularly terrifying for the Romans with their love of order and precision and their neat certainties of rank and lines of command.

The barbarians held no war-meetings. They would attack on the spur of the moment. There was much exhilaration in suddenly bursting forward after months, or years, of contemplation. They guarded their reputations zealously; going out of their way to appear totally incomprehensible to the traders who dealt also with the Romans. In such a way the Romans knew about them, and were mentally exhausted come the time of battle. Being curious by nature, the Romans spent countless hours speculating on what might be the true nature of the barbarians camped by the frozen river in winter or else by the perfumed stream in summer just a short distance from the walls of the town. In the great amphitheatres, the temples, the baths and the private houses, it was the only topic of conversation.

The barbarians were incomprehensible. Even though they were of the same human dimensions as the Romans, they could, nevertheless, have come from the moon, or from a planet hovering above in the night sky. There was much speculation as to where they had come from, and how they could live in such an animal state, without ever putting down roots, without ever being warm or satiated. The barbarians guarded their incomprehensibility zealously—they knew it was their main weapon.

*

Strangely, our discussion in those days by the frozen river in the wilderness of Narbonensis as we reclined on our horses at nightfall was not of the Romans but rather it was of the other barbarians (whom we had heard tell of from the traders) who were also in Septem Provinciae and who were laying waste to Roman towns and cities in vast numbers. This was something of a revelation to us as we had never imagined that there would be others, apparently like us but who spoke a vastly different and inferior language and who were engaged in similar occupation to ourselves.

Apparently these other barbarians spoke only by way of grunts and a few words which they used to describe everyday activities such as eating and sleeping and making love. The Levantine traders amused us for hour after hour with stories of how primitive these other barbarians were and how basic and elemental was their way of life. Needless to say, these other barbarians had none of the rich inner life that we had and they had no concept of a metaphorical way of life. We could only begin to imagine the poverty of their lives.

They were, however, more ferocious than us (according to the traders) and would eat their food raw, having never bothered to learn to practise the very rudiments of cooking on an open fire. Their hair was covered with rancid butter and many of the men were two metres tall in height. We heard tales of a primitive ferociousness, which made us listen intently. They kept their equally fierce women and children with them, which was incomprehensible to us; we preferring to keep our women and children a few kilometres behind us so they might be in no danger, and so we could better concentrate on the life of the mind.

We had even been told that these other warlike barbarians had been known to attack true and pure barbarians like us in a show of ruthless ferocity and that we were considered by them to be soft barbarians, having over-cultivated our minds, our powers of speech and our love of metaphor, rhythm and verse. This was a revelation to us as we considered ourselves to define all there was to be defined by that lovely and dignified word 'barbarian'.

As none of us had ever laid eyes on these other barbarians, they became objects of great conjecture—endlessly more fascinating than the Romans whom we had seen, understood and conquered (and would in the future, again and again). The Romans, it was generally agreed, possessed the most amazing array of machinery but they lacked an indefinable quality which rendered them useless against barbarians. The Romans (according to the traders) thought that we were other than we were. Primitives, they called us. They saw themselves as the holders and maintainers of Reason; they did not suspect we too had our own, but much more poetic, logic. It suited our purposes that they were misled, though on the other hand it was a source of perpetual grievance that they did not respect us; and it disturbed us that the Romans saw ourselves and the other barbarians as being one and the same. Why you might as well say the same about moths and butterflies!

Another trader, one who plied his trade up and down the ice-laden seas of the far north, had said that he had seen and traded with yet another strand of barbarians many years before. These were clean-shaven, were of large and handsome proportions and had long blond hair, beautifully combed, and wore hairpieces with clasps that were inlaid with Damascene silver. This was ridiculed and immediately rejected as coming from the imagination of a mead-soaked mind.

How could these too be barbarians? The world was apparently being overrun with barbarians, when we had in the past assumed there was only us. What could all this mean? Was the whole world either on the move or camped by frozen rivers besieging each other? Would the Romans too one day turn into barbarians? Would they one day besiege us? Would they give up their cities, and return to the natural world? Where had all these *other* barbarians come from?

It was a question which occupied our thoughts for end-less nights. It was possible, said one barbarian reclining on his horse in the darkness, that these unusual barbarians were ones who had mingled with the Romans and who had started to cultivate their soft and uxorious ways. Such things had been known to have happened. Why the natives of Southern Gaul themselves—they of the language that pertained to music, the language that went up and down with startling results—had become mini-Romans after a fashion, adopting wholesale the love of water, of comfort and of luxury.

One of the traders had told us, amazingly, that he had seen with his very eyes a young barbarian chief who had taken to dressing in tunics of silk and gold and was parad-ing around not on a horse (the sign of a true barbarian) but on two legs—and carrying himself with propriety and elegance what's more. Astonishing things were happening all the time. The new ways of the young seemed bizarre to us—we who had for a long time been wedded to the notions of the proper ways for true barbarians to behave. It appeared to us there were a lot of impostors around. Unscrupulous types who called themselves barbarians to get ahead with the Romans. Such publicity could only be bad for us, weakening our position as barbarians, for how were the Romans to tell between us? How could they tell between a pure barbarian, a vicious uncultured barbarian and a clean northern barbarian?

It was disturbing indeed to hear of a barbarian dressed in silk and gold. Why would any barbarian, we asked our-selves while inclining on the necks of our horses by the frozen river, want to give up the simple yet demanding pleasures of life as a barbarian? To become a version of a Roman, an imitator, one who would never be truly accepted as an equal by the Romans, an object of fun? The senators would snigger behind their hands at the sight of a pretend Roman. We at least would never descend to that level. We knew the Romans respected our ability as warriors. The traders had told us that even our name— 'barbarians'—whispered in the great bathhouses would be enough to make the faces of the senators bloodless and would be enough to send them scurrying home to polish their speeches with which to greet us. We could sit and wait outside the walls of their towns for an endless progression of days. Time has no meaning for us, unlike the Romans who, the traders tell us, are obsessed with dividing each day into segments—segments which then rule what they do.

What was disturbing was that if one barbarian could descend into the ranks of being a pretend Roman then perhaps we too could be tricked into abandoning our hard-won gains. The life of the open plain, of the frozen river, of the smoky campsite, of the focused and steady mind, was worth preserving. The Romans, after all, were a sedentary, building-enclosed race who missed out on the fresh air of the windswept plains and the bracing awakening to the delicate sound of fresh snow falling on your face in the early morning. They missed out on the endless travelling. They missed out on the peaceful certitude of laying siege, for they were always the besieged—beset by their doubts, whereas pure and true barbarians have no doubts, no insecurities...And if one of our number gave in to worries and anxieties it was because he had not yet become, after a lifetime of trying, a true pure warrior barbarian. The Romans sleep on cushions: we sleep on our horses—and thus we have the advantage of a living thing with all its warmth under us.

There was something traitorous and undermining about the suggestion that a barbarian might aspire to be a Roman. It would be a perversion of nature, a turning backwards to become so soft and mentally weak. But then, what was it that made a pure warrior barbarian?

It was agreed after nights of tortuous thought, and some discussion, that while a definitive list would be difficult to establish, the pure barbarian had the following qualities: a love of metaphor, a passion for gold, a respect for silence, a love of the physical life, a fondness for music and verse, and a philosophical turn of mind.

On cold nights a lone bard would chant verses to keep us warm. When the snow fell one of our number would beat out a tune which would mimic the falling snow...And so we prided ourselves on our differentness from the sedentary Romans and from the mindlessness of the other barbarians who were only interested in savagery unredeemed by the power of the mind. During the long nights, trying to sleep on our horses, we would turn over and over the beginning of a perfect metaphor: something so exact and yet so simultaneously poetic that everyone who heard it would shudder involuntarily.

Over the course of many months of cold nights which by slow degrees transformed themselves into warm and fragrant summer nights we contemplated our old familiar conundrums. We were searching for a system that was large enough to contain all that we wished to think of; something that incorporated a reason for the rocks and rivers, grass and stars.

After the first few months of our siege of this isolated walled town in Narbonensis, the Romans sent us via the traders many armbands of different colours. The meaning of the colours, explained the traders, was a way of displaying rank. It was as though the Romans were trying to organize us. The armbands were left in a pile until the wind blew them back in the direction of our children and womenfolk. They may yet have a use for them. Still in spite of everything, self-doubt started to cloud over and we were thrust into a gloomy interlude of profound melancholy. It may have had something to do with the length of time we had been laying siege: a couple of seasons had already passed us by.

But whatever it was, our lives changed for the better when we were visited by a couple of Greek merchants. In exchange for a cartload of golden aurei and silver denarii coins of the old style, we received from them some stolen axioms they claimed to have picked up legitimately in Crete, some paradoxes from Ionia and a logic machine from Athens called a syllogism which they showed us how to work. The merchants explained that the logic machine was a way of arguing that led to the truthfulness of a claim being tested. In exchange for our hard-won and bloodied coins they left us with an example which we were well satisfied with. It was this:

Antoni Jach

All living creatures breathe and make a sound.

Barbarians breathe and make a sound.

Therefore barbarians are living creatures.

We were thunderstruck. Not only did the logic apparatus enable us to build our own thought-patterns but it
resembled our bardic verses which we listened to each night
and it contained something of the quality of our songs with
their deep and rich humming sounds which were so hypnotic; a repetition of similar-sounding words in an endless
loop which gave us unlimited pleasure. Any barbarian who
could create such a pleasing loop was venerated above all
others.

We could not wait to investigate the workings of the
Greek logic machine. One of our number, he who was called
the cantankerous one by virtue of his nature, came up with
the following thought-pattern, in the Greek style:

Beards grow on the faces of barbarians.

Our wives and children have no beards.

Therefore our wives and children are not barbarians.

The consternation amongst our number was loud and
immediate; everyone spoke at once, and the cantankerous
one had to be defended from the threatened blows and
drawn knives.

If our wives and children aren't barbarians what are
they? Do they therefore not exist? But we can see them.
We know they are flesh and blood. We visit their camp and
commune with them at times.

Harmony was restored by the one dubbed the consoler,
he who had healed many similar disputes in the past. He
said the following:

—Our learned friend has used the logic machine in a faulty fashion. All that needs to be done to fix the problem is to amend his lines thus:

Beards grow on the faces of warrior barbarians.

Our wives and children have no beards.

Therefore our wives and children are not warrior barbarians.

This formula proved to be satisfactory to all, but it showed how dangerous was the apparatus we were using; it had the potential to lead to bloodshed. If it proved to be too dangerous we would have to dispose of it and return to our traditional ways.

Verse died out when we discovered the many uses of the logic machine. There was no longer any need for verse or song. The bards were inconsolable. However, many ordinary warrior barbarians tried their hand at the new constructions which led to the problems. The following one led to bloodshed:

All Romans love water.

Barbarians love water.

Therefore Romans are the same as barbarians.

The battle raged all night and by morning many were bleeding and damaged; some were dead. Though the following thought-pattern restored calm:

All Romans build machines.

Barbarians build no machines.

Therefore Romans are not the same as barbarians.

How could both conclusions be true? Obviously we had been sold an imperfect form of reasoning. This logic machine is an imperfect engine: it makes nothing happen.

It was agreed upon by popular assent, that only skilled practitioners should be allowed to use the logic machine due to the dire consequences of it falling into the wrong hands.

Nevertheless the appearance of the thought-pattern of the love of water and the sameness between barbarians and Romans was disturbing and left us thinking for a long time afterwards. Late at night while inclining on our horses while the chill winds swirled around us one of our number suggested that as we had become necessary to the Romans we were therefore superior to them. We were curious to hear his reasoning and pressed him to proceed. He added that in our destruction of Roman cities and towns we provide Romans with a chance to be more Roman than before by giving them an excuse to rebuild what used to exist— they only being Roman when they are building and thus their dependency on our necessary destruction making them dependent on us. We therefore needed a new name to denote us as *mightier-than-Romans* but no word currently existed and no-one could think of a suitable word. A long and profound silence ensued, with each barbarian in our number considering the meaning of this speech.

To tell the truth, we were now starting to lose interest in this siege. We were hungry to become travellers again. The siege was now in its second summer and the Romans showed no sign of surrendering. But on the other hand there was time enough for mental pursuits. During the day we pretended to busy ourselves with various tasks: mending carts and shining our daggers with pig's fat. We executed our duties as barbarians in a coldly efficient way so we could earn the privacy and usefulness of nightfall with its round of rumination and contemplation. Some of the young bloods were eager for a fight but the patience of the barbarians is legendary and nothing will happen without a spontaneous irruption.

Another thought-pattern was raised late at night by one of our number in an endeavour to provoke us:

All barbarians are great travellers.

We are currently stationary.

Therefore we are not barbarians.

Loud uproar and protests ensued, but no bloodshed this time. We were getting used to the nature of the thought-patterns. We had come to realize that the saying of a thought-pattern does not make it true.

After a long silence, a voice was raised:

—And if we are not barbarians, who are we? We are not Abyssinian traders, we are not Levantines, we are not Greek merchants, we are not Romans, we are not the *other* barbarians, therefore we must be barbarians.

When the Greek merchants returned in search of another cartload of coins there was a suggestion from one quarter that their heads should be sliced from ear to ear for the trouble they had caused us but our curiosity for what new device they might bring us got the better of us and we decided they should be allowed to come and go freely, but we told them we wanted new instruments from them on each visit. Their logic machine had made the time pass quickly. Their logic machine had given us more pleasure— and pain—than the inert golden and silver coins which after all had to be dragged from camp to camp. Coins were plentiful after all; wherever Romans were there were coins in abundance.

The merchants said they had something called *arithmetic* to sell us. But the cost had increased since last time. Due to increased costs from the originators, the Greek philosophers, and due to the increasing dangers of travelling through borderlines they were going to charge two cartloads of silver denarii and gold aurei coins of the style minted under the reign of Augustus. The Greek merchants explained that it was only through the wonders of arithmetic that the Romans had managed to build edifices and machines of such awe-inspiring capacity. So the bargain was struck: on the word of honour of the barbarians we would exchange two cartloads of pure silver and gold coins of the old style for the secret of arithmetic.

On receipt of the two cartloads of coins the elder merchant, the one with the rheumy eye, took a stick and drew the following pattern in the sand:

We stared at the diagram for a long time while the merchants busied themselves and prepared for departure. We didn't want to betray our ignorance by asking inappropriate questions of the merchants. They had such a confident air when it came to knowledge, and the diagram had a certain inexplicable power that drew us to it. What it meant we did not know, but it looked like a purposeful diagram, it looked as though it contained necessary information. So we bade farewell to the merchants without disturbing a hair on their weathered heads. We wished them well, and said we hoped to see them again bearing gifts from the edges of the earth. But we warned them that by the time they returned we might have moved into a new cycle of destruction and restless movement. Even so they should seek us out—the Romans could tell them where we were to be found.

Many nights passed in silent rumination as we puzzled over the secret meaning of the circles in the sand, and reflected upon one crucial piece of information that the Greek merchants had let slip: namely that the philosophers who had sold them the sign had claimed that the sign had created itself one day as an arrangement of pebbles in the forecourt of the Academy. It must be a supernatural sign. A long time passed. We slipped into lassitude at the thought of our own ignorance. It was humiliating to contemplate. Here we were, fully grown barbarians, of a warrior caste, unable to come to terms with a drawing in the sand.

We protected the pattern in the sand zealously. We did not let either wind or rain efface its subtlety. Initially we stood in awe in front of it. The arrangement seemed perfect. We grouped barbarians in the same arrangement and a handsome youth who had never grown hair was brought from the camp of the womenfolk and asked if he could explain the meaning of the pattern. He said he could if he would be allowed sufficient time to think about its meaning. So we placed the youth under guard and he established a vigil day and night over the precious sign. There were doubters who felt angry that we were cheated out of our coins, but the overwhelming feeling was of belief.

Then one clear night of a quarter moon the youth

announced that he had something to tell us. He said he had found a possible answer to the conundrum. The diagram in the sand could represent a way of building. That if you stood the diagram up, so to speak, instead of seeing it as flat then you find the that the lightest weight would be on the top supported at each descending stage by a solider and more substantial base. This could indeed be the secret of building. And to follow that up, he said, the pattern showed in one glance that one plus two plus three plus four equals ten and by drawing and redrawing patterns in the sand you could estimate in groups of ten the cumulative number of anything. We were all dumbstruck. It did indeed seem possible. We were delighted. We brought the youth into our company and even though he was very young he became the principal guide through our search for the nature of things. We called him the youth-of-wisdom. Verse was banished from night-time activities. Henceforth we would discuss numbers.

A siege is a long affair—and so we had countless nights to discuss the problematic nature of the world. We were becoming eager to attack the Romans but the exact time never seemed propitious. We spent many nights during the first summer while inclining peacefully on the necks of our horses discussing the possible value of the next offering of the Greek traders, who had no trouble finding us as we had remained in the same spot. We introduced them to our youth-of-wisdom.

They somewhat reluctantly offered to sell us a magical substance which was concealed in an earthenware jug covered with a lead stopper in exchange for three cartloads of pure gold aurei coins minted during the reign of Augustus. They claimed the substance was magical because it had the power to transform itself: it could change from liquid to solid to air upon provocation. But while we were discussing over a series of nights whether or not we should invest in the magical substance the Greek merchants vanished into thin air. They had obviously had enough of our indecision. They may have feared for their lives.

So we did not have a chance to discover what this substance was. Once again we called upon the youth who was the keeper of wisdom beyond his years. This time he answered at once that the substance was water; that magical substance that could turn into ice or steam upon provocation. Then it became clear, but our lives were poorer for the revelation, something mysterious had disappeared, a matter for discussion had evaporated. We decided we would use the youth-of-wisdom more carefully in future. We were becoming more and more distracted. Maybe we were straying too far away from our real purpose in life. It was decided that at some stage we would have to attack the Romans. We were becoming overwhelmed by the realm of thought. It was time to do something practical.

One of our number—the shortest and most unkempt— whom we had dubbed the foreteller due to his gifts of prophecy was asked when the attack should begin. He replied that a certain confluence of events had to take place: firstly, a white cock would appear with one leg missing; secondly, our horses would cease to leave footprints in the sandy soil; and thirdly the ashes from the fire would arrange themselves in the shape of a crescent moon for three nights in a row. Then, and only then, would we attack and be in mindless perpetual movement once again—like the wind or hail which no force can keep out. It would be a relief, we decided one moonless night, to leave the life of the mind with all its accompanying perturbations behind us for a while; to once again be swept up into the physicality of the world; to once again be mindless as we used to be in our hot-tempered youth.

With the return of cold nights the mind-tricks of the youth-of-wisdom fell out of favour and we asked the long-forgotten bard to once again recite the verses which his father's father had taught him in order to keep the icy wind blowing off the frozen river from going through our very bones. He himself had forgotten some of the words, and had even forgotten the meanings of some of the sections but he could remember the ancient rhythm well enough. His voice sounded like a drumbeat announcing a war, and by this means we kept ourselves warm throughout the bitter winter. When warmer weather comes we will attack, we said to each other as a way of keeping our spirits up.

But by slow degrees we drifted back again to the problems of arithmetic. The diagram in the sand might be a useful way of assessing our strength as a fighting force, one said. So we sent one of our number into the mass of the encamped barbarians behind us. He was armed with the stick the Greeks had left us and he carried a miniature replica—sand on bark—in the same configuration of the diagram. His task was to draw numerous dots in the sand in the same shape as a way of counting the number of warrior barbarians who lay behind us.

When he returned after a very long time and started to sketch out, in the form of patterns, the number of barbarians behind us, he spent many days at his task covering every millimetre of ground until he had nearly reached the walls of the Roman fortifications. He complained there wouldn't be enough sand in the whole of Gaul to sketch out the mass of barbarity behind us. And he said, by way of explanation as to why he had taken so long, that at first he had been distracted by his wife and children and then continuing into the crowd had become dazed and confused by the smells and the sounds, the different languages spoken and the varied customs the further he had penetrated into the mass of barbarity. He said that he had no idea that there could be so many barbarians in the world, and even when he gave up, in order to return, barbarians stretched as far as the eye could see, the campfires sending up a watery glow.

Finally we challenged the youth-of-wisdom to prove by arithmetic that the wind was heavier than water. He replied that if you add sun to water you end up with wind; therefore the substances are all the same anyway, so the question is invalid. This was a reply that we liked very much and that particular grouping of words—the question is invalid—struck a cord with our barbarian imagination...and once again the youth-of-wisdom was back in favour and the bard was inconsolable.

One disturbing thought that was often alluded to but rarely spoken of directly was the following: that we barbarians, by exercising our minds rather than our bodies, would eventually by slow degrees end up as Romans. This

suggestion perturbed us greatly for a while but was overtaken by the question of the seasons. Why did snow have
to follow the shedding of leaves, and why did heat have
to follow the return of little birds? Why could there not be
one continuous state? Why did the moon decline in power
and return after a short space of time, flushed and resonant in its own triumphant roundness? We did not know
the answers. Though we kept the questions from the youth-
of-wisdom because he had become by now a little too sure
of himself. He had forgotten he was dealing with warrior
barbarians.

In the second summer of heat-filled days of our siege of
the Roman city, one of our number—the one with the scar
running down the side of his left cheek—was continually
complaining of his weary limbs and failing eyesight and it
was he who suggested tentatively that it would not be such
a bad idea to prolong the siege indefinitely, especially considering that the place we were camped in was so pleasant
in the heat, near a majestic river and surrounded by slop-
ing hills, with such a fragrant air and with olive trees and
grape vines that had been planted by the Romans nearby.
He said we should settle down in this particular place. From
the Roman point of view it would still be a siege, and we
would naturally be prepared to fight at a moment's notice,
but we could start to make life a bit more comfortable for
ourselves. We could cultivate the grapes and plant crops. If
we wanted to we could agree that pure warrior barbarians
did not need to be perpetually on the move and that, after
all, as we had been stationary now for two summers the

stationary was becoming our normal state rather than that of frenetic movement.

This speech threw us into consternation. Indeed it was very pleasant here we all agreed. Especially in the hot and fragrant months. That much was indisputable. With the aid of the warmth, our children were growing up into fine young barbarians. Our womenfolk—who had started to make semi-permanent structures (with the aid of the Greek pattern-in-the-sand which showed that you put lightness on top of weight) in which they gossiped and slept and kept each other warm—seemed to be content enough.

The scarred one suggested that at some stage we might prefer not to sleep on our horses, in readiness for battle, but might prefer to sleep on the ground by the campfire, or even to sleep with our womenfolk. This brought on a wave of even greater consternation and loud murmurings including the suggestion that was distinctly heard from out of the darkness that a quick knife through the sinews of the throat would put paid to such heresies.

How could we give up the life of the mind that our current lifestyle affords? How could we give up our stumbling search for the goddess of poetic logic?

At times the need for sleep overcame us like a powerful drug, but most times the nights were ours and we could be our true selves rather than having to hold up a facade of purposeful activity.

We would gaze up at the moon on cloudless nights and tell each other elliptical stories with strange portents and work on the unending, imperfect and impossible search for the perfect metaphor. The moon was like a broken drum;

it gave off a heart-rending sound, but bit by bit as time goes on parts of it fell away just as loudness gives way to softness in all natural sounds. The half-moon is like the ear of a warrior barbarian.

For how could we give up our cause? The cause that had set us on our round of continual momentum. If it wasn't for love of gold and movement we would never have set out on this journey. When we were young we were shown the glittering coins and told by way of grunts and cuffs around the head that the pursuit of gold and endless destruction would be our destiny. For we needed a reason for movement and room to live. The desolate and windswept lands of our birth could not sustain us for ever. The soil is poor, often covered in ice and snow. Once we started to travel as young men we acquired a taste for it; our skins grew as hard as stone and we ceased to feel the cold.

Of course you need a just cause to live a warlike life; you need to believe in something. What would be the point of settling down? To surrender the life of a barbarian? To live a life of luxury, a life of softness? How could one cease to be a warrior? How could one just simply give up? The Romans dissolve in fear at the mention of our name. Their only answer is to build higher and thicker fortifications. But we still insinuate ourselves little by little into the cracks in their minds. We've seen it happen before: a huge force of Roman soldiers in neat little groupings vanish into thin air at the first sound of barbarian warriors, barbarian women and children. Our publicity goes before us. We only have to maintain our reputation for random savagery to terrorize the ordered, well-disciplined minds of the civilized. For what the civilized can't bear is disorder. Refusing to fight in formation, refusing to be led is incomprehensible to them. So even when we have few in number conjoined with a belief in a just cause we can overcome many.

The Levantine traders have recently told us about barbarians who have travelled far south to the land the Romans call Hispaniae in search of gold and slaves and that they have captured so much and so many that they are virtually immobile. They say we should go there too. That once you cross a difficult mountain range you strike dry and dusty plains where the sun is fierce and warlike. In those dry lands barbarians have found so many gold coins in a Roman garrison that they are unable to move. They can't bear to leave even a small part of the great wealth and have been immobilized for the past two summers. Only one barbarian has returned to tell the tale and he is being sheltered in the camp of the traders; he is delirious with the heat of the sun and the exertions of his journey; he has many silver denarii coins and many gold aurei coins, of the ancient kind, to prove his tale.

There is something very attractive about the idea of travelling south immediately towards the sun; but we couldn't do that to the Romans. They would be bereft. After all we have been yoked together like man and wife for these past two summers.

We will attack the Romans one day. We will be true to our word. It will be satisfying to take apart everything they have constructed. We will meticulously take apart their walls stone by stone...if we can rouse ourselves to action.

Maybe we have become too distracted, as has been claimed, by games of the mind? But why is *activity* any more purposeful, or useful?

We have heard tell of the Romans' bathhouses, their amphitheatres, their bakeries, their temples, their multi-storey dwellings. All of their buildings are an affront to nature, and to the natural world. The sky serves as a roof for all who lie down beneath it. There is running water in every stream, grapes are here to be squeezed dry. The olive tree provides both food and shelter. Why do they have this need to build? And if they did not build maybe we would not have a need to destroy? Why do they waste their time?

Some time soon, of course, we must attack the Romans. They have been waiting patiently for us for so long. They have been worthy enemies—never panicking, never doing anything untoward. We will get round to it one day. But just at the moment the sun is shining, we are basking in its warmth and our world is full of contentment.

*

The word is passing through the camp that the Levantine trader has returned. He says the *other* barbarians are coming. The warlike ones. They have already cut off our retreat at the back and are encircling us. They are coming at us with a bloodthirsty ferociousness. They are laying siege to us, and will one day attack. They say we have gone soft, that we are no longer pure barbarians but rather they are, and we are aspiring Romans. Of course, all this is false. They say we have made a pact with the Romans; that we are merely *pretending* to lay siege so we can rest awhile, and the Romans are merely *pretending* to resist; whereas deep down we are in bed with each other, as you might find with servants and masters. But the other barbarians are coming anyway. We feel the noose tightening around our necks. We may yet have to attack the Romans, and probably with much haste.

And yet in the midst of our fear of the approaching other barbarians we are gripped with an overpowering and disabling nostalgia. That is what *we* used to be like. We used to be impetuous, warlike, ruthless... We are being pursued by our former selves who will devour us as soon as they catch us. Our past is about to overtake us. We will be cannibalized by our own former ambitions. The reports are all despairing. Many of our number have been massacred at the rear. They are attacking, as we used to, with a mindless ferocity. They are attacking with such confidence, with such reckless disregard for their own safety. We have been so focused on what lies ahead that we had no time or inclination to look backwards. We have had no time to protect our backs. What seemed so important in the past is no longer important. We are being thrust into the present at a great rate. We did not believe anyone would dare to attack us. Who after all would attack pure and true warrior barbarians?

The only way out is forward. We have finally decided. We will attack the Romans tomorrow. You cannot reason with barbarians...

seven | The Romans

We have our speeches ready. We have them in tripli-
cate. We memorize them in the *caldarium*, on our
way to the *tepidarium* and on to the *frigidarium*. We have
oiled our gestures in preparation. We have worked on our
posture so we may impress them with our general
demeanour, so they may see us as people of stature and
status. We have worked long into the night by candlelight
to master the content, the tenses and the appropriate tone—
neither too overbearing nor too servile—with which to
address the leaders of the barbarians and their retinue. The
wrong word or the right word in the wrong place would
be enough to undo all our intentions. We have given up
so many worldly pleasures so our speeches may be luminous, persuasive, inventive, declamatory, engaging...We
have neglected our children, neglected our health so that
our speeches will be more resonant, more meaningful, more
glorious. We dream of speeches in our sleep. We silently
enunciate each word. We cannot get away from the task.
We will sway them with the power of our rhetoric—we who

are masters of the pause, of the absent word, of the full-blown metaphor. We will render them dumb with our eloquence. We have not been studying the arts of rhetoric for the past thirty years for nothing. We are armed with our words, armed with our attitudes, with our general bearing. They will be overwhelmed, poor savages, with our sense of assurance, our sense of calm, our composure in the face of threat. We will meet them without weapons, with just our words to bolster and protect us. We now want the day to arrive. We are impatient for the test. We are almost ready for them.

Our scribes are working overtime incorporating our daily changes. There is always one word that is more *felicitous* than another, there is always a phrase more shining, a pause more poignant, more heart-rending, more delicate, more caressing—like water falling from ledge to ledge in a moss-covered valley, like music. We are never satisfied. A speech is always a temporary solution, a transitory state between the potential and the actual. There is always the possibility of being misunderstood. For what is a speech without a listener? What is a human without an animal to compare ourselves with? What is the measure of self without contrast, without opposition? How can we see black if there is no white? How know happiness, without misery? How hear sound if there is no silence?

Doubtlessly, they will arrive at the gates of our city any day now to discuss the terms and conditions of war. We bathe daily in case they may come today. We are daily anointed with seven oils, are perfumed and we practise answers with each other and with our wives and mistresses in case there are any possible questions that may arise. We are prepared to defend ourselves with speeches in defence of Roman civilization and the world order we have created, and we hope and trust we have as much success with them as we have had with the Gauls who were eventually seduced by our control over nature.

We make water run uphill, downhill and through man-made channels over vast distances. We clear mountains if we need to. We build multistorey dwellings with central heating. Our machinery is of the highest sophistication. Our theatrical events are exemplary. Our skills of rhetoric are highly developed. There is nothing we cannot do. Except fly. We cannot fly. But we do not need to fly. Our system of organization is second to none in the whole of the known world. We are lovers of order, luxury and sensual experience for it is only in the harmony of an efficient order that we can freely indulge ourselves and our substantial appetites.

We seduced the Gauls effortlessly with the example of our lives of comfort and luxury but above all with our concept of the city: no longer need they all live separately on their isolated farms, they can all live together, share in company and have their needs met. The farmer can become a baker or a candlestick maker. They can all live on top of one another as houses grow upwards to get better views of the open land they have left behind. They can enjoy the fountains in the city square, marvel at the comfort of water. They can participate in a general conversation rather than continually talking to themselves on some bleak and desolate plain. They can feel part of something that is larger than themselves, more enterprising, more ambitious. If they subsume their individual will to the will of the whole, they can feel a sense of belonging. Even the humblest slave can feel a part of the majesty of the imperial hegemony. If every member knows his place, everything will go smoothly. If everyone works together to maintain the social order, all shall go well. We can all sleep peacefully at night.

Our womenfolk have prepared garlands for the leaders of the barbarians and their entourage and have prepared tunics of fine silk—but without the purple stripes of senatorial honour—so their leaders might dress like us and thus have no jealousy and, therefore, no need to destroy us. We await the barbarians with anticipation, our thoughts are on them. Everything we now do is tinged with the knowledge that they are resting just a short distance to the east of us by the banks of the frozen river. We focus on them as if our lives depended on them.

The speeches we have written are good speeches. Our wives and mistresses have told us so. They are worthy of senators. The proconsul of the region has let us know by means of a messenger that we are to be ready at any moment day or night for the entry of the barbarian entourage. We are to pay them the respect they deserve. We are not to look askance at their rough manners or rude dressing. We are to pay them the respect of being worthy adversaries. We are to disguise our true feelings. We have been coached in the use of a blank smiling facade by the greatest actor in our region—a Phoenician who knows many things. We are to charm them, to flatter them. For they too can have a place in the working out of our imperial destiny. Barbarians too have their place in the Empire, our proconsul has written.

The proconsul does not expect Roman-born senators to fail. He has told us so in the form of a message delivered by a bloodied soldier who said he had been savaged for sport by bands of marauding ex-barbarians dressed in the outfits of Roman soldiers who had been hired to defend the outskirts of the Empire—the limes—against fiercer more implacable barbarians. How strange. Barbarians employed by Romans to defeat barbarians. We have even heard of a man of barbarian birth who has risen to the position of a Roman general. Why won't the world stay still? Why must we live in a time of uncertainty?

The proconsul has sent a second message via a disease-ridden messenger that he will visit us on his tour of the region; and that we are to be ready, night and day, to receive him. We have been working on a new set of speeches for our proconsul. We have crafted a speech of welcome for him if he happens to be in a good mood, and we have crafted a second in case he is in a sour mood. We have crafted other speeches in case he is melancholic or choleric or phlegmatic or sanguine by nature. We hope he doesn't come too soon because his set of speeches is not yet ready. And then after writing them we will still have the task of memorizing them via the technique of the memory palace where every imagined room contains a word which leads to the next part of the speech. The rooms of the palace contain notions of hospitality (the kitchen), of loyalty (the main chamber) and of comfort (the bedrooms) and so on until the speech is fully unravelled. We have trained our minds as athletes train their bodies—through constant repetition. We have minds that are stuffed full of words, retrievable at a moment's notice.

Our proconsul expects us to succeed in our encounter with the barbarians. He has reminded us via a letter that warfare is very much a matter of willpower and to overcome we must be prepared to face many defeats along the road to victory. Even though we have never met him, we senators have agreed that he is a wise and just ruler and worthy of our love. He would not mislead us or harm us or better himself at our expense. We are fortunate to have such a leader who will visit us one day when he deems us worthy to receive him. He reminds us constantly, via letters marked with the imperial seal of the proconsul, of the thoughts of Marcus Aurelius and he exhorts us to give up our life of pleasure to revel in the life of the mind. He reminds us that there is beauty in thought and happiness in self-denial.

We have memorized our speeches for the barbarians word by word for they are almost upon us. From the watchtower we can see the many camps of the barbarians—extending for as far as the eye can see. They have taken over the whole plain, excluding nature from our sight. Such a mass of warm and breathing humanity and savagery. As each season ends, more barbarians camp on the plain and by the river. Their reputation for savagery is legend. Rome has already fallen once in recent times, burnt to the ground, which threw us into the deepest despair, for how can the children in the provinces feel safe when the mother city has been trampled upon? The fall of Rome engendered a new reign of doubt. We, the sons of the defeated defenders of Rome, have never been the same since. We carry the burden of our parents. Our mission is to burn out the weaknesses of our forebears and to right the wrongs suffered by them. We cannot fully rest until we have accomplished our task. We may, of course, never rest. But, no matter…we will endure anyway.

Our speeches are on the themes of civic duty, the discipline of the individual, and individual sacrifice for the collective good. Our phrasing is immaculate, our gestures apt, our linen freshly ironed and perfumed. By now we have practised so many times that at night our dreams resound with the words we have so lovingly created: Our duty becomes our pleasure, our pleasure our duty.

We are creating a banquet for them. Our chefs are on stand-by day and night. We have created a most delicate and exotic menu for the barbarian chief and his entourage. The slaves are stamping on the purple grapes at this very moment; squeezing out the life juices to create the most glorious wine ever likely to be tasted. The calves are being slaughtered at this moment. The grain is being harvested to turn into loaves of warm bread as we speak. The olives lie in their vast vats awaiting consumption. The blood and guts of the chickens fall on the stone floor. The flies have been banished from the vast kitchens. The waiters have been brushing up on their expected duties. The chief chef has been to see the sibyls to get their blessing. Everywhere there is an air of expectation. The slaves are in the corners sharpening the blades. Even in the heat of midsummer there is a frenzied activity.

The Layers of the City

We are oiling ourselves anew with imported perfumes from Asia Minor so they may see how civilized we are. They will be impressed by us. They will see our clothes, our gestures, they will hear our grave pauses and listen to our sparkling eloquence. When they leave us they will abandon any thoughts of destroying us. They will have learnt to respect us. They will see the wonder of what we have created and they will leave us in awe of how we have trained nature to our own purposes. We have diverted mighty rivers, turned others into ponds, directed water to fields which were once barren so that flowers and crops may grow. We have built aqueducts, viaducts, sewers, paved roads and created conformity over a land mass where once natural chaos reigned supreme; flattening hills and in other places constructing a hill overnight so that there may be a place for the sibyls and the augurs to reside. We have regimented the rivers so they are now loyal legionnaires that do our bidding. We have improved upon the Hellenic legacy. We have brought order to the land.

Though at the moment the barbarians are the only ones benefiting from the crops we have grown outside the town's high walls. We are sovereign over water—so they will probably attack us with fire. Rome was ill-prepared. There was no deputation of senators to meet the leaders, there was no forethought. Whereas we carry the experience of Rome's destruction with us; we have been preparing for this day all our lives. All our lives from the moment we were born we were raised to face the barbarians and at different times in our careers when we were most ready we have been seeking them out and they have disappeared into the air.

But now we are ready. Our speeches are consigned to memory. Everyone in this walled town knows their place, everyone has a role—that is the civilization we have brought to this formerly rough and immature place. We shall be prepared. Those rude creatures have no inkling of what's in store for them. We expect them any day now. We have a permanent watch. We will be alerted at the first sight of the entourage.

We have prepared an entertainment for them. Our engineers have created scenery which moves across the ceiling mimicking the movement of clouds, we have created the illusion of waves with water and lightning, we have created a scene of hay being blown in the field. Our musicians are busy mimicking the sound of wind passing over a frozen river. We have constructed this set inside our banquet hall so they can eat and drink and pass away the night with an entertainment on the theme of Nature. We have actresses dressed as mermaids and actors dressed as sailors being lured onto the rocks by the siren's song. The cast have been rehearsing for ever and they are getting impatient to present their spectacle to the barbarian chiefs. The actors are starting to squabble amongst themselves. They are plotting, I have been told by my principal spy, to do away with the director and get a new one from Rome. They are not used to such a long delay between preparation and execution. We have asked the versifiers to send a representative who will compose and recite an ode for the barbarians but the versifiers cannot agree on a representative. They have told us that they will either all come or none of them will come, so we have banned the versifiers from the entertainment for being troublemakers.

We will present speeches to the barbarians on the benefits of order and civilization. They are barbarians because they do not understand. But words won't have to do all the convincing: we will show them the meaning of the good life; we will show them the comfort and luxury of Roman civilization. What does not appeal to their reason will appeal to their senses. We will ambush the poor savages in this way. We will take them on a tour of the many bathhouses. We will show them the Forum, the markets, let them smell the fresh bread, show them the watchtowers that oversee everything, the apartments where they can admire the ingenuity of central heating, show them our adding machines and our many implements of warfare. We will let them see how we have conquered Nature. They will come over to our side. They will ask to be part of the imperial system, with all its trappings. We have a role mapped out for our barbarians. They can fight for us against other barbarians. We will provide them with uniforms and pay them every month. All barbarians, just like the Gauls before them, are aspiring Romans anyway.

We speak often in the baths, and in the civic square, and in the vast arena where the gladiators fight the lions and we ask each other if the barbarians could have built what we have built. The answer is always no. They are primitive, without organization, like children. But then, how could they have been so successful? The question is always left hanging. Unanswerable. Though in moments of lucidity we can grasp that the other side of our own lightness and our reason is a dark side: a rootless, violent, unmanageable side. Only through discipline, through a sheer effort of will have we secured a civilization that will last. Our temples and arenas will last for centuries, our legal system and our social structures will last forever.

Our speeches are ready. We expect that any day now they will send us a deputation to arrange the terms under which they will attack us, and the conditions under which they will fight. It is only reasonable to expect a visit. But they did not come yesterday, and they may not come today. Our wives and mistresses will laugh in our faces at the waste of time in writing speeches. Why write when we could have been getting drunk, carousing and amusing ourselves in the usual ways? Why write when no-one is going to listen? Why have we wasted all those days and all those nights, exchanging one inadequate word for a word which is less inadequate when every sensible person is sleeping? We may be humiliated once again.

As each week passes we are becoming more and more uneasy. What if our speeches are not to be used, ever? So many fine phrases, rich comparisons, multilayered argumentation. How can we face our wives and children, we who have invested so much of our waking time in speechmaking, if it all comes to nought? We will see our wives gathering in the corners of the city square—and our mistresses gathering outside the Baths of Diocletian—with hands over their mouths whispering and laughing at us. The ordinary people, the plebeians, expect so much from their senators. Even the Gauls look up to us. What shall we tell them? That the barbarians will not listen to our speeches? That they cannot be bothered, do not have time for that sort of thing, that our elegant words are worthless? That our lives spent composing speeches have been wasted? That we speechmakers should have dug a well instead? Built a school? Made writing tablets? Become bakers? Spent a life outside rather than inside? Created something practical, done something useful? That we should have made something with our hands instead? Maybe even made a loaf of bread that our children could eat. That would be a task at least of dignity. The purpose is obvious. Flour, salt and water is transformed into a corporeal substance. And if the barbarians invade and capture us what need will they have for speechmakers? What will we senators do? We will no longer have a role to play.

We are obsessed with the barbarians. We talk of nothing else. In tender carnal moments with our wives or mistresses there is an image which invades our consciousness: the image of barbarians asleep on the backs of their horses by the frozen river—with their wives and children huddled under animal skins in the corners of their carts trying to escape the rudely untameable winds. These images fill our thoughts night and day. Perhaps we are already prisoners. Perhaps we were taken prisoner two to three winters ago when they first arrived. At first just one or two arrived, installing themselves, without haste, by the banks of the frozen river; scraggly, unkempt, like bit-players in a play for the common crowd. It was as if those barbarians had wandered on stage unsure of what they were doing there, blinded by the intensity of the stage braziers. Then more came, gradually over a period of months. And then their womenfolk and children arrived in their broken-down carts, camping at a distance from their menfolk. The only ones with any energy left after their long journey, according to the traders, were the children—chasing sparrows, playing with knucklebones in the dust of summer, impervious to the cold and the heat. Who knows how far they have come? Over how many mountain ranges, and through how many mighty rivers? Just to persecute us.

It was so different when we ourselves arrived twenty-one years ago. We saw the Gauls initially as barbarians, which is odd to think of now, because now we see them as such a reasonable and pliable race. Spend too much time with Romans and you become a Roman, that's what the Gauls say. Though not in the truest sense—only in the sense that you want to accumulate more and more things: a better, bigger house, more slaves, a country villa, more mistresses. In short, all the accoutrements of civilization. The Gauls saw our air of authority, our sense of dignity, our sense of civic pride—*authoritas, gravitas, civitas*—and were obviously and rightly impressed. They put up some resistance to be sure. But in the end they could see we were a superior civilization—tamers of water. We put the grape to work as well, and produced wine in abundance, and of superior quality. We planted crops which flourished. Everything we touched turned to gold. And when we started to build upwards to the heavens—towards the domain of the gods—they were awestruck. And then when we built the walls of the city—to distinguish between the light of civilization and the darkness of animality—and asked the Gauls which of them wished to come within the city limits and work for us as slaves, many, not surprisingly, agreed to do so. The smell of oxen on revolving spikes cooking over huge fires was too much for them. The sound of full-bodied laughter was too much for them. The sound of the lyre. The sound of water lapping on the soft skins of the men and women in the Baths of Diocletian was too much for them. So many of them agreed willingly to be slaves. So they could be near us. Touch us. To see if we are real. Our wives and mistresses agree: the Gauls covet our love of hierarchies, our overwhelming judgement, our magisterial sense of taste, our technological advancement. They admire our sense of duty, of justice, of generosity. They want to be us, you can see it in their eyes. They want to play with our toys—to be themselves in charge of water and of fire, once only the possession of the gods but stolen by Prometheus for our benefit. We are the beneficiaries of theft, so we are now entrusted with upholding the law. We have a flexible sense of justice. We are custodians of what used to be their land and is our land now by virtue of our ability to cultivate and to build. No-one who does not cultivate or build upon land can own it. We have instituted taxation in order to remind everyone of the communal nature of life. No more is an individual alone, partaking of solitude: now everyone can be a citizen partaking of the rights and responsibilities of being part of a modern state. The barbarians do not understand these things, and that is why they are barbarians.

But will the barbarians respect us as well? We want them to respect us, to notice us, to pay us attention, to give us a sign that we are more than just their enemies. But instead, looking out from the watchtower, all you can see is this brooding sullen mass completely flooding the plain. A future world perhaps, where everywhere you look there are primitives covering every stretch of land. An undistinguishable crowd huddled by their meagre fires. We could be irrelevant to them, that is our fear. They have come, not to attack us but to sit on the edges of our mind. They have come to subtly poison everything we do; to overthrow us from our equanimity. Like a gigantic herd of cattle just morosely chewing grass, they are waiting malevolently for us to make the wrong move. They do not notice us. They do not respect us. This is what is corrupting our pleasure with the poison of doubt.

As the weeks have passed and changed into years, our wives have decided that the barbarians secretly wish to be Romans. We don't know, but what we have decided is this: that they are tied to us in some strange, unaccountable way. How the world changes, we said to each other in the *caldarium*. One moment you are a free man, and the next you have a monkey on your back; you didn't ask it to hop on, it just arrived out of the blue, with no fanfare, with no warning. A monkey who at first glance appeared to be a momentary diversion, a figure of fun, but who then quickly changed into a demanding shrew who would not let you alone and took up all your waking moments, and invaded your dreams as well.

Our mistresses have decided that these barbarians are in awe of us, for after all we know which grapes to mix to make the best wine, we know the art of rhetoric, the art of geometry, the art of astronomy, the art of conversation, the art of flattery, and of flirtation. We Romans have ventured to the edges of the known world—and conquered. We have subdued all the races who have stood between us and our imperial destiny. Rome was becoming too small for us, too crowded, too dirty. We needed more land so that every soldier could have a parcel of dirt when he retired. We have triumphed by the force of our willpower alone. Not even the mighty Greeks, in spite of all their philosophers, in spite of their magnificent sculptors, have succeeded in achieving as much. We have become connoisseurs of the finer things in life: we know how to eat and drink in style, something the Greeks never knew how to do. We have surpassed them in our appetites. We entertain ourselves with our elegance, our wit. We are lovers of painting and sculpture. We are attentive to beauty in all its forms.

We knew how to amuse ourselves in those days, before the arrival of the barbarians: drunken nights, food in abundance, surrounded by the sounds of laughter and song, while some poor fool, a Numidian slave, amused us by juggling braziers of fire while balancing on a rolling barrel. It's harder these days, of course, with the barbarians camped a short distance from us, on the other side of the city walls, camped by the frozen river, ageing imperceptibly, their poor children scrounging for food, their womenfolk sheltering from the winds in their roughly made carts...What do the barbarians think of? we ask each other on our way to the *frigidarium*. Do they not value momentum? They have been camped motionless for so long that by now the hooves of their horses must be sprouting roots that are sinking into the ground. The Abyssinian traders—

those strange creatures who dare venture between Roman, Gaul and barbarian alike—tell us the barbarians are great travellers. Why then do our barbarians not move on?

We have known about the barbarians ever since we were children, of course. They were creatures conjured out of the thin air at night in order to frighten us to sleep. They were presented to us as the creatures of punishment. If you didn't eat your food the barbarians would get you, if you didn't go to school the barbarians would get you. So we have grown up with them all our lives. Our parents have told us of the destruction of Rome and as we turned into adults we heard stories of the devastation caused by them: great cities put to the sword and monstrously turned to ashes. They are creatures of immolation ready to sacrifice everything in order to appease their anger, according to my dead father. And yet the first few of the advance guard, whom we saw from our watchtowers, looked so haggard, so scruffy, so woebegone, so dispirited, so miserable. It's possible we could have done something about them in those early days—years ago now—when those first miserable creatures arrived. We could have mounted a pre-emptive strike, but we had no way of knowing how thick and deep was this crop of newly minted barbarians. But we did nothing; the name itself, *barbarian* overpowered us. And our curiosity overcame us. We had heard about them all our lives but had never seen them until a few years ago. They had always descended on someone else's, a cousin's or a nephew's city, with devastating consequences, and now here they are finally confronting us. We have spent a lifetime avoiding them, yet also a lifetime of looking over our shoulders to see if they have grafted themselves onto us like shadows of the late afternoon. And now here they are—we can avoid them no longer. They are truly our dark side. They are our disease. We have to cut them out of the body to save the rest of the body. They are the legs and arms we have to amputate; arms and legs that have taken on independent life.

We have no way of knowing how many barbarians are camped by the frozen river, though the Abyssinians have told us that more barbarians are arriving every month, bloodied, covered in scars and festering sores, surly and truculent, barely given to speech at all. They speak in grunts and use, only when they have to, guttural indistinct words whose meanings are lost back in the folds and creases of ancient time.

In the midst of our nightly entertainments one of our company only has to lean over and whisper the word *when?* for you to see a palpable shiver ripple across the room like a field of wheat in the face of an imminent storm. Our night-minds are full of these, *our,* barbarians. When we half wake in the middle of the night, the faces of our wives beside us take on the appearance of those accursed barbarians. Our lives are no longer our own. We have been overtaken by something growing inside us. We have been impregnated. Our thoughts are no longer our own. Our thoughts have been purloined. We have been invaded from within. In distressed moments, anxious moments, we privately wish the barbarians would finally attack—just to put us out of the misery of waiting, the misery of having our thoughts nightly invaded, the misery of being dependent on their movements before we can move. Unless we make a pre-emptive strike. But it is too late for that. We don't know how many of them there are.

We discovered yesterday that we are now surrounded by a vast mass of truly uncountable, unknowable savages. Though we cannot rely on the Abyssinians to tell us the truth. They will only tell us what suits their purposes. We often repeat to each other while reclining in the hottest of the three baths, the *caldarium*, the story of the first day that we saw from the watchtower two barbarians arrive on horseback, their beards caked in mud, their long filthy hair, the torn animal skins they use for clothes barely covering them, their muscular bodies exposed to all the elements. We laughed at them. It was preposterous that two of these primitives could hold us to ransom, would threaten to lay siege to our fine city. They already looked woebegone and defeated. But gradually more of them arrived, and then much later their womenfolk and children arrived—a more miserable bunch of brutes you could not imagine.

They have been put here—we said to each other while crossing from the bakers through the city square and on the way to the Baths of Diocletian—for the purpose of placing our lives in a context: so that finally we can measure how far we have progressed in contrast to their rude state of being. We were glad to see them initially. At first just out of idle curiosity because we had heard stories over the course of a lifetime about these creatures called barbarians who had destroyed cities with utter ruthlessness but we had not until two to three years ago laid eyes on them. At first we half-welcomed them—something to take our minds off the multiple worry and misery of marriage, concubines, children, ageing, faltering health and governance. Curiosities out on the plain. Out of harm's way. Like rich men's fools whom you pay to distract you for an hour or two before going on with the pressing concerns of accountancy, civic planning and matters of law.

But when the Abyssinian traders—they who are so skilled in the use of many languages and they who are sufficiently chameleon-like to appear to barbarians and Romans alike as being not altogether untrustworthy—told us that there were thousands of barbarians camped outside our walls, but only on the eastern side, with more arriving each month, then it was still not too late. We were not yet surrounded, we could still attain supplies from the west and in those early days we lived like kings with food and wine in abundance supplied by the Gauls who did the dangerous task of tilling the fields far from the protection of the city walls. The barbarians apparently were, in their calm and measured ways, tending to their sores and scars and resting on the backs of their horses. But one day we sensed they would awake from their slumber—and it filled us full of dread because they are not like us. Supernatural beings, utterly different from us. The traders had described their appearance and their habits: rough-hewn faces, with misshapen noses and mud-covered beards. They never wash and their animal stink is unbelievable.

So how could they call themselves human? we asked each other on our way through the narrow streets to the Senate. Did they not aim to be civilized? Did they not long for the soothing comfort of warm water on tired bones?

Did they not long for the luxuriousness of oils and perfumes, the sweetness of spices, the aroma of burning frankincense, the sound of soft music and the taste of rich wine? How were these rough creatures made that they did not desire comfort? Which faulty craftsmen can we call to account?

We might hold them with our speeches. That is our plan. When the leader of the barbarians arrives with his retinue to arrange the terms under which we will fight, we senators will present our speeches one by one until they are swept away with the beauty of our eloquence and the cleverness of our craft. Then we will entertain the leader of the barbarians and his entourage in the finest manner known. We will bedazzle them. There will be food in abundance—roast peacocks, chickens' gizzards and roasted lizards—and the finest Falernian wine shipped in from Rome. Our lyric poets and songmakers will entertain them. We will schedule a gladiatorial spectacle—man against lion, man against wild boar, man against man—for the entertainment of our opposites: those rude creatures from the lands of the howling winds and never-ending rains. We will dazzle the rude beasts with the beauty and cleverness of our women. There will be no escaping our hospitality. Our finest storytellers will entertain them with stories of courage and adventure. There will be no escaping our magnanimity. They will be seduced by our mastery over all things natural and unnatural.

We will tell them how we have trained water to run upwards, how we have trained monkeys to speak, how we have constructed war-machines the likes of which no other culture has ever imagined, let alone built. We will tell them, and tell them and tell them until they are numb with amazement. The leader of the barbarians, poor dumb beast, will be amazed by the splendour. He will step out of a world of darkness into a large banquet hall full of light, mica, saffron, perfume and wine, and be overcome. Our esteemed philosopher from Corduba, the capital of Baetica, will impress him with his grasp of the nature of things, the very nature of being. Our engineers will impress the leaders of the barbarians with their understanding of the way mechanical objects work, their knowledge of the principles of thrust and pull. And the poor dumb beasts will not escape without an appreciation of the might, the power, the splendour of the Roman world—at least as it manifests itself in this part of Narbonensis. We will argue our case and the barbarians will go away. That will be it. They will torment us no longer, with their taciturn silence, their disregard for bodily comforts, their rude and insolent passivity. They will leave with a heightened knowledge of the splendour and greatness of Imperial Rome. They will discover they are outsiders with only a supporting role to play; they can never be the main actors. They are lower than the Gauls; they are lower than the so-called *bagaudes* (those highly trained Roman rebel soldiers); they are mere unknowing, unthinking savages. We will shock them with our sophistication. They will retreat like wounded wolves with their tails between their legs. The main roles on the world stage have all been filled—by Romans.

*

But today we are in a great state because the Abyssinian traders have told us that the barbarians have no leader, they do not send delegations to discuss the conduct of war, they attack whenever they feel like it, and they are as patient and as clever as Romans. These are things we have not considered before. True warriors only fight after having sent a delegation and agreeing upon the terms of war. We are heartbroken, we are bereft. Maybe they will never hear our poignant, impressive speeches. Maybe it has all been in vain. The Senate is disbanded for the day. Some of our number have gone home to bed, others to the Baths of Diocletian, others to their mistresses and others go home to take poison.

We are convinced now. They will overrun us. The vestal virgins told us so in an early-morning consultation before the sun was up.

—Tell us what to do? we ask the vestal virgins.

—The only way to avoid a bloodthirsty end is to make a sacrifice to the gods so the outrage of the gods may be appeased, we are told.

—Why are the gods angry with us?

—It is because the gods feel ignored, we are told.

So we have turned our backs on the vestal virgins and we have consulted the astrologers instead. They say our end is not so certain, there is room for doubt, but that the omens do not look good. We must avoid letting the citizenry know so there is no panic. We must go about our daily routine as if nothing out of the ordinary is about to happen. The banqueting and feasting, the carousing and seducing, even the law-making must go on as before. We senators must present a united front, especially to the Gauls, who may take advantage of any sign of weakness and thus attempt to overthrow us at the first opportunity.

The barbarians will put our city to the torch. They are lovers of fire. They are here to destroy our civilization. Out of jealousy they will lay waste to what we have created. We are the builders of the world. No other civilization has built as much, nor been as successful. We have organized the world in a way no other civilization has ever done before. We want to transfer all of these words from our speeches that go around and around in our heads and will not leave us alone. We want to be done with *those* words. We want them to fear us, and respect us. We want to make them understand their place in the scheme of things. But maybe they do—all too well. Maybe that is the problem.

We must be rid of them now, as a matter of urgency. They have gone too far. We shall attack them in the morning. They have plagued and beleaguered us long enough. We shall act now while there is still time. We have sent out the traders to ascertain their strength.

There is no more time. We have no more time. We are done for. Some of us go home to sleep, others go home to slice their wrists in a warm bath in Stoic style. We are done for. Unless starvation gets them first. Unless disease destroys them. Maybe it is time to make a sacrifice to the gods...

So we returned to the vestal virgins before the sun had risen but they turned their backs on us, and we have ended up with the astrologers again but they can add nothing new to their forecast and so we have turned to the philosopher

Antoni Jach

from Corduba, the Moor with the dark skin, the recessed eyes and the drooping eyelids who can only say in a mournful tone that what will be, will be, and that life will go on long after we are all dead and we are but transitory. He is of no comfort so we have turned to our wives and mistresses but we can tell them nothing of our distress. They have turned their backs on our sorrowing faces, preferring gaiety instead.

We have come up with a plan—to strike first. We have amassed our weapons of war. We have covertly ascertained our fighting strength. Now we are in black despair...

Perhaps they will starve, camped out there on the frozen plains, we say to each other in the oiling room after the warm bath of the *tepidarium*. We have heard it happen before: the siegers starve while the besieged have plenty to eat and drink, as we do. We can last another year without any great privation. Our granaries are full to bursting, our wine vats are overflowing. Perhaps we will not act. Perhaps we can do nothing anymore...except make speeches. Perhaps our willpower leached away while we were sleeping.

*

Yesterday, we decided that our speeches will not do, and now I am sick at heart. We will have to write new ones. My wife is inconsolable (she will not stop talking she is so anxious, she has lost all her gaiety, she has heard something), my mistress is melancholic (she has lost all her desire), my children are miserable (they push their food around, refusing to touch it), our slaves are disconsolate

190

(they have fallen into a languid stupor, are slow in doing the simplest of tasks and answer back), our animals are in decline (sores are appearing on their hindquarters), the populace refuses to pay its taxes, and even our freshly baked bread tastes stale. The word is that it is we, the senators, who are to blame. It is always the senators who are to blame. We are said to be lazy, indulgent, corrupt and vice-ridden. We have lost all energy to deny these claims. Those prominent citizens who decry us walk the streets unpunished. We are in the hold of lassitude.

We have received a deputation of upstanding citizens who have implored us to fix the problem of the barbarians. We senators are charged with failing to get rid of the barbarians. We are charged with failure to act. We should have done something, when there was still time before the hundred thousand or so barbarians had time to assemble. We cannot explain that it was our curiosity that prevented us from acting in a timely fashion, having never seen barbarians before—the upstanding citizens would not understand that.

We are told we have let everyone down. We should be ashamed of ourselves. We have been too lenient towards the barbarians. We should go out and punish them for daring to stand up to Imperial Rome. It is upon our heads and the heads of our families. Even the Gauls no longer respect us. There will be an insurrection at any moment from within the walls of the city. Our allies have become our foes by small degrees; especially when they see signs of weakness. Time is no longer ours to command, we are told. The upstanding citizens are refusing to pay any taxes or to commence any of the multiple building projects that have been agreed upon. They want the return of their country estates. We have been warned that the plebeians are ready to rebel at a moment's notice. They want firm leadership, removal of the barbarians, a decrease in the price of grain, more festivals and the end of taxes being sent back to Rome.

We have been told that one of our upstanding citizens— Maximinius, the surveyor—has already left saying he will make his way south to Hispaniae, and others who have the means are planning to desert at the first opportunity. If upstanding citizens leave, everyone will attempt to flee the city and there will be chaos. There is a malicious rumour circulating about Maximinius that claims he has deserted to the barbarians saying he would prefer to live as a free man amongst barbarians than live as a taxed and enslaved Roman.

My personal and favourite servant was knifed this morning upon leaving the *domus* by a deranged citizen. The city is starting to fray around the edges. There is hysteria building. My bodyguards are looking more nervous than ever before. On every street corner you see disputes erupting over trivial things: a shop-owner beaten to death for failing to serve a full jug's measure of olive oil; public confusion caused by a broken pipe gushing water in the city square. Even water is getting away from us now. We who have been so good at training water.

Hardly anything reaches me anymore: neither smell, nor sound, nor sight. Life is losing its piquant flavour. It dissembles moment by moment. The sundial is losing its power to order the days. What need have we of Time when the barbarians are camped by the frozen river, coiled up yet ever ready to spring? No longer does the beauty of our surroundings have any effect: the sunlight in the olive trees; the sparrows around our open doors; our children writing on their wax-covered tablets; the philosophers—old and battle-scarred—under the colonnades telling us how to live our lives: to renounce Epicureanism and take up Stoicism's balance, order and restraint as a way of life; the smell of the sea—either imagined or real—wafting through the breeze; the allure of ancient Greece—the source of wisdom, of laughing voices, the wellspring of tragedy; the beauty of Grecian sculpture—its calm, its repose, its sense of timeless order. My former philosophy teacher argues that you feel life more keenly when you are staring at great danger, and that he is grateful to the barbarians for making him realize that he too has to take stock of his situation and not just live each day as it comes.

We go—my friend, a fellow senator, and I—occasionally at dusk onto the ramparts and then we climb the steps to the watchtower. We can see the vast amount of smoke from their campfires. The start of them is only a short distance away. There must be a hundred thousand of them out there. We can feel their poverty, their desolation, their loneliness, their compressed, contained power. Occasionally their smoke drifts our way and we are surrounded by it, smelling the roasted flesh of animals, of fish.

I turn to Marius and ask him if he is ever homesick. He replies he is and that is why he spends so much time in the watchtower. He is not really focusing on the barbarians at all. He is in fact desperately trying to forget the barbarians. He is looking over their heads towards Rome, towards his childhood in Ostia, his mother now dead, his younger brother now dead, his father dying, his sister married with three children of her own and a country villa in the surrounding hills, his older brother a renowned senator, a man of the purple stripe, a man of the people, providing honest service. He is ready to return to Rome. His stay of duty has come to an end; he has served honourably his twenty-one years in the western provinces and he is now ready to return to the seven hills of Rome to receive the respect that is due to him as a diligent son of Rome. If it wasn't for the barbarians he would make the journey tomorrow. He would pack up his wife, his primary mistress, his secondary mistress, his children, their dogs, camels, parakeets, monkeys and horses, his one hundred slaves, his personal guard, the ten maids of his wife, the five maids of his primary mistress, his sculpture of Hermes by Polyclitus that he brought all the way from Rome by cart and oxen, and just go. Too many enemies to leave anyone or anything valuable behind. He would leave as quickly as is possible, considering the great weight he is pulling along behind him.

—Something gnaws away at you, he says in a low voice, until you can stand it no longer, and what you used to hold dear loses its meaning and the future comes into view in its many-hued colours and you see yourself placed in a future landscape that has possibilities. The essential greyness of life dissipates, like fog clearing from a valley when the sun finally reaches it at two in the afternoon. And it can all happen in an instant. You can be in the middle of the most outrageous commotion—the children are crying over petty injustices, the maids are tearing each other's hair out, one's personal guard of gladiators are fighting in the wine-cellar, your wife is attacking your arm with a pair of scissors while your mistress wails in an adjoining room threatening to poison herself if you do not take more notice of her—and a thought can flicker across your mind that can change the way you view everything. It all becomes clear what you must do. Not what you *should* do, or *ought* to do but *must* do. You must return to Rome. Devastated as it still is after the sacking by the barbarians many years ago, it is still Rome. It is still the greatest city in the known world. It is still home. The way is now clear. You had not realized that before. Your stay of duty is over—you need not renew it. You have been so bowed down with duty that you had not realized that time was passing you by, that even your face was changing year after year until you caught a glimpse of your mirrored image in a broken piece of glass and were startled, then horrified, then revolted by what you saw. While you weren't watching you had become another person. You realized you did not like yourself anymore. You would have to flee yourself. You have become, while you weren't watching, a civilized barbarian.

—You have to do what you think is best, Marius, I reply.

—The only barricade to free passage is the barbarians, he continues. The greater difficulty—the way I see things—has been overcome. The rest is negotiable. With a cartload of gold and silver coins from the reign of Augustus I might

be able to buy a safe passage for myself and my retinue...
What do you think?

—I think we are all trapped here.

He turns to me and says:

—So will you stay here till you die?

And I reply:

—I don't know, Marius, I don't know. I may turn into a barbarian myself. Give away the purple stripe of the senator for the beard caked in mud of the barbarian. Give away everything I have accumulated in exchange for a cart, a broken-down horse, just my family around me, and a sense of peace. My mind has been an occupied country of late. It has already been invaded by barbarians. I have none of my own thoughts. I am imprisoned already.

—It's the deceit, that gets to you in the end, he says after a long pause. The number of lies needed to stay in high public office gets larger every year. And then you have to service those lies with more lies, and you have to remember to cover your tracks, and cover your back because there is always someone ready to strike you down when you go out into the public arena, and in the end you just want to retire to tend to your garden. It's too much for any one person to bear.

And we look out silently across the vast mass of barbarians, stretching far away into the distance for as far as the naked eye can see, and we wonder what Mithras, the sun god, has in store for each of us: what trick, what ruse, what adventure, what stratagem?

—And then, says Marius, if we get past the barbarians there are always those Roman mercenaries, the *bagaudes*, who are in the employ of the barbarians, to get past, and then there are the numerous wild beasts in the endless dark forests to avoid...So, then I ask myself softly: why not stay here in Narbonensis where the air is fresh, the olives are sweet, the wines are fragrant and the plains and hills are so beautiful? But then again at other times I say to myself it would be good to leave all of this and the past behind. Even forget about Rome. To escape. To see Carthage before I die. You and your retinue could come too. We could leave this city behind. We could escape from the barbarians via the western route initially, then travel southwards into Hispaniae and finally cross the Mare Internum at Gades and make our way to Tingi in Africa, then via Caesarea to Carthage where we could rest our weary bodies and minds until our bodies obey their final destiny, obey the pull towards completion in the same way a falling stone longs to hit the ground or else an athlete longs to rest or a thirsty man longs for water...But who knows, maybe in Carthage there are barbarians as well. Maybe we will just take our own barbarians with us, in our baggage? Maybe we can never throw them off our backs, their short, sharp daggers perpetually held to our throats? Maybe we need the barbarians to feel alive? To see ourselves as we really are? Carthage. Lately, I cannot get the word out of my head. From the first time it was planted in my head I was keen to harvest its promise. I have kept saying to myself these past twenty-one years that in a few more years I will have done enough to have some time to myself away from the noise and confusion of public and private demands. I have heard tell it's the most beautiful place in the Roman world.

Particularly at evening, with the sun descending into the
harbour. Many fine buildings. I have heard the women there
wrap their legs around you by way of greeting, and they
will not let a foreigner go. And the heat! No more frozen
winters. We could find ourselves anew. Start over again
with new identities. Become Carthaginians, rather than senators, with all the weight of Roman civilization, of propriety
of order, of measure, upon our shoulders; with all of the
hidden and secret contractual arrangements we take on by
being part of a civilized nation. We could throw off the
yoke of the role of a provincial senator in a Roman town
in Narbonensis and become like children again. See how
sensually they play with each other, so roughly, so
unashamedly. They do not fear, are not frightened of themselves when they wake in the middle of the night. They do
not share our terrors. Their faces are not bowed down and
broken. They are content to be themselves. They do not
hide their anger. They are not confused about who they
are. They do not suspect others. We could reconstruct ourselves. We could become master craftsmen, or jewellers, or
even the highest calling of all, a sculptor? We could fashion bracelets and necklaces out of bronze, of silver, of gold
too. Our days would be filled with sunshine, our children
and those of our mistresses would run around at our feet
playing happily together, content to be warmed by the sun.
We could plant some vines, or better still some olive trees
that would last a millennium and be useful in a minor
way...I will endeavour to deposit my retinue as I travel.
To simplify. Once past the barbarians, en route to Carthage
I will loosen the ties of a hundred and fifteen slaves. At

Barcino, fifty can go free, at Corduba another fifty. Eventually, all who serve can go free. Except for the slaves driving the cart with my sculpture of Hermes. That will go wherever I go until I die. It is the most lovely thing I have ever seen. Finally when we reach the safety of Carthage, my personal guards can go free as well. Everything that was born deserves to have a space in which to draw in oxygen, as would a fire that is getting hungry. I am tired of all the landscape my eyes can see—I have seen it all before. Whatever used to be fresh now has the mould of decay upon it. Even the pale sun struggles in vain to warm me. I have had enough of serving other people, of living other people's lives for them. All who serve can go free, and become humble makers of little objects appreciated by only an astute few...I may become a sculptor in my old age. A sculptor to rival those masters of calm and order, Praxiteles and Polyclitus...But then again, we could leave both of our substantial retinues behind and we could go, just the two of us to Carthage. What do you say? We could become goldsmiths and make delicate objects under an awning in the street in the sunshine.

*

But that was yesterday. Today we are in a great state because the word is that the barbarians are ready to make a pact with us. An Abyssinian trader mentioned it to a joiner who mentioned it to a carpenter who mentioned it to a scrivener who was overheard in the massage room of the Baths of Diocletian by a senator who passed the word on through the ranks of senators. Our first thought, naturally, was that it was a trick, a ruse, a stratagem, of the first magnitude—worthy only of Roman contempt. But now we are not so sure. As we pass from the gymnasium to the *tepidarium* to the *caldarium* and finally to the *frigidarium* we confer with each other in hushed tones so that the plebeians may not overhear us. The word is...a pact between the Romans of the walled city with the near-barbarians of the frozen river against the *other* barbarians who are ravaging the rear forces of the near-barbarians. Nothing is implausible we say to each other while we are being boiled alive by the heat of the *caldarium*. The idea is— according to the trader who mentioned it to the joiner who mentioned it to the carpenter who mentioned it to the scrivener who was overheard in the massage room of the Baths of Diocletian by a senator—that we should open the huge public gates of the town to the barbarian forces as a sign of trust and that we should join forces against a common enemy. The other barbarians, apparently, are fiercer and more warlike than our near-barbarians who have become ascetic due to the sedentary nature of their siege for the past three years. The near-barbarians have become like us: dwellers. They have lost their edge. The word is... they are no longer ruthless. They spend their time reflecting upon their lives thus far, occasionally speaking. They have become like babes in the woods. Or have they? It is said the near-barbarians need our protection. Or do they? Is this not another cunning mind-game served up guilefully to further perturb us during our restless nights when we toss and turn substituting one less inadequate word for a merely inadequate one?

The Layers of the City

The word is that the near-barbarians are prepared to give up their own gods and worship ours. We can choose for them—they will become followers of either Mars or Jupiter or Mithras, or any other god we can name. According to our sources, they are worn down with their life of privation and would dearly love to exchange their tunics made of the skins of wild rats for the soft silk with a purple stripe of the Roman senator. They would like to exchange the smell of rotting meat for the fragrances of frankincense and myrrh. They would like to exchange the fierce winds blowing off the frozen river for the heated room. They would like to exchange the disorder of the campsite for the order of the stroll from the Forum to the theatre, from the bathhouse to the amphitheatre, from the water-tower to the temple.

But then the information is not necessarily reliable, coming as it does via word of mouth. Only now we have one more piece to throw into the jigsaw puzzle of conjecture. It is hard to believe that the near-barbarians, *our* barbarians would so change their orientation overnight. One thing is certain, we are not about to open the public gates precipitously. It would take many months of argument and discussion. Though if *our* barbarians truly did need our help then that might be another matter. After all we have been together these two years or more. Perhaps they have become more like us than we realize. The world is now confusion writ large.

Tonight we are back writing our speeches. We must get the syntax, the pauses right. Marius is at his desk. He says he can no longer remember what is true and what is false.

He says he can no longer remember the speech he gave last week or the one before that. His memory palace has fallen into disuse: it's fit only for thieves now. He says he is working diligently, in the old rhetorical style of which people are still fond. He says the other senators expect lies, so lies may as well be forthcoming. He says he is creating beautiful new lies, embroidered in the old flowery style which we all still love. His rhetoric will be full-blown, with enough wind to puff a four-sailed ship across the oceans, or it will be worthless. He says the populace expects too much of their senators: they expect integrity, forthrightness, wisdom and eloquence. The first three are impossible, the last one is only just possible, given proper diligence to the task of writing the speech, he says. He is becoming more melancholic with each day. He has decided to stay. We are truly encircled. A cartload of gold coins in the old style will not do the trick, and besides there is still this talk of a pact in the air—it is all we can cling to.

We senators have finally decided to do something. We have scheduled a grand debate for tomorrow. Every senator will be allowed to speak about the situation we find ourselves in. The debate will last a week. We will then decide what to do. We could make a pact with the barbarians and then invite their leaders to hear our prepared speeches, though they may need some revision by now for, like fresh bread, speeches too can go off. Without warning we could throw open the city's gates, and let all of the barbarians enter. They would doubtlessly come in stupefied at the sights surrounding them, and fall under the sway of our superior culture. We could show them the great public

Baths of Diocletian which are modelled on the ones in Rome. We could show them the comfort of water.

Where does their great hatred come from? Where does their need to destroy come from?

—Because the ordinary people cannot be trusted we have to tell them lies, says Marius. Because we want them to think better of us than we think of ourselves we have to tell them lies. Because we want their trust we tell them lies. Because, finally, it's for their own good we have to tell them lies. In the end the people, like the barbarians, are aware of their own inferiority. They want someone to be superior—that's why there are senators.

I am back writing speeches because there is nothing else to do. And I realize, with a sickening thud, that there will not be a day now between this day and when I die when I will not be turning over some thought or other to turn into a speech. And that the very day the barbarians vanish into thin air—if they ever do—then there will be more speeches to write: one to welcome the proconsul, one to welcome the season of spring, one to anoint a new building and one a speech of thanksgiving for the fertility of the land. There is no natural pause in this occupation; just as the sun is diurnal, so this is too. The wheel has been set upon the millstone; the water turns it endlessly, the chaff needs separating from the kernel.

Lately I have taken to wandering through the narrow city streets without thought for my personal safety. I have left my bodyguards at home. It feels good to just wander without knowing where I am heading. Simple things give me moments of pleasure: a child twirling a flower around to catch the glinting of the sun; a beggar hitting his clothes bringing up clouds of dust; the commotion inside the market where the slaughtered animals are held up for display, blood trickling down the insides of arms; the simple movements of a peasant girl as she crosses the square, swaying from one childish hip to the other, caught up in her own world, the sun burning a swathe across her naked shoulders. And then a thought interrupts me. A new topic for a speech comes to mind: we shall build taller and grander than ever before. When your nerves are about to fail there is nothing better than to start a public project to bring the populace together. We could create a building on a gigantic scale which will dwarf everything else—say, a new arena. We shall commence the demolition of the old one tomorrow. That is actually the way out of our dilemma. It will give us something to occupy our thoughts, between the moment of waking and the moment of sleeping. It will take our minds off the threat of the near-barbarians and off the far greater threat of the other barbarians. Forgetfulness is to be much praised, especially in one who has been raised to remember.

Given the fragility of life, given the tempestuous nature of current events, given the extremes that beset us, we shall build a new arena with a ring of life-sized sculptures of senators surrounding the uppermost floor looking inward at the games. In this way we may not go unrecognized into the future. In years to come our statues may be discovered, when we have long since gone. Our statues will be dug up—one with a broken nose, one with a broken arm, one without a jaw; but it will still be us, something of our spirit will be caught, if the sculptor is good enough. And if not, we will pass on unrecorded and unremarked upon. Our legacy will live on, however. Other people will build houses on top of our bones. Buildings will be burnt down, new ones will be built, but underneath all those new people will be the bones of the Romans, mingled with the bones of barbarians. Those succeeding generations will not be able to escape us. We will have left them our gift.

But now the commotion is rising. There is noise on all sides. We have been told they have smashed our aqueducts and we will soon be without water. There is fire outside the walls. Now it is finally happening. The word is...the barbarians are coming.

eight | The Arrival

It is said by reliable sources that the Abyssinian traders of Southern Gaul carry their solitude with them like a second skin. While they move in small groups for reasons of security, constantly forming new alliances as suits them, they remain as individuals unable or unwilling to escape from their own profound inwardness. Only occasionally on their feast days have we witnessed them attempting to break out of the straightjacket of their inner selves by drinking mead until their eyeballs are bulging and about to pop out and by indulging in an activity apparently reserved only for feast days: the eating of a warm steak cut from the side of a live cow.

It is also said, but we have no proof of it, that for sport they encourage their young men to steal the cubs of panthers and leopards to give to their younger sisters for rearing. It is only when drunk that the traders speak more than is absolutely necessary and on such occasions one of them might attempt to describe fantastic creatures that none of us had ever heard of or seen.

The Greek merchants on the other hand could not be more different: they are men of learning and culture, confident in manner, alert in thought and both voluble and acerbic when the opportunity presents itself. They are always up-to-date with the latest trinket of knowledge or bauble of logic but they are also easily amused by their own clevernesses. They delight themselves with puns and witticisms and love to hear the sound of their own voices as much as any Roman. We look forward to their visits as they bring the scent of familiarity with them, inadvertently making us homesick for our native Rome and its seven hills. They are not without courage, plying their trade between ourselves and the barbarians with a studied nonchalance. There is something in their bearing, perhaps a certain *gravitas* that may protect them in their dealings with the barbarians, though this very quality would doubtlessly prove to be worthless upon coming face to face with the *other* barbarians. But considering how the province of Gallia Narbonensis is such a wild place, it is always with a spirit of longing that we open the heavy gates to the dusty Greek merchants and pounce upon them, eager for an excuse to hold a banquet, eager for their stories. They bring with them the perfume of a shared past: learning, culture, knowledge.

When they look at our architecture, our sculpture, our ceramics or our glassware the Greeks delight in telling us that we are imitation Greeks. They never tire of telling us that we are camped on Greek land and that Hellenic civilization has, centuries before, laid claim to all of the lands that we can see and all of the winds that blow and all of the rivers that meander lazily across the swathes of wheat and the olive groves and through the fields of dense oak trees. In fact, according to the merchants, if it wasn't for the Greeks bringing their olive trees with them hundreds of years before, there would be no olive trees in the whole of the diocesis of Septem Provinciae. They confide in us that just as the Greeks were supplanted by the Romans then we too will eventually have to make way for the barbarians for they have something more powerful than civilization: they have barbarism.

Even the merchants' mangling of the Latin language we find amusing. For when it comes to the gift of languages the Abyssinian traders are far quicker; better at turning any situation to their advantage and much more accomplished in the transformation of the sweat of their brows into gold. The Abyssinians have the reputation of taking any risk that is asked for; if they can be persuaded, that is, that there will be sufficient recompense at the end of the day.

So while we are moving along the corridors of the Baths of Diocletian, complaining about the numerous false alarms of imminent invasion and endlessly discussing the vexed question of how to arrange a meeting with the barbarians, it is obvious and natural that our thoughts turn to the Abyssinian traders as a means of providing contact. For while we understand and like the merchants as men, we cannot trust them to succeed in matters of importance in spite of all their learning. They have spent too much of their time living in their heads, revolving through the 'weeping philosopher' Heraclitus's notions of fire and water and the eternal flux of the Universe. They are too *other-worldly* for our plans and we require practical and efficient go-betweens. We know the Abyssinian traders are totally untrustworthy and loyal only to the highest bidder, but provided we can pay them enough, we feel confident that they will succeed in any task they are given. They are as hungry for success as the Greeks are complacent in their lesser abilities.

*

On the next working day while our heads are still clouded with alcohol we call in the loneliest Abyssinian trader we have ever seen: an ancient trader who has provided us with good service in the past, a man who has no name, who is wizened, with one good but cloudy eye and one eye which does not see, whose brown translucent skin hangs around him like a sack. We confide in him that we have a plan that will secure him an honourable and comfortable old age—an expression he has obviously heard many times before. Numerous gold and silver coins of the old style, we say, will guarantee him a happy old age in which he can sit surrounded in a state of honour by his grateful family. He spits in the dust, impatient with our prologue. He does not trust us—his eyes are moving restlessly sideways—nor should he. We do not like him. We know he has no family. He is only a necessary functionary. It lessens us to deal with him. We feel somehow soiled, but we can use his utterly alone and dangerous will to succeed.

All he has to do, we patiently explain as though talking to a child, is to organize some of his men to take cartloads of grain and wine to the near-barbarians every day for the next thirty days, studiously avoiding however the seventh day in every sequence, so they can have a taste of absence, the surfeit of anything dulling the taste of its presence. Each time the cartloads arrive the Abyssinian is to tell the near-barbarians that they have to choose five leaders to serve as a delegation for two meetings with we Romans.

The first meeting will be a public occasion to coincide with the first of the harvest festivals, the Consualia, to be held in the open-air theatre within the city walls in thirty-one days time. The second occasion will be a private affair outside the perimeters of the walled city in the natural amphitheatre near the running brook in thirty-two days time. This second meeting will be with a delegation of five senators. The purpose of the first meeting is purely social— they will be guests at a spectacle presented in their honour.

The purpose of the second meeting is to decide what can jointly be done about the mutual problem of the *other* barbarians; those savages who are so completely warlike and unused to the rules of war that they pose a permanent danger to both Romans and the near-barbarians alike. The trader can hint obliquely at the possibility of the barbarians being hired as an auxiliary Roman army, a federated force as they are called—as has happened elsewhere, notably in Hispaniae—to defend the city from the other barbarians, but he is not to give any undertakings beyond that.

We have been warned about the superstitiousness of the Abyssinians by the philosophers and the historians of the Senate and it has come to our attention on previous occasions when we have engaged the traders to do our dirty work that a proposed deal could be broken on the spot by the sight of, say, a senator wearing a red stripe upon his toga, red being the sign of bad luck, or else by the sight of a chicken crossing a room—that also being a sign of bad luck. There are, also, certain days of the year when the traders do no work but lie around, eating nothing, sipping only water in a state of silence for days on end in accordance with a religious observance. But when we have need of someone whom we can guarantee will be successful, then we always choose an Abyssinian; their profound loneliness, the intense despair in their eyes, their shifting sense of unease making them ideal subjects for purposeful nefarious activity.

We explain carefully to the ancient Abyssinian that on the twenty-ninth day he is to take five specially made golden armbands to the barbarians so they can choose amongst themselves who their leaders will be; the armband being a sign of leadership and the wearing of the same being a sign that the barbarians have agreed to the safety of the senators in the second of the two meetings. The barbarians will naturally be safe within the walled city, Romans being men of honour, men of their word.

The Abyssinian returns on the evening of the sixth day with the reply that the barbarians will meet with us on the two occasions as outlined. They claim their granaries are overflowing and as they have no need of extra grain—whether this is true or not we do not know—they now ask for cartloads of freshly baked wheat bread and barrels of fermented barley and hops rather than wine, which they cannot abide.

Before the arrival of the thirty-first day we have hardly slept; what with the necessity to polish our speeches to their highest sheen so the barbarians will be impressed with our rhetorical powers, or else due to our desire to spend time with our wives, mistresses and children in case we do not return from the natural amphitheatre with the running brook—having met with treachery and its cousin duplicity; together with the apparent necessity of the city to show its gratitude to its senators by numerous banquets and festivals of entertainment and farewell. Normal law-making has fallen by the wayside as we move into a cycle whereby day slides into night without our noticing so caught up are we with the outpouring of emotion and what seems to be genuine affection, from at least the Roman part of the population, at the knowledge of our impending self-sacrifice.

Marius and I have our speeches polished to perfection. They would shine even if an earthquake overtook us; even if lightning struck us; even if the river Rhône burst its banks and swallowed us. Our speeches are full of subtlety, strength and wit; they contain profound sounds full of long bass notes which will appeal to the barbarians; the meaning is embodied in the rhetoric.

There is much to do in preparation for the arrival of the barbarians. There are 20 000 tickets to sell for the vast open-air theatre where they will be appearing and with the public's expectation of a peaceful settlement to the siege we now have an acceptable reason to add a new tax—

a Pax Barbaricum, or *Peace with the barbarians* tax. We have to suggest the order of the evening's events. The speeches of the senators will come first, that is only natural, but after that, what form of spectacle? What would be fitting for barbarians? A Greek tragedy? Too serious. A Roman farce? Too light? A licentious entertainment? The citizens would love it, but what would the barbarians think? Would the barbarians want to see magic, juggling, a display of tightrope walking? The poets have been banned due to their continuing outbursts of riotous and drunken behaviour in public places, so there will be no poetry. The lighting still has to be arranged. It is obvious that flaming braziers illuminating the night sky would impress the barbarians, they being creatures of darkness and solitude. We stress to the Director of Spectacles and Mass Rallies that the effect of the night on the barbarians and on the plebeians has to be overwhelming; in the end we leave the nature of the entertainment for him to decide. There is an orchestra to hire, with lots of drums; we know they like the sound of drums. The populace has to be informed how to behave with the leaders of the barbarians; they have to be treated with dignity and respect.

But how then to deal with the proconsul? He may or may not approve of our strategy for dealing with the barbarians. We will inform him by messenger—after the event. There is still a possibility, albeit distant, that he might visit us unexpectedly; that is if he can find a way to penetrate the mass of warm living bodies between him and us. Our proconsul is a good and wise man; he will not have forgotten us. Though there is probably little he can do for us now. His generous cupped hands are probably overflowing with barbarians, even as we speak—cascading out like so many rivulets. We fear the power of Rome cannot aid us in this time of quiet desperation. What is the purpose of an empire if it can't defend itself from challenges? To have power that is only useable in peacetime is to have no power at all. Catastrophes grip the vestments of the powerful as moss clings to a rock. But we are comforted by the thought that our leader thinks of us, his unworthy subjects, and he represents us in his dealings with the emperor. Our only certainties come from feeling we are part of an empire. Though we have heard disturbing news, via the Greek merchants, that Romans, both plebeians and from the middle class alike, are living with barbarians as pretend-barbarians.

—The world is obviously turning upside down, I say to Marius while we are being massaged with the seven oils of Christendom, when Romans wish to become barbarians. I can understand barbarians wishing to be Romans but not the other way round.

On the evening of the twenty-ninth day the ancient Abyssinian pulls us out of an evening of feasting and general orgiastic behaviour with the news that the barbarians have taken to each other with knives and spears because they could not agree as to which five would have the honour of wearing the golden armbands and, rather than despising the armbands as trickery to inculcate disorder, they were much impressed with the finery of the objects and with the notion that five of them who are used to being warrior equals could now be superior to the others and order the other warriors to do things they did not want to do. Some of the barbarians—the trader had overheard them talking to each other in their strange and primitive language—were worried that the close proximity of the barbarians to the Romans for the past three years had weakened their erstwhile warlike qualities and turned them into second-rate Romans rather than first-rate barbarians.

We do not, at first, know what to think, but the five of us who have been delegated to entertain the barbarian leaders on the first evening at the theatre and then subsequently meet with them outside the walled city by the running brook reluctantly tear ourselves away from the delights of young perfumed flesh to convene a meeting in a room off the Senate chamber to discuss the ramifications of the news. We do not know whether to be jubilant or despairing at the trader's news. We do not even know if we can trust the Abyssinian. We have no way of knowing whether or not he is now working for the barbarians, they having paid him more to work for them.

So we try to think in a rational manner, our heads so befogged with alcohol that it takes the utmost effort to force our minds to concentrate. Marius is confident that it is all for the best, but the rest of us are not so sure, arguing that our salvation over the long term lies in a deal whereby the barbarians form auxiliary Roman units, with the promise of becoming Romans in the future if they perform successfully. We have heard of barbarians even becoming senators, in Rome of all places, in exchange for duty and loyalty—though it reportedly caused a scandal amongst the populace when it was discovered. The experience of Rome has been that the most vicious and effective warriors against other barbarians are always those who have been born as barbarians themselves.

Marius, who has drunk less than the rest of us, confidently orders five suits of armour to be made as quickly as possible—but with the proviso that one is to be be made of gold encrusted with diamonds while each of the other suits is to be of gradually lesser quality, with the fifth suit being as shoddy and as uncraftsmanlike as a Roman can make it, so that anyone at a glance can see the status of the wearer by merely looking at the armour. We are bewildered, seeing no reason for this gesture. It is only the confidence of the gesture that sways us to trust that he has something in mind. When we ask him to explain, all he will say is that he has a plan.

On the evening of the arrival of the barbarians we five senators are attempting to keep our nerves under control as it is not only the barbarians who will judge our speeches but twenty thousand citizens angry at increased taxation, but also looking forward to a night of spectacle for which they have paid dearly. We have been told to expect trouble from the Gauls. They traditionally express their displeasure with their rulers by shouting during entertainments and spectacles.

At the sight of the five barbarians outside the main city gates wearing the specially made golden armbands we throw open the gates in a spirit of trepidation. Is it a trick? Will the general mass of barbarians use the opening of the gates to rush at us and overpower us?

But that is not to be. The only thing that is overpowering is the smell of the five barbarians. They smell primarily

of dead animals with an after-smell of fire and pine nee-
dles. As they come closer we can detect that their bodies
smell of fields, of rivers, of poppies, of sunlight and snow.
But the lingering odour is the smell of rotting carcases
overpowering any of the pleasant smells they bring with
them. It is all that we can do to prevent ourselves from
recoiling in disgust. But we keep a civil face, as Romans
should. As for their appearance, they are huge in physique
and covered in animal skins. Their long hair and beards
are all matted with a mixture of blood, urine and mud.
Their powerful horses snort restlessly.

We make gestures of greeting, but they say nothing so
we urge them to follow us the short distance into the theatre. We have specially-made bronze chairs for them just
in front of the orchestra, but when we encourage them to
dismount they refuse, preferring not to leave their horses—
their long warrior broadswords gleaming in the reflected
brilliance of the braziers. The barbarian entourage rides
with a lack of concern into the orchestra whose members
have to run or else be trampled on, one horse managing
to put its hoof through a drum. They wait with the patience
of dead men throughout the duration of the speeches, which
are as brilliant as anticipated. But the barbarians are not
impressed, occasionally leaning over on the necks of the
horses as if seeking solace and comfort from their steady
breathing.

Ostensibly our speeches are speeches of welcome for the
barbarians and speeches marking the first of the harvest
festivals, the Consualia. But in reality, once the prelimi-
naries are out of the way, our speeches are masterpieces of

rhetoric, expounding, as always, the consistent Roman virtues of duty, loyalty, justice, generosity, clemency and piety. There are homages paid to the four superior gods, Janus, Jupiter, Mars and Quirinus and the one superior goddess, Vesta, who have looked after us since time immemorial and who have provided us with bountiful harvests, which are for the time being, at least, in the possession of the barbarians.

The speeches emphasize the need for all to follow the middle way, to avoid the extremes of existence: arrogance and self-negation. We invite all in the audience, Gauls and barbarians alike, to see themselves as part of the Roman family with the emperor as the head of the motherland. We invoke Aristotle's notion of composure, and looking over at the barbarians we can't help but notice how composed they are—almost asleep on the necks of their horses, locked in their bodies in a self-protective strength, fearless in the midst of what must be utterly foreign to them. We emphasize, as much for the sake of the Gauls and the retired Roman veterans in the audience as for the barbarians, the gifts that Roman civilization has brought to the rude, uncultured territory of the province of Narbonensis in the diocesis of Septem Provinciae: the gifts of banking, of investment, of a civil service, of a treasury that runs efficiently, of a social order, of a sophisticated network of roads and communication, of a mighty military machine capable of protecting the region's inhabitants from the many attacks of a dangerous world.

At the end of our speeches there is loud applause, probably from the professional clappers, but to our experienced ears there is neither warmth nor enthusiasm nor love contained in that applause. There is no expressed gratitude proffered by the sullen mass of citizens and plebeians and neither is there, unfortunately, any interest shown. We realize later that we should have provided Abyssinian traders as interpreters for the barbarians so they could better appreciate our eloquence. But what with all the other planning that was required—the need to sell so many tickets which in the end turned a tidy profit and started the Director of Spectacles and Mass Rallies on a course of thinking about ways of capitalising on other *Welcome to the barbarians* spectaculars—this most important matter has been overlooked. At least at the end of the evening's speeches—so luminous and stirring, so tender yet masculine in their cadences—the populace, even if they do not care for the sentiments expressed, can at least begin to comprehend that their senators stand for some eternal values beyond the ordinary venality of modern life.

The plebeians in the audience seem bored by the speeches in spite of the eloquence, the command of rhythm and the daring use of language. It is only when the spectacle commences, when the jugglers, the fire-eaters, the tightrope walkers and the fifty lewd comics wearing giant phalluses on their heads come onto the stage urinating profusely onto the heads of the orchestra members, then defecating from openly displayed backsides for the delight of the crowd that the barbarians and those who have fallen asleep start to pay attention. At least our part in the evening has finished and as our heartbeats start to slow to a normal pace we are able to sit back and notice the beauty of the warm coal-black night, later accentuated by the burst of flames licking the huge stone wall of the theatre coming from the burning of twenty-seven straw puppets on a pyre, a tradition of sacrifice emanating from Rome, going back so many centuries that its particular meaning has been lost to us now.

We five senators who gave speeches are disturbed that our lengthy, noble eloquence has been taken so much for granted, for what use is a rhetorician if you cannot sway a crowd and bend it to your will? We turn to each other during the short interval and ask: Why do the populace not love us and respect us? Our numerous spies in the audience inform us, on bended knees and with bowed heads, that our speeches were greatly admired by citizens and Gauls alike and the Greek merchants come over to congratulate us on the *almost* Hellenic quality of our rhetoric; but all we are left with is a profound feeling of emptiness. We have finally delivered our speeches of welcome to the barbarians, speeches that have taken three years of toil, privation and disturbance, speeches which are supposed to guarantee our security, but so what? Nothing has changed. No-one is interested in what we have devoted years of our lives to achieving. We know well the Roman reward for failure for the senatorial class—a warm bath, slit wrists and a vapour room for suffocation—but we have not finished yet: we have a feeling that there are still a few more scenes of the tragi-comedy of life still to be played out.

What will the barbarians think of us now? Apart from the nobility of the speeches and the commanding dignity of the final sacrifice, the rest of the evening's spectacle was full of lewdness and obscenity with a smattering of skill thrown in by the tightrope walkers and the acrobats. Some of the orchestral instruments were destroyed by the barbarians' horses and the orchestra did not see the humour in being urinated on from the stage—compensation claims will flow from both of these occurrences. The evening's entertainment, unfortunately, turned into a public spectacle of what is normally reserved for the private viewing of the noble class. It delighted the plebeians in the audience but what will our savage guests make of it all? What was the Director of Spectacles and Mass Rallies thinking of when he commissioned that monstrous disgrace? We will deal with him in due course. The Roman navy, we are told, is in desperate need of oarsmen. Our softly spoken director may have to chance his arm surrounded by rougher types. It may strengthen his character, teach him obedience.

In private we agree with each other that as senators we have lost the respect of the people. We can instil fear in a total population but we are unable to invade the minds of our people and command respect and admiration. What is to be done in this regard? Pass more laws, put more prisoners to death in the arena, lower the price of bread, proclaim more holidays? There is nothing to be done.

At the end of the evening the barbarians depart with a look of weariness and distance on their faces; they are unreachable, unknowable, half men, half beasts. Their horses move slowly towards the great gates of the city. The barbarians move off like drunken men slumped forward on the necks of their horses letting the horses carry them on without a sense of concern for their own safety. We

remember the Greek merchants saying that the barbarians
lacked a concern over their individual well-being because
collectively there are thousands of them, hundreds of thousands, millions of barbarians, and one individual life by
way of contrast is of little importance. We gesture in a sign
of amity and say that we will meet them the next day in
the natural amphitheatre where the field curves down into
a rock face near the place of the running brook.

Tomorrow we shall attempt to negotiate terms and conditions of an alliance. They can become allies of the
Romans, forming a defensive chain between us and the
other barbarians at whose hands we all have much to fear.

The first part of our plan has succeeded well enough, in
spite of the disappointment with the reception of the
speeches and the lewdness of the spectacle: with the
appearance of the barbarians there is still the possibility of
an agreement and those poor rough and rude souls could
not help but be impressed by the power and the splendour
of the Roman Empire. Besides, all twenty thousand tickets
sold quickly at a tidy profit for the city's coffers; the populace were amazed at the sight of the primitives, delighted
by the spectacle and there was no rioting at the end of the
performance so they must have had their money's worth.

We five senators, however, are nevertheless disconsolate
at the loss of face suffered at the hands of the common
people, many of whom are Gauls who depend on our
beneficence and munificence for their livelihoods. We have
successfully taken them into the Roman family and we
could incorporate our barbarians as well. We console each
other with the suggestion that the common people would

not know a magisterial speech if it was placed on the table in front of them; they having nothing with which to judge speeches by. What they failed to appreciate is the purity and truthfulness of the speeches. They cannot see the late nights and early mornings that have gone into the crafting of the speeches; the endless writing and rewriting, the acknowledgment of the inadequacy of one phrase needing to be replaced by what turns out to be only a slightly less inadequate phrase. What is doubly annoying is that the plebeians can appreciate other art forms—the transparent blown-glass amphoras or the equestrian statues of our finest sculptors—but when it comes to speeches they are at a loss. Somehow our rhetoric has failed to move them. Where in our speeches was the mesmerizing quality of the finest speechmakers whereupon at the end of each speech the crowd is ready to lay down its life in the service of the State? Were our speeches overpowered by the lazy and cheap anticipation of mere jugglers and tightrope walkers, comedians and lewd types wearing horns upon their heads? Why could not the crowd appreciate the finery and cerebral delights of one well-chosen word after another? Why did they have to be so utterly and disgustingly *plebeian* in their tastes?

In the late hours of the night, as we lie on the massage tables being seductively stroked, I turn to my fellow senator and say:

—You know Marius, as I sat watching those primitive, half-human, half-animal beings on their horses I couldn't help but feel that I was looking at a part of myself, an almost completely forgotten part of myself. The more I

looked at them inclining forward on their horses the more
I could see a part of myself located in their sullen, impas-
sive, speechless manner.

*

The next morning we come laden with gifts for our barbarians. A cartload of gifts for those who will be waiting
for us at the natural amphitheatre by the running brook.
But when we arrive they are not there. We instruct our personal guard to haul out of the cart the five suits of
armour—one gold encrusted with jewels, one silver
engraved with warrior scenes, one bronze polished to a
reflective sheen, one linen decorated with a dusty strip of
cloth and one made of the skins of dogs sewn so skilfully
together that no seams are showing. In this fashion we wait
under the noonday sun with the ancient Abyssinian who
has offered to be our interpreter as a sign of good faith.

This is the most dangerous time: to be outside the walled
city without protection—except for our personal guard of
Moors and our huge swords which unfamiliarly slap against
our bare legs. There is the omnipresent danger of wild animals as well as the danger of all manner of barbarian—they
seem to have transmuted like a field of butterflies into so
many strange and rare varieties that they have become
impossible to comprehend.

While we are waiting for the barbarians we press Marius
for an explanation of the five suits of armour. At first he
is reluctant to enlighten us but as the sun progresses
through the sky and at that point when extreme anxiety
starts to tip over into boredom he decides to tell us the

tale of the five suits. The suits, he explains, are to be given to the barbarians to decide who will wear which suit of armour. As with the armbands there will be much bloodshed as they will be unable to decide who will have the status of wearing the golden suit of armour. The barbarians will be thrown into turmoil and will subsequently sue for peace. The Abyssinian spits contemptuously in the dust and walks away.

When the sun has reached its zenith, Marius tells us as a way of passing the time, that the previous day, before the spectacle for the barbarians, he was speaking to one of the Greek merchants who had just returned from Carthage which, he said, was currently overrun with barbarians and Roman slaves. The merchant had been speaking with a Levantine shipowner in Carthage who had told him that the barbarians were everywhere throughout the length and breadth of North Africa and there were now so many tribes of barbarians that it was hard to keep track of them. That, plus the fact that no two people called the same group of barbarians by the same name, make it difficult to tell if the various groups of barbarians were multiplying or if merely the different names they were being called were multiplying at a dizzying rate.

What was adding to the confusion was that there were groups of *bagaudes* roaming the countryside, selling their services to the highest bidder. Their loyalty was only to their brothers-in-arms. They had given up the rights of Romans so that they could give up the duties of Romans. One of their number had told the shipowner that he would rather die a free savage than an indebted Roman. The

Levantine added that one thing he had noticed about the barbarians, having spent time amongst them, was that they had no memory, time had no meaning for them, they lived always in the present—in a string of todays. And he added that barbarians had neither birthplace nor birthdate, a remark that caused us to involuntarily shiver even though the sun was still hot.

The ancient Abyssinian is becoming agitated, walking to and fro in a menacing fashion, so we throw a handful of gold coins into the dust to placate him, which he collects assiduously. He asks us in his characteristic wary and bitter manner why the gold content has decreased in the coins of the Roman Empire. Even the coins are going soft, he says, biting one to prove it. We tell him that as far as we know the gold content has stayed the same since the reign of Augustus, but we add that with the passage of time teeth grow softer and so the general impression of the misguided public is that the coins are softer. He replies that Romans do not always tell the truth; even the barbarians are more straightforward than Romans and he spits once more in the parched dust. So we raise a broadsword to him and tell him to be off, to climb the short incline and return with news of the whereabouts of the barbarians, and in future to display more respect towards his betters or else his life will end in an untimely and spectacular fashion.

When he has gone, and making sure we are out of earshot of the Moors, I turn to the others and say in all truthfulness that the gold content in coins has been declining since the days of Marcus Aurelius and that under Augustus the silver denarius used to be pure silver but this is no longer the case. Even Nero, I say, debased the silver coins during his time by adding five to ten per cent of alloy to each coin. You cannot even trust the emperors these days. But our lives would not be worth living if the general population finds out about the debasing of the currency; that, combined with the weekly addition of new taxes designed to raise money to fight the barbarians, would be too much for their sensitive souls to bear. For the sake of the welfare of the general population it is necessary to be protective of the truth. You must not be too generous with it. Truth is a luxury you spend in good times not bad.

Everyone has to make sacrifices in bad times. Why, we even have our finest architects designing missiles and missile throwers these days. Every artist, except the drunken poets—who are totally untrustworthy—has been pressed into the service of the State. Even an architect can build a weapon. One of our number says that he had word yesterday afternoon that fifty new catapults have been recently constructed, each capable of throwing 40-kilogram steel balls. We have two hundred *talons* already in place along the main wall facing east, each one capable of picking up a barbarian attempting to scale a wall and throwing him to his death. We have likewise thousands of vats of burning fat ready to pour down the sides of the walls upon any who dares attempt to scale the heights. Our machines might save us yet.

We are starting to feel complacent and lazy in the mid-afternoon sunshine: time has passed and we are still alive. The Moors guarding the perimeter are restless, giving discrete signs that they want to return to the safety of the walls. But we are starting to relax, our heartbeats are slowing down and we start to notice little by little how beautiful the place we are standing in is—the barbarians having denied us excursions into Nature for the past few years; with the colourful stream flowing lazily to one side of us, with a little waterfall spurting from out of the side of the moss-covered rock, we lie down in the dirt, reclining on our elbows and throwing pebbles into the stream to pass the time.

—What is it to be human? Marius asks.

As the afternoon turns to evening we realize the barbarians will not come. When we turn around with the intention of throttling the life out of the ancient Abyssinian with our bare hands we discover he has vanished into the dry south wind. We have been betrayed. By the Abyssinian? By our barbarians? We do not know. Our anger has no direction, and so we have nothing else to do but to return to our fate as the laughing-stock of the city, before the wolves of the forest set upon us, leaving the cart and the suits of armour for the barbarians to find. Already the night-air is bitterly cold. But our anger is red-hot, like a newly minted sword.

Turning back in the direction of the city's gates we notice a man being brought roughly towards us by our personal guard. He is a bloodied messenger with a halo of flies around his head, who hands us a missive before being allowed to fall into the dust, exhausted. The message is from Rome informing us that the proconsul for Septem Provinciae has been kidnapped by the barbarians, or by rebel Romans with grievances against the state, one month ago and is now presumed dead.

So our leader—the one whom we have looked up to, respected and cherished—is dead, has been dead for two months, or is possibly still alive? Our emotions move from grief to anger to bewilderment. We do not know what to think. The past few days' events have been enough to destabilize us; this knowledge shakes us further. We decide that at the first opportune moment we will write luminous speeches of grief to recite to the citizens, the half-citizens, the aliens and externals; in fact to all those who live within the city's walls. It will be a symbolic moment in the life of the city. A moment to acknowledge the might, power and splendour of Imperial Rome. There will be a flood of tears let loose by the general populace, enough to top up the emptying reservoir. Our reputation as speechmakers can be restored with one glorious display of artistry. There is much you can do with rhetoric.

We decide there and then to call a day of mourning. A hundred animals, including all of our imported animals— the hippopotami and crocodiles from Arabia, the lions and tigers from Syria, bulls from Ache, camels and gazelles from Cyrenaica, bears from Britannia, leopards and wild asses from Africa—will be sacrificed in the main arena as recompense to the gods. We will organize the grandest display yet held in the arena. We will deliver our highly crafted speeches of mourning to the sorrowing crowd before the afternoon's entertainment in a display of *authoritas, gravitas* and *civitas*. We will make our own ungrateful population of savages listen to us and respect us. We have been presented with what seems to be one last chance to win their hearts and minds—and what better way than through a mourning ceremony coupled with the entertainment of sacrifice. Our leader's death could not have come at a better time.

As we enter the city's gates we ask each other who would want to kidnap and kill a proconsul? The barbarians? For what reason? To humiliate the Empire? To humiliate its senators? To attack the order, dignity and serenity of the State? But then, you cannot reason with barbarians. Who knows what passes through a primitive's mind?

On returning home we find our womenfolk disconsolate, our children, who are ashamed of us for failing to resolve the situation, refusing to eat. Our children have been told by their mothers that the barbarians will overrun us and when they ask us directly if that is true, we have no answers: we are all emptied out of responses, the old lies will no longer do anymore, we have moved into new territory.

*

The following day finds us in the curia deciding what to do. We are in the process of agreeing that the known world is in chaos—managing each day is like trying to keep wet sand from slipping beneath your feet at the water's edge—when the Abyssinian trader skulks in behind us on silent feet. We have already agreed that we have been humiliated by the Gauls, by the barbarians and by the trader and that something will have to be done by way of vengeance. We set upon the ancient Abyssinian as soon as we catch sight of his meagre presence and fling him to the ground roughly.

He says with some dignity, blood curling from the corner of his mouth, that he has information that is of more value than his life. In exchange for a large purse of gold coins of the old style he will tell us our future. We did not know he had the power of divination but there is something in his manner that demonstrates to us that he knows something of importance and so we dust him off, carry him to a chair—he is so light I find him as easy to pick up as a child—and give him wine to drink, which he promptly spits out on the marble floor.

We warn him solemnly that he is talking for his life so he had better speak well. He says he is so old nothing much matters anymore except the pursuit of gold and silver, but the reason he slipped away yesterday was because he was overcome with curiosity at the failure of the barbarians to appear, the near-barbarians being honourable men of their word, and he was starting to fear for their safety, having heard from his men of vast numbers of *other* barbarians in the region. When he arrived in the camp of the near-barbarians he was amazed to see the five barbarians still wearing the gold armbands discussing matters by way of an interpreter with *another* delegation of barbarians. But the most amazing thing—and this is why his life should be spared—was that these new barbarians didn't even look like barbarians: they had long red hair that had been newly washed and flew freely in the breeze. These others had no beards—the presence of which usually meant 'barbarian'. They had, sitting above upper lips, distinctive thin red moustaches. They wore linen shirts under vests made of the skins of animals. They were exceptionally tall and looked like athletes rather than barbarians. Each one wore a large belt buckle, decorated with demonic faces that kept his vest of skins fastened at the waist, a charm necklace, and each had hanging from a belt a broadsword with intricate lace iron-work around the handle. These indeed are the *elite of savages,* says the ancient trader. He confesses he has never seen barbarians before who looked like this. In spite of their appearance they are warlike, he has been told by one of the elders of the near-barbarians. They have apparently been trained from infancy for war and their womenfolk are as deadly as the males. It is reported that each of these elite barbarians would fight like ten men. The women are also tall and fair with strong shoulders and a lack of regard for their own safety. They raise their children by throwing them into campfires and seeing how swiftly they can extricate themselves. They show no affection for their own kind, according to the elder, merely tending to their children as if they are wild things, so the children grow up to hate and look forward to the days when they will be the ones dispensing anger, violence, death and destruction upon the world.

We are truly astounded at the news. But the trader continues. These barbarians are not the *other* barbarians we have all been so concerned about—these are *new* barbarians, only recently arrived from the north-east and eager to prove themselves. But the point to consider, and this is why his life should be spared, is that he has discovered that the near-barbarians and the new elite barbarians are meeting to consider an alliance against the *other* barbarians, the ones who were so completely warlike that you cannot reason with them, and subsequently against the Romans and the Gauls.

We are astonished and perplexed. Our slaves pour more wine for us as we slump back in our chairs. Is the whole of the known world being overrun by barbarians? we ask out loud. What has happened to civilization? Is there no Greece, no Rome to confer a swaying influence of reason and order and stability? Has barbarism become the way of life and is civilization a mere aberration whose time is coming to an end? What if even more barbarians are to follow on the heels of these newcomers? What is the point of building aqueducts, viaducts, bathhouses and sewers if they are being built for succeeding generations who know only the lessons of destruction, rather than the lessons of construction?

The interpreter for the new barbarians, says the trader, is a Greek doctor turned merchant whom the trader had managed to talk to briefly. There is much money to be made from the newer style barbarians. They are the cleverest barbarians the doctor has ever met, but they are no less ruthless for all their intelligence, just more effective. According to the doctor-turned-merchant these are the first barbarians he has met who can be cleaved apart from their horses and they are the first of a new breed of barbarians who are curious about machinery. They are always paying the doctor to spy upon the Romans and steal the secrets of their machines. These new barbarians act honourably with traders and merchants, always paying more

than agreed and guaranteeing their safety. The Greek
doctor-turned-merchant said that they behave with dignity,
charm and grace; even the sound of their language is elegant as opposed to the grating and leaden sounds made by
the average barbarian. And the doctor added that there are
waves and *waves* of barbarians, all belonging to different
areas, coming from the north-east, pushed out by over-
crowding, starvation, disease and a love of adventure. He
said they are looking for *living space.*

After the Abyssinian trader has been paid handsomely
in thirty gold coins of the Empire, all tied together in a
leather purse scorched with the sign of the Roman eagle,
we whisper to our personal guard of Moors to show the
trader to the door and kill him in the street as a means of
ensuring his silence about such matters and as a warning
to the Gauls, returning the coins to us at their earliest convenience.

We are confused and perplexed, we need to discuss matters quietly and sombrely. Marius speaks first:

—We will attempt to establish the facts. These new barbarians are barbarians who wear no beards, who are clean,
who walk instead of living on top of their horses, who wear
jewellery, who take an interest in machines and who are
honourable in every way.

He pauses for a long time letting the implications of
what he has just said permeate our minds. Then, he continues:

—If these new barbarians are barbarians, *who are we?*
What room have they left for us? What role do we still
have amongst the Gauls? If the Gauls have the new

barbarians to look up to, why do they need to look up to us? Perhaps our role has finished in Narbonensis and it is incumbent upon us to return home—if we can, in fact, find a safe passage home. Our tour of duty has ended, but we may yet not reach a deserved and honourable old age free from anxiety and cares.

And he pauses again for a long time. The Moors return and place the gold coins and the leather purse all covered in warm sallow blood upon the table.

Marius sighs deeply, looks through the open door into the far distance, fondling the warm coins and says:

—There is no more need for Romans now that barbarians have become us, and we have become barbarians. Our stay of duty is over. What will become of us now that we no longer have any role to play?

nine | The Departure

We are disappointed with the Romans. They are hardly behaving like Romans anymore. Their so-called entertainment was not entertaining, their speeches were boring. That is what we told our fellow barbarians, while the chill wind came off the nearby river as we inclined on the necks of our horses. The Romans have let us down, and the weather is starting to change. They do not deserve to be called Romans anymore.

We are becoming restless again; we long for the ground rushing beneath the hooves of our horses with the wind blowing our long locks. But we decide after much discussion that we cannot let the Romans down; we cannot be less than the barbarians they imagine us to be and so we are condemned to maintain our siege. We cannot desert them. Besides, we are providing a useful service by providing a buffer between them and the waves of barbarians descending from the north-east.

So having resigned ourselves to our fate, you can imagine our consternation the next day when we hear bloodcurdling cries coming from the direction of the walled city. We presume it's bloodshed and destruction; they're familiar sounds. We can see and smell the fires of the burning city. Our worst fears are confirmed later that same day.

In the evening the Greek merchants arrive with a tale of woe. The other barbarians had descended upon the Romans in the early hours of the morning from the west, something the Romans were not prepared for, putting the citizens to the sword and the city to the flame. Being the *other* barbarians they would not listen to speeches. The Greek merchants also have brought with them many cartloads of stolen Roman property to sell to us, including the purple-striped togas of the senatorial class. For cultured men we are amazed at how mercenary they have become. We buy nothing of the Romans' clothing or goods from the merchants, out of respect for the dead and dying. We are eager, however, to hear more of the merchants' account of what has befallen the Romans. During the attack, we are told, a number of the senatorial class with their wives and children managed to escape from the city via secret tunnels that took them into caves in the countryside. Several senators had mentioned to the merchants in the past that in the event of an attack they intended heading southwards into Hispaniae with the goal of Africa as a safe haven from barbarians of all types. They had learnt to live with us, the near-barbarians, they had told the merchants, and had even become a little fond of us (which makes us feel proud).

We grieve at the fate that has befallen our Romans but after a long while we realize we are finally free of the Romans and we are thus free to recommence our nomadic way of life. We have not precipitated our freedom, that has been done for us by the newer style barbarians. Later still the realization dawns upon us that we have not been attacked by the other barbarians and, upon questioning the Greek merchants—who seem to know everything—we are told that our reputation amongst the other barbarians is fearsome. The other barbarians told the merchants that there was nothing to be gained by taking on such ruthless opponents (again we feel proud that our reputation has spread before us—no doubt encouraged by the merchants and traders who, we have slowly come to realise, make great profit out of spreading misinformation about rival groups).

We decide, by general consensus, that the dead Romans do not deserve to have their city besieged anymore. The siege is over, the travelling will begin again, and we are starting to feel happy at the prospect. No longer will we let the grass grow through the hooves of our horses, no longer will our womenfolk live their sedentary lives of mending garments, finding food and raising warrior children who are conducting ever more deadly activities as they grow older.

We are slowly adjusting to the change of circumstance. We have been still for so long we can no longer remember what it is like to move. In making preparations to depart the blood is starting to circulate again in our bodies. We are starting to feel like barbarians again. We will move southwards over the mountains and into Hispaniae. The merchants and traders tell us that this region holds fewer barbarians and there are even Romans in Hispaniae who have never seen a barbarian before. We can start anew, just like at the end of the great cold when the birds start to sing again. We can find new Romans, ones who have never seen barbarians before and we can become *their* barbarians. We shall find a new walled city in Hispaniae with *worthy* Romans living peaceably within and we shall lay siege to that city, so they can discover barbarians for the first time and thus know the meaning of fear and respect and we shall rediscover our lost certainty and our lost identity.

The Romans, *our* Romans, have let us down by being conquered by the other barbarians and by fleeing. We did not realize our Romans could be defeated so easily. We have always looked up to them. They of course ended up taking us for granted, with their supply of baubles and trinkets; they were treating us like savages rather than men of thought and reason. In the end they did not know who we were. They no longer had any fear of us and therefore no longer had any respect for us either. They needed us, however, as a buffer. But in the end even that did not work.

So now we will teach them a lesson: we will no longer be *their* barbarians. We will desert their ruined city. We will no longer pay homage to their dead spirits. We will leave their city to the mercilessness of the other barbarians, the clean and beardless barbarians, the barbarians of the far north, the stunted barbarians from the far east with their flat noses and broad foreheads, for we are travelling southwards, to the virgin lands of Hispaniae, to resume the life of pure and true barbarians. They will be bereft when our fleeing senators discover, if they ever do, that *their* barbarians have deserted their ruined city. It will be their *reward* for taking us for granted. They do not realize how lucky they have been, for all those long years, to have *us* as their barbarians for we are the last of the barbarians to follow a code of honour in our dealings with the Romans. Certainly on overwhelming a city, we kill all of the menfolk, piling body upon body in the city square as is our custom, but we leave the women and children alone. We do not rape the women and put the children to the sword as is the habit amongst the other barbarians, the beardless barbarians, the northern barbarians, or the stunted barbarians.

This new crop of barbarians is more completely warlike than our generation. We were brought up in a different fashion. Certainly as young children we were made to walk over the hot coals of the campfire at regular intervals to test our hardiness and to prepare us for a life of valour but our parents were merely doing what their parents used to do; it was all for the best; it was for our education. And we were the first of the barbarians to throw our children through the fragile ice of first winter to see if they could survive. It was for their benefit of course; we wanted them to be hardy so they could survive the later perils of barbarian life. We did not want them to be soft. It was a natural way of life back then. But now that we have decided to travel it is physically painful to have to wait for our womenfolk and children to load the wagons. We have so many cartloads of *things* that we never used to have before.

In the past we would have left everything behind us. But now remembering what it is be hungry and to be thirsty we are becoming more cautious. We will take all of the grain the Romans have given us by way of bribes and we will take all of the barley beer, the mead and even the wine, though none of us drink it. We will empty our vast granaries into carts and we will load special carts with the mounds of ancient gold aurei and silver denarii coins. The traders and merchants will be sad to see us go—we have been such good customers of theirs, always behaving honourably towards them, never killing them or robbing them as is the custom elsewhere amongst the other barbarians, the beardless barbarians, the northern barbarians and the stunted barbarians with the flat noses. There is little honour left amongst barbarians. We barbarians, we the pure and true barbarians, the ones who love metaphor and song, are getting a bad name all due to the activities of our fellow barbarians. We need a new name to distinguish ourselves. The noble word 'barbarian' will not do as it did in the past, as no-one knows what it means anymore. The Romans are confused; even we ourselves are confused. We are suffering from a lack of language. The word still has one use though: to throw terror into the hearts of those who do not know us.

How petty the Romans seem to us now—considering how impressive they used to be. We are taking the cartload of armour that the Romans left for us. But now we are aware of their tricks. They wished to sow once more the seeds of disharmony amongst us as they did one time before with the armbands. We will keep the suits of armour as mementoes of our Romans but we will not distribute the suits as that would lead to discord. We do not need to imitate the

Romans with their love of status, their love of order, their desire to build. It is of course easier to destroy; it is what a barbarian grows up to do; it flows through mother's milk.

Besides, we will make our own Romans in the South. Hispaniae will become our playground, our unconquered land, full of virgin Romans who have never seen a barbarian before, but have heard of us. Our reputation floods their night-thoughts. We will start anew. We are flushed with exhilaration at the thought. Our adventure begins again; raise the cry amongst the full width and breadth of barbarians.

We are finally moving. We notice we have bodies again. We rue the wasted sedentary years. What were we thinking of back then, to conduct such a long siege? We misled ourselves, thinking our fealty to our Romans would be rewarded. We fell in love with them gradually over a long period of time without realizing it.

Every city on our journey southwards is a flattened scar of rubble, broken pipes, walls knocked down brick by brick; inhabited by frightened communities, usually Gauls who are trying to live amidst the still-burning rubble. We are amazed at the devastation wrought by these other barbarians. The amount of effort involved in completely destroying a walled city is beyond anything we have ever ventured to attempt. These other barbarians are indeed ferocious. There are many fires burning and the people of the ruined cities are continually on the move, so much so that the roads are often choked with Gauls and Romans fleeing from these other barbarians who make *death, annihilation and hatred* their battle cry. They are obviously determined to obliterate. They have a hatred of *things,* as we used to.

On our journey south-west through Narbonensis towards the Pyranaei mountains we come across a city which is a smoking ruin. What has taken a hundred years to build has taken only a few days to destroy. The walls of the city have been taken apart brick by brick. We wonder once again at the hatred expended on those bricks and we say to each other as we install ourselves once again outside the walls of a ruined city that these other barbarians truly have a hatred of walls and bricks. Why else would they have expended so much energy in destroying this particular city? Even the reservoir and the extensive network of aqueducts have been destroyed. The city is uninhabitable though there are a few Gauls who have ventured into the former city scrounging around in the ruins without hope or dignity, looking for sustenance. These other barbarians even hate water, we say to each other, late at night, inclining on the necks of our horses. We settle down as we used to in the past—but we were happier back then—by the banks of a broad river with our vast ranks of barbarians, a mass of humanity greater than eyes could see the end of, stretching way beyond the horizon. We are amazed at how quickly the world can change, we say to each other, from certainty to chaos.

*

We are settling back into a sedentary life, besieging a ruined city, when the shortest and unruliest of our number points out to us late one night that he has heard from various traders and merchants who have slowly been returning to this recently destroyed city that it is no longer safe to stay in this area because new waves of barbarians, even more ferocious than the last waves, are descending at a great rate from the north-east. So urgently we discuss the necessity of departure and reluctantly we proceed to prepare to depart once again, even though we are just starting to enjoy the comforts of a peaceful settled life with our womenfolk and children around us to keep us company and tend to our few bodily cares and wants. But the report of the unruly one is deeply unsettling and we agree that at first light we will have to leave our newly found plain by the broad river and once again prepare to resume the nomadic life.

With the passing of time—a few seasons have passed already—we are starting to feel bereft without our Romans. If only they had been spared! If only they were still safely ensconced behind the walls of their beautiful city and we could thus have a reason to settle peaceably into old age in a place with such pleasant surroundings—with a mighty river to keep us company and by the passage of its flow to be reminded of our erstwhile love of travelling.

But it has become obvious that a sedentary life is not to be our fate and so after a few nights we are ready to depart, once again going south-west through the country-side towards the mountains. We are torn between the allure of continual movement, when we feel young again, and the comforts of the sedentary life when we feel at peace with the world. Each state is a giving up of the other. We are likewise torn between a loyalty towards our old Romans and a desire to see new Romans, to impress them with our skills, our talents, our very *barbarianness*.

At the site of each obliterated city we turn to each other and ask: How could barbarians do this? Especially the reservoirs. We do not understand how anyone who has ever been thirsty could destroy reservoir after reservoir, but it is obviously no longer beyond the limits for these other barbarians. To destroy a reservoir with all its life-sustaining water would not have been tolerated when we were young. The elder barbarians would have kept our high-spiritedness in check, but now it is obvious that the other barbarians do not live by any rules; nor have they a code of conduct to govern their behaviour with the Romans or with each other.

Our womenfolk are very upset at our intention to cross the mountains and venture into the unknown world of Hispaniae. They say they have grown used to the sights and sounds of the province of Narbonensis. We are impatient to test ourselves in new lands. We tell our womenfolk that we will cross the mountains and settle just the other side so we can return quickly if that proves to be necessary. Amongst ourselves our secret plan is to voyage to Hispaniae and to find our Romans—the senators who have escaped—and encourage them, if indeed they need encouraging, to once again build a walled city as they did in the past which we could then once again besiege to the contentment of both parties. Or failing ever finding them, we will search out a new Roman city and lay siege to the first one we find. If we can only find our first Romans—the ones who were originally so impressed by us—then we can once more be the ferocious barbarians of old. In the early days of our siege our Romans accorded us so much dignity and respect.

The Greek merchants in the past used to tell us about the golden city of Corduba, capital of the province of Baetica in the diocesis of Hispaniae. We will find it if we can. We hope it is a walled city so we can lay siege to it in traditional barbarian fashion. There are considerable misgivings at the thought of the dangers that lie ahead of us, but we say to each other late at night that we used to long for the unknown and once we cross the mountains of the Pyranaei and arrive in Hispaniae then our spirits will revive. We used to be fearless barbarians after all.

*

Now that we have finally arrived in Hispaniae—the way over the mountains was hard, our journey long, the passes treacherous, the snow and ice making our passage hazardous—we have seen no-one, neither Roman nor barbarian. The Greek merchants call this region of Hispaniae by its Roman name, Tarraconensis. The ground we are travelling across is more arid than Narbonensis, the sun is hotter, the trees provide no shade and our faces are getting burnt. At least we are travelling again, even our horses are grateful. We are starting again to feel like our old barbarian selves instead of pretend-Romans as some of our number call us dismissively. Even our womenfolk, they who are usually so miserable, are happy to be seeing new sights, smelling the scents of new trees, feeling the following sun on their long flowing hair with our children running alongside the carts in the dust for long periods of time.

We are starting to leave our thoughts of the Romans, the ones who may have escaped, behind. We no longer think of them except to wonder out aloud while we are stationary, late at night, beside a dried-up river bed, if they are still thinking of us. We ask each other: for those Romans, the senators in particular, who escaped and travelled southwards, was our place in their minds immediately occupied by thoughts of other barbarians? Or a more disturbing thought that came to us only after a long period of time: did our Romans know which group of barbarians attacked them and put them to the sword and the flame? Did they feel that we, who loved them in an odd sort of way, betrayed them by invading from the west, squeezing the lives out of their bare throats? We are much disturbed by such thoughts. We wish to resurrect their bodies, if indeed they have died, to tell them we did not let them down—we remained faithful to our side of the bargain until the end.

The thrill of life is in instilling fear amongst others. We cannot be fully barbarian if we do not quickly find a Roman settlement—preferably one that has not already been saturated by a proximity to barbarian ways. Where shall we find new Romans, ones who still fear barbarians?

What else is the purpose of the journey forward if there is no end-goal in sight? With each new movement forward we are finding ourselves marooned more and more in unfamiliar desert. We are unaccustomed to the aridity of the place and we are becoming disheartened, having gone around in circles, or so it seems, coming across the same dry riverbed and the same clump of shadeless trees over and over again. We are reminded once again that we were better off before: at least we had a climate we liked, an enemy we were sure of and a place, a patch of earth that we could call our own.

We are unable to find any Romans or merchants or barbarians. We are truly in a desert. Even our much vaunted metaphor-making has been leached away by the excesses of the sun and the ravages of the years. Our love of metaphor and verse belong now to the past. They were different barbarians, younger ones, who sought night after night to turn thought into gold. We have become disillusioned by all that.

Though one night, inclining on the necks of our horses, one of our number happens to mention those erstwhile nights of metaphor-making and those days when the Greek merchants sold us secrets of the Hellenic world and we decide at that moment to send out a search party at first light to retrieve the youth-of-wisdom from within the vast mass of barbarianhood straggling behind us, in order that he might retell us those secrets—we vaguely remember the word 'arithmetic' but not what it means—and via this method remind us of our former selves.

We are starting to tire of our life in the natural state as wanderers, even though initially it was that desire to be a wanderer—together with our sense of running out of living-space, our homelands having become overcrowded with savages wanting to share our food and land, and also being young and looking for adventure—that made us take up the life of a barbarian. We have realized that we are happy neither travelling nor being still and, worst of all, we are starting to feel less like barbarians with each passing day. There is no enemy to fight, no-one to besiege and no-one to pay us the respect of fearing us. There is no-one, apart from ourselves, who regards us as barbarians and therefore we feel unsure as to who we are. Only the Romans are capable of holding up a mirror to us that will reflect us back as we wish to be shown.

At moments of weakness we envy the Romans their buildings and their sense of the past. They know who their ancestors are, they even have statues made to remind them. We on the other hand have no idea. In the dryness of Hispaniae we envy the Romans their reservoirs and aqueducts and we discuss endlessly the possibilities of joining with the Romans as a federated army of barbarians in order to fight against all of the other barbarians who are destroying the good name of barbarianhood. What we long for above all is certainty. We have been travelling for who knows how long in Hispaniae without seeing any Romans; nor have we seen any stray groups of wandering traders. We have come across wide gravel roads with kerbing obviously built by the Romans as well as other signs of civilization such as massive stone bridges running across either flowing streams or dried-up riverbeds, depending on the season. We occasionally see local farmers who run from our sight. But the land appears strangely unoccupied and strangely quiet, like it's been hit by inexplicable devastation—a vast wind which has scoured the land carrying away all its inhabitants. Perhaps disease has wiped everybody out, or perhaps there is a simpler explanation—other barbarians have been here before us putting whole provinces to the torch.

We look forward to the day we can plant ourselves, like trees taking root, outside a walled city. When we set out in our youth, after adventure and glory, we did not realize there would come a time when we would be surfeited of travelling, our bones would ache constantly, craving rest, our eyesight would deteriorate and pleasures would be few. But we have now travelled through many changing seasons of hot and then mild weather with an increasingly dissatisfied company of barbarians. We have searched for signs of life, occasionally seeing clouds of dust or smoke a long way off on the horizon, causing us to turn to each other and say: If only they are *our* Romans! We are turning all our hopes on Corduba.

We could not bear it if we were to arrive and find the capital of Baetica was a humble village by a dried-up riverbed, unworthy of besieging, providing no excuse for settling into a long and prosperous existence. The city would have to be worthy enough to provide us with a reason to stop travelling. Many of our number are dying along the way dispirited by constant disappointment and the extremes of the climate: the fierce sunshine during the day followed by the bitterly cold nights. Our homelands are not like this. We were born of ice and snow and sleet. We were creatures of fog and mist and mud. This persistent sun beating on our heads is enough to turn our thoughts inside out.

Our grain is running out after the numerous seasons of wandering through the lonely Hispanic deserts; our mead has run out and we're now drinking the wine which we dislike. We're confused as to why we have not sighted anyone. We thought Hispaniae was more crowded than it appears to be. Maybe we have slipped off the known world and we've slipped into a nether world which is unoccupied.

*

One day, in the era in which we have given up hope, we chase a cloud of dust and catch up with a group of Moors who are transporting carpets and pottery jugs full of African olive oil. We are overjoyed to see them and even though we have no language in common they are able to indicate that a large walled city is ahead of us but in a more southerly direction; we have apparently been travelling too far west.

As we journey on there are signs we are getting closer to a settlement and we hope that we have not set out from Narbonensis in vain, and that the walled city ahead of us— perhaps it is Corduba, perhaps another city—will not let us down. We say to each other late at night while inclining on our horses that if it is indeed the capital of Baetica then it should be a mighty city worthy of a long and fruitful siege. We have become so anxious with day-to-day matters that no-one enquires about the search party that was sent out to find the youth-of-wisdom. As we grow closer to the city we increasingly start to encounter traders who speak words that we are unable to understand but at least they are able to point the way to the city—though whether we are being misled is something we are unsure about. We decide we will kidnap the next band of traders and force them to take us to the walled city.

We hope that the city is well protected with noble Romans who have heard of, but have never seen, barbarians in the flesh before, then all will be well. They will send us grain and wheat bread and barley beer to prevent us from attacking. But if the truth be known we hardly have the strength to take the life of a goat, such is our state after years of pointless wandering with our number declining steadily from the heat, the unfamiliar surroundings and what the youth-of-wisdom has referred to as 'past-sickness'—a longing for times gone by.

We are going around in circles in the desert. The heat is making us delirious, making us uncertain of our bearings. Clumps of trees start to look familiar. Late at night with the chill wind swirling around our horses we try to work out where we have been. The one called the silent one is the first one to speak and, as we have not heard his voice in a very long time, everyone listens. He says, in a rough and grating voice that's unpleasant to the ear:

—We started out as barbarians because we did not know any better, and because we found we were good at it, very good at it in fact. We came to Narbonensis in a spirit of adventure. We were greatly feared by the Romans, our reputation had preceded us apace. The Romans greatly respected us as fearsome warriors who were unreasonably and unpredictably violent; but then they got to know us more and more and saw that we would willingly take their grain and barley beer and would even accept their invitation to visit and be entertained. In getting to know us they respected us less. That coincided with the possibility that our role could be replaced by the other barbarians, those completely warlike ones, who reminded them of us, the first barbarians they had ever encountered, the first barbarians they had ever needed, the first barbarians they had ever loved. With the destruction of the walled city we had no alternative but to leave. There was no longer anything for us to do there. So although we are going around in circles in this primitive desert, it is necessary for us to be here. We cannot go back to Narbonensis. There is nothing for us there. There is no space in which we could exist. It is overrun with *barbarians*. (He spat the word out.) At least here in the desert when we finally encounter our walled city, we have the possibility of starting out again with a community of virgin Roman senators and citizens who will see us as we truly are.

His words make a lot of sense and he is accorded much honour in the days and weeks to come. He has spoken the truth. The silent one has followed a course all his life of wisely refraining from speaking when he has nothing to say so that when it comes time for him to speak everyone listens attentively.

The next day we see to our surprise a cloud of dust coming towards us. As the cloud grows closer we attack as in days gone by: our long matted hair flowing behind us, our broadswords raised, our hearts beating faster. But we find to our amazement a group of covered carts filled with frightened artisans, their wives and children and, upon further investigation, we find it is a company of Roman goldsmiths, together with cartloads of equipment to make coins, and a Levantine who is acting as their interpreter and their guide. The Levantine tells us that the two master goldsmiths, who look so alike we cannot tell them apart, are originally from Ostia, a trading port near Rome, and they are travelling from Italica in the south to Barcino in the north, a town we had not encountered on our journey.

We are delighted to have the company of cultured, gentle and thoughtful Romans and we are pleased at our good fortune in being able to communicate with them via the interpreter. We are distressed to hear that many cities in the south of Hispaniae have been destroyed by all shades and types of barbarians. Many cities are burning, disease has broken out due to the lack of fresh water, the barbarians having destroyed many reservoirs and aqueducts along the way. We persuade the goldsmiths and their families to accompany us southwards, on pain of death, and while they are initially frightened of us they eventually relax in our presence and are able to answer our many curious questions relating to what ordinary Romans think of barbarians. Naturally, Romans on the whole are frightened of us— which pleases us. But what is less pleasing is the admission we manage to prise out of the goldsmiths, once they learn to trust us, that Romans on the whole regard us as *savages*.

After many nights of feverish discussion, the like of which we have not known for many years, a wild idea enters our heads: we will become our own Romans. We will mint our own coins and become masters of water as a sign of our power. We have cultured, machine-loving artisans to assist us in our transformation which will begin as soon as we can find a fertile valley to settle in. Through talking to the master goldsmiths—identical twins (a sign we take as an omen of good luck)—we are able to see how we could ourselves be turned into water-lovers. With the knowledge of the goldsmiths, who have talked with engineers in their youth and know the secrets of building and the hypnotizing of water, we could divert a river to build our own reservoir. We could besiege a local river until we captured water. We could become the owners of water. We could have traders negotiate with the other barbarians on our behalf. It will be an end to uncertainty. We could mint our own coins. The goldsmiths agree to help us when they are forced to stare into the face of an alternative darkness.

The realization that we can become our own Romans seems to be some sort of solution to our problem of the lack of Romans and a walled city to besiege. Walled cities must surely exist in Hispaniae but in many seasons of fruitless travelling we have not been able to find any. We will start with the minting of coins. The goldsmiths, whom we have grown to like, have unwittingly shown us possibilities we had previously been blind to. Renewed hope makes us feel like pure barbarians again. We will remake ourselves. The goldsmiths patiently explain to us over a period of days that in order to mint coins for us they need an image for the reverse side and an image for the obverse. We cannot think of a suitable image so we ask them to suggest something, which they do: the face of the ruler for the obverse side and a warlike scene befitting the nature of barbarians for the reverse. We patiently explain we have no ruler. The master goldsmiths explain that they need a face to copy, so we show them the body of the last barbarian who died, and one of the twins dutifully copies the visage. We have endless cartloads of gold aurei and silver denarii coins which can be melted down and recast for the making of barbarian money. The way, for once, seems straightforward; it only requires the presence of a fertile valley with a river running through the middle of it for us to settle down and commence the transformation.

The desert eventually turns into a plateau which declines to a fertile valley with a mighty river running through the middle. From the heights we can see a settlement way off in the distance. We do not know if it is Corduba or not. The goldsmiths say they do not know the name of the city: they have lost their bearings. We are overjoyed at the discovery. Perhaps we need not turn ourselves into Romans after all. We can go back to our simple barbarian way of life, far away from the cares of Romanhood. We can lay siege to a walled city once more. But as we approach we are distressed to see the remains of what was once a great city ruined no doubt by a ferocious barbarian anger, as ferocious as anything Nature can itself provide by means of fire, flood or earthquake.

Again we spend many feverish nights discussing what we ought to do. We could move into the ruined city, bury the dead, rebuild the reservoir, mint coins, which could be used to defend us from invading warriors of all kinds—in short, become our own Romans in their absence—or else we could go back to what we know best: laying siege peaceably and contentedly outside the ruins of the former city. We have heard stories from the master goldsmiths, which we find hard to believe, of Roman soldiers behaving like the worst of barbarians—undertaking punitive raids upon small barbarian settlements, slaying men, women and children and putting all of the settlement under the sway of fire. We tell them they are mistaken—that the behaviour described is that of the *other* barbarians, but they assure us it is true, which enrages us to the point we have to remind the twins that first and foremost, in spite of our Roman-like eloquence, we are still barbarians.

After we have settled in the fertile valley for a while outside the perimeter of the site of the former walled city we order the goldsmiths to commence their coin-making. It gives us great satisfaction to finally see the newly minted gold and silver coins coming out of the heavy presses with the image of the face of a dead barbarian on one side and a warlike scene on the reverse. The sway of the coins is such that we cannot help but look at them again and again, fondling them and imagining the secret power that resides within these simple objects. As we pass around the gold and silver coins we turn to each other, smile and say:

—If only our Roman senators could see us now. How proud they would be of us!

And we look forward to the day when the Romans will return to rebuild their former city so that we can get on with our old way of life, of the continual siege, in harmony and contentment. Late that night, as we incline on the necks of our horses outside the walls of the former city and after a long period of silence, we start to ask each other how the Romans had managed to become such great builders. We wonder if they too had started as barbarians, way back in the distant past, or if they had always been

Romans. There are no immediate answers to our questions and we stay motionless in the semi-darkness for an eternity until we remember that we have once again our youth-of-wisdom on hand—our search party found him living a peaceful married life with a wife and many children at the rear of our vast number—and we implore him to give us any information that might help us in our quest for the answers to the many riddles of our existence.

The youth-of-wisdom clears his throat and walks—he having given up sleeping on his horse many years before—into the centre of the circle of our horses. Through the purple light of the night sky, he says, and I quote him accurately at this point, word for word, so that you may know:

—The Greek merchants at the time of giving us arithmetic all those years ago also gave me secretly, in exchange for seeds and thoughts that I had managed to collect over many years, what they called the ancient secret of civilization, and thus of building, of good order, of law, of society and of the taming of water. The Romans, they said, had stolen the secret of civilization from the Greeks.

And then he lapses into silence for a long period of time. When he is ready to resume speaking, the moonlight is shining onto his face so we can see him clearly. He says that ever since he was given the secret he has memorized the words over and over and secretly scratched the pictures he was given in the dust before wiping them over so that no-one else would see. But now he is giving over the secret because in the case of his death the secret would be lost to we barbarians, formerly of the country of snow and sleet and now more lately of Narbonensis and the province of

Baetica in the diocesis of Hispaniae. The youth-of-wisdom
says he has repeated the words every single day since the
Greek merchants told him the secret of civilization.

The youth-of-wisdom says to us:

—Repeat after me:

Alpha, Beta, Gamma, Delta,

Epsilon, Zeta, Eta, Theta,

Iota, Kappa, Lambda, Mu,

Nu, Xi, Omicron, Pi,

Rho, Sigma, Tau, Upsilon,

Phi, Chi, Psi, Omega.

Leaning over, the youth-of-wisdom proceeds to scratch
in the sandy soil the following figures with the point of
his sword by the moonlight:

Α Β Γ Δ Ε Ζ Η Θ Ι Κ Λ Μ Ν Ξ Ο Π Ρ Σ Τ Υ Φ Χ Ψ Ω

He says:

—With these letters, the Greek merchants told me, you
can do anything.

The youth-of-wisdom says we should use the power of
the letters to pass the time. He says we can build anything
we want with the letters. They are blocks that can be placed
beside each other—exactly in the same way the Romans
place blocks of stone beside each other in order to make a
wall.

We decide there is much sense in what the youth-of-
wisdom has recounted to us. We will learn to use the power
of the figures in the sand to see if they will bring us everything that the Romans have in their possession. In the
meantime while we are learning to scratch in the sand we
agree that we will, in true barbarian fashion, lay siege to

the ruined city and wait patiently for the return of the Romans.

To pass away the night we repeat the words we have been given. Words, apparently, that have been handed down from generation to generation, the words that seem so right, so musical; the words that seem to hold within them the spirit of the dead and the power of the living.

We chant the words in unison, as the night-sky turns into the pink softness of morning light. Repeating and repeating we say:

—Alpha, Beta, Gamma, Delta, Epsilon, Zeta, Eta, Theta, Iota, Kappa, Lambda, Mu, Nu, Xi, Omicron, Pi, Rho, Sigma, Tau, Upsilon, Phi, Chi, Psi, Omega.

ten | The Awakening

You pull yourself out of the dust of ages—it is in your mouth. You are very cold. You have no idea how long you have been in the dust. You haul yourself up the side of the wall with considerable effort. There is minimal lighting. You hear the sound of what might be rats. You walk slowly up the walkway until you reach the front gates. They are locked, but you notice an emergency button which you push. A security guard arrives eventually. He is rude and brusque, initially, as you would expect him to be. You tell him you passed out. You can tell he doesn't know what to make of you. He looks confused, unsure of what to do next. You tell him the whole of civilization flashed before your eyes in the moments before losing consciousness. This statement makes him even more edgy. He thinks you might be a madman and he doesn't want to be trapped in such a place with a crazy man, you can tell. He's very young, with a scar on his left cheek. You say you live in the Marais, you'll walk home, it's OK, it's not far. You walk up the steps, but turn halfway up to thank him for letting you out of your prison of the past. He says Wait, but you keep walking. You can tell by his body language that he doesn't know what to do, so you take control of the situation. You walk confidently up the remaining steps and out into the forecourt of Notre-Dame staring at the facade of the medieval building. You enter the cathedral for comfort's sake. There are people everywhere, incense, singing—a Gregorian chant fills the whole space. You have stepped into medieval Paris. You stay for a few minutes but feel you do not belong and thus leave. You make it to your temporary home and feel instantly better as you turn on the lights and the heater and the CD player; Johann Sebastian Bach's *Brandenburg Concertos* spring to life. The music is a solace. You are back in the real world, you have been on a journey. You decide you will not research or write anything ever again. You need to let go of the words you have been reading, all the words you have ever read and all of the words you have written. For words once they've been read can undo everything you've ever thought. You start to shiver. Words in a certain order will undo you every time. Better to be without words for a long time so that the present can write over the past. Your nervous system can't take the incursion of memory. Your imagination has always been too active— you are in no need of any further stimulus. You determine to let the past go. There is nothing anymore that you can do about the past of your forebears, your past of Romans and barbarians. The past is *over*, you finally realize. If you don't let go the past it will devour you; there is nothing more certain. Better by far to go about daily life as if you are in a trance, as if you are a sleepwalker, with

The Layers of the City

diminished consciousness and diminished responsibility—in that safety lies. You do not need to read—reading has brought you to this state—nor do you need to think too much. To be a sleepwalker. To be safe. To be disengaged from the world. You can no longer take responsibility for being a Roman or a barbarian. Your mind is too fragile for that. You have to learn to deal with what's only on the surface layer. You need to rebury the past beneath the many layers of the city. The present must be allowed to write over the past.

Bibliography

Author's Note

There are a number of books that have been very helpful in the creation of this novel.

For the period of the barbarians:

Maurice Bouvier-Ajam's *Les Empereurs Gaulois* (Paris: Tallandier, 1984); Thomas Burns' *A History of the Ostrogoths* (Bloomington: Indiana University Press, 1991); and Hans Delbrück's *The Barbarian Invasions* (Lincoln: University of Nebraska Press, 1990).

For the period of the Romans:

Geza Alföldy's *The Social History of Rome* (London: Routledge, 1988); and Michel Meslin's *L'Homme Romain* (Paris: Hachette, 1985).

On the nature of Adolf Hitler:

Joachim C. Fest's *The Face of the Third Reich* (Harmondsworth: Penguin, 1979); and Allan Bullock's *Hitler: A Study in Tyranny* (Harmondsworth: Penguin, 1967).

The Layers of the City

For reflections on Marx, Talleyrand, sacrifice and the gods:

Roberto Calasso's *The Ruin of Kasch* (Cambridge: Harvard University Press, 1994) and his *The Marriage of Cadmus and Harmony* (London: Vintage, 1994).

For the comments quoting the poet Paul Valéry on family life:

A History of Private Life, volume 5, edited by Antoine Prost and Gerard Vincent, translated by Arthur Goldhammer (Cambridge: The Belknap Press, 1991).

For comments on Heraclitus:

Fifty Major Philosophers, A Reference Guide, Diané Collinson (London: Routledge, 1987).

For Jung's comments about himself:

C.G. Jung's *Memories, Dreams, Reflections* (London: Flamingo, 1983).

For information about the Chernobyl disaster:

Viktor Haynes and Marko Bojcun's *The Chernobyl Disaster* (London: The Hogarth Press, 1988).

And for inspiration, the poetry of Constantine Cavafy and Rainer Maria Rilke and in particular the following books:

C.P. Cavafy's *Poems by C.P. Cavafy*, translated by John Mavrogordato (London: Chatto & Windus, 1978); Rainer Maria Rilke's *Sonnets to Orpheus*, translated by M.D. Norton (New York: Norton, 1962); Rainer Maria Rilke's *Selected Poems of Rainer Maria Rilke*, translated by Robert Bly (New York: Harper & Row, 1981); Rainer Maria Rilke's *Duino Elegies*, translated by J.B. Leishman & Stephen Spender (London: The Hogarth Press, 1968) and in another translation by David Young (New York: Norton, 1978).

Also consulted were the following books which were useful for my research into the various periods.

General Bibliography

Beck, Francoise & Chew, Hélène 1989, *Quand les Gaulois étaient romains*, Découvertes Gallimard

Aurelius, Marcus 1964, *Meditations*, Penguin, Harmondsworth

Courcelle, Pierre 1948, *Histoire Littéraire des Grands Invasions Germaniques*, Libraire Hachette, Paris

Mamou, Yves 1980, *Paris Sous Terre*, Editions Nesle, Paris

Michel, Pierre 1981, *Les Barbares 1789–1948*, Presses Universitaires de Lyon, Lyon

Michelet, Jules 1846, *Le Peuple*, Hachette, Paris

Mumford, Lewis 1973, *The City in History*, Penguin, Harmondsworth

Scarre, Chris 1995, *The Penguin Historical Atlas of Ancient Rome*, Penguin, Harmondsworth

Pryce-Jones, David 1981, *Paris in the Third Reich*, Holt, Rinehart Winston, New York

Riché, Pierre 1953, *Les Invasions Barbares*, Presses Universitaires de France, Paris

Roux, Jean-Paul 1982, *Les Barbares*, Bordas

Sarris, Andrew 1969, *Interviews with Film Directors*, Aron, New York

Seneca 1969, *Letters from a Stoic*, Penguin, Harmondsworth

Tacitus 1972, *The Annals of Imperial Rome*, Penguin, Harmondsworth

Thierry, M. Amedée 1856, *Histoire D'Attila et des Successeurs*, Didier, Paris